EBURY PRESS

TIGER SEASON

Gargi Rawat is a senior news anchor and environment reporter who has worked with NDTV 24x7 for the last two decades. She was educated at the Welham Girls' School, Dehradun, and St. Stephen's College of Delhi University. For many years she has been a regular face on the channel and has filmed several documentaries and environment-related programmes. She worked on the first-ever news show on wildlife in India, *Born Wild*, and anchored its Hindi version, *Safari India*, for the Hindi channel NDTV India. Gargi has also been editorial head for some of the best-known environmental campaigns carried out by NDTV, including 'The Greenathon', 'Save Our Tigers', 'Protecting India's Coastline' and the 'Banega Swachh India' campaign. She received widespread acclaim for her award-winning documentary series on the state of the river Ganga. This is her first book.

Celebrating 35 Years of
Penguin Random House India

TIGER
SEASON

Stripes, safaris and sparks

GARGI RAWAT

EBURY
PRESS

An imprint of Penguin Random House

EBURY PRESS

USA | Canada | UK | Ireland | Australia
New Zealand | India | South Africa | China | Singapore

Ebury Press is part of the Penguin Random House group of companies
whose addresses can be found at global.penguinrandomhouse.com

Published by Penguin Random House India Pvt. Ltd
4th Floor, Capital Tower 1, MG Road,
Gurugram 122 002, Haryana, India

First published in Ebury Press by Penguin Random House India 2023

ISBN 9780143459361

Typeset in Sabon by Manipal Technologies Limited, Manipal
Printed at Thomson Press India Ltd, New Delhi

www.penguin.co.in

To my parents, my biggest cheerleaders

1

'If we see Mallika today, it's a legit sign from the fates, and you will not get married just now.'

We were sitting in a jeep, in the middle of a very quiet jungle, waiting for a tiger to show up. It was a sweltering hot day, and I could feel the sweat slowly trickling down my back. We could sense the deep drone of the jungle—the rhythmic hum of wilderness, the low buzzing of insects, birdsong near and far and a steady breeze that rustled the leaves and grasses—around us. The gentle gushing of a distant stream overrode these sporadic interludes.

Jaya, to whom my comment was addressed, was intently peering into her camera lens. She now turned around with an irritated expression.

I had sprung these comments on her while we—a reporter and camera person news team—were waiting, yet again, in the middle of the jungle for a wild predator that had remained elusive for the last three days.

'Just what is that supposed to mean, Sunaina?' exclaimed Jaya. 'What does one thing even have to do with another?'

I shrugged my shoulders, unable to rationalize why I felt a sighting of Chambalgarh's most famous denizen should help decide her fate. In my own mind I was simply looking for signs from the universe, to tell her something I didn't want to. Sometimes, when faced with tough decisions, I sought signs and symbols, even unconnected, to give me an answer.

Usually, this was to do with a decision I was not inclined to make. All this made no sense to anyone else, and in this case it wasn't even my decision. But what Jaya had told me had been bothering me from the moment I heard it.

The long wait here had made me think about the news she had broken the night before. She was considering a proposal for her marriage arranged by her parents, whose only justification to have their daughter wedded was that 'it was the right thing to do'.

But why was I agitated?

We had been colleagues for four years, friends for three and had gone on countless shoots together for NNTV, the news channel we both worked for. I knew this was a bad idea for her.

We'd grown reasonably close and I had felt we were on the same wavelength. So I just could not understand why she was willing to throw away a promising career. Over the years I had witnessed colleagues and friends whose careers had been sacrificed on the altar of 'getting hitched, bearing children, running households'. In my estimation, they had basically sold themselves short and it would catch up with them one day. I hated seeing it happen.

'Look, I know you feel pressured to get married to someone in your community, especially since your elder sisters went their own way, but don't do it! You're not some sacrificial lamb who has to give up her future.' I said this as forcefully as I could in that special 'quiet' voice that one adopts in a jungle.

All this while Jaya was fiddling with the camera and tripod set up at the back of the jeep, ignoring me.

We were stationed next to a patch of tall grass, with a riverbed and the jungle beyond. There was a narrow stream trickling between the rocks, pooling in places.

We had been informed by our guide that the most famous tiger in the park, Mallika, had last been seen resting on the river bed.

'Take it as a sign from the heavens!' I continued. 'Do you know there are people who worship Mallika? They consider her a jungle goddess, a *devi*. If she appears now, I'm telling you, it is a sign you should not get married just now!'

For a moment, silence intervened.

Jaya turned to me, irked. She rolled her eyes and whispered, 'I won't have to give up everything, just this job, but then I can be more flexible, take projects, make documentaries like I've always wanted. And the family will be happy, especially my sisters.'

I was exasperated.

'Seriously? You think you can become a documentary film-maker while married to some engineer in the Indian

Railways? That's not going to happen and you know it. You'll be moving around from one small town to the other, managing the house, socializing with other wives. And then you will have little kids and it will be all over.'

I knew I was being harsh but couldn't help it. Over the years, Jaya had come to be a friend I cherished and I didn't want to see her making short-sighted choices, which I knew were going to leave her unhappy.

This dusky, charming girl, full of life and zest, with her frizzy black hair and bright eyes, was destined to go places. Like me, she was driven, passionate about work. She also had an infectious sense of humour that made her a fun companion.

To marry for the wrong reasons would destroy her.

Jaya Deogam belonged to a tiny and fast-shrinking tribal community, the Kols, who were from Jharkhand. Her two older sisters, like many others of their generation, had chosen to marry outside the cycle of endogamic pressure. Her brother, however, had followed tradition and married one of their own. Sadly for him, the marriage did not work out, and he found himself divorced within two years. For Jaya's parents, therefore, it became a matter of clan pride to ensure their youngest child married within the fold.

For all her bravado, I knew she would be miserable if she sacrificed her dreams for the sake of a good match.

And, let's face it, the 'good match' was only theoretical. Who knew what would happen once she was married?

I also knew Jaya's own guilt of not meeting family expectations was what was propelling her decision. Her family was well regarded in the community.

Her ancestors had played a significant role against their British overlords in 1857. They had staunchly supported the rebellion led by their hereditary liege-lord, the raja of Porahat, and it had taken the British two years to quell. This family history was something that generated much pride within the family.

The same pride was now pushing my friend to step up where her other siblings had seemingly failed.

I was simply unable to stand by and watch this happen to someone I really cared about.

But whatever Jaya may have responded with was cut short by the booming distress call of a sambar deer close by. The sound, a sharp, loud bark of this antlered beast, resounded against the rocks in our vicinity. This large species seldom calls except when it is gravely threatened. We could see the sambar standing at a slight distance, in the grass, its head up, front leg raised in the air. The first 'alarm' was followed by a sharper, more nasal shriek that reverberated through the jungle canopy. The sambar stamped its front legs, turned around and ran.

Within seconds, a langur in a tree nearby also gave its distinct warning call, a loud, sharp yelp, which they make when they have sighted a predator.

I was no longer thinking about Jaya, her marriage, siblings and tribe. I was frantically scanning the grasses and treeline around us to detect some movement that could signify that a tiger was on the prowl.

The jeep lunged forward to reposition itself and my breathing accentuated with the change in gears. Jaya too was desperately checking her camera settings as our guide and driver moved the jeep for a more panoramic view.

I felt on edge, and the constant shift of the gearbox, the braking of the pedals and the sound of an ageing chassis were adding to my stress. The monkeys continued their chattering and occasional hooting, but they had stopped the alarm call. The sambar had stopped calling as well. Maybe the tiger had settled down? Not a good sign as I couldn't spot it!

The vines on the banyan tree to our left suddenly moved and I jerked my head around for a closer look. It was only a peacock dislocating a broken shoot that dropped on its way down to those grey thick roots.

Everything was silent again and my heart sank. Time was running out. We had been filming for three days in this vast expanse of green with not so much as a sighting of even a sliver of tiger stripes.

I looked back to see Jaya scowl at me, her mouth pursed forlornly. In any case, we would have to be out of the park soon, and our team of driver and guide were becoming restless.

'We have to leave soon,' said the driver, Lakhan Singh. 'I don't want to lose my driving permit.'

I wish you would, I thought to myself unkindly but did not say it aloud. I was irritated and stressed. It also wasn't the best-kept jeep in the world, and he hadn't done much to help us in our quest anyway.

'*Chalo* then, let's go,' I said resignedly after another few minutes.

He switched on the engine and, with one final look around, the jeep took off on the dirt road. Lakhan Singh had to swerve round the almost 180-degree bend in the track, only to brake suddenly. We nearly fell and just about managed to steady ourselves.

I was on the verge of scolding Lakhan but was rendered speechless.

There she was!

It was Mallika, sitting languidly, sprawled across the breadth of the road, barely metres away from where we were positioned. We hadn't seen her because of the curve in the road and the tall grass had blocked our view.

I gripped Jaya's arm, only to realize she was already filming.

The most overwhelming sensation at that moment was the hush of stillness that had descended around us.

Here was perhaps the most famous tiger in the world, the greatest ambassador of her species. I felt a swell of emotion rising but suppressed it as it reached my throat.

Lakhan Singh and Faiz, our guide, appeared even more excited than I was. Relieved, perhaps.

I had to hold Lakhan Singh's shoulder to calm him down as he took photos with his phone.

Then I carefully took out my own phone to get some pictures as well.

For a tigress of her age, Mallika looked in good form. Her coat had yellowed with the onset of summer, and apart from a missing canine, there was little that suggested she was seventeen years old, by no means young for a species that seldom survives beyond fourteen years in the wild.

No other predator in the wild had been filmed, photographed or documented for as long and as much as Mallika. By observing her, scientists and writers, film-makers and photographers had learnt much about the behaviour of tigers in the wild.

She had brought up no less than twelve tigers to adulthood, and her progeny now inhabited different parts of the Chambalgarh jungle in Rajasthan. According to some, even farther afield.

It was with good reason that Mallika had found such fame; India retained almost 70 per cent of the world's wild tiger population, and within the country, Chambalgarh was considered the most accessible tiger reserve of them all.

And its most famous inhabitant was Mallika, the grand dame of the park.

Tourists and journalists had given her many titles, each according to their experience of her behaviour. Some called her 'the lady of the mountain', basing their name on her frequent sightings atop the most prominent hill of Chambalgarh.

Others referred to her as 'bear slayer', following on her determined onslaughts against the formidable sloth bears that grant tigers only a cursory respect. One story claimed that a sloth bear had killed one of her cubs, sparking her lifelong, deadly feud against them. A particular video of her wounding and then killing a large sloth bear after a prolonged encounter had even gone viral on YouTube.

She was a photographer's delight. Over the years, magazines had carried various prize-winning photographs of her—on a hilltop, looking down on the vast expanse of the forest, swimming across the lake with three cubs and fiercely facing down a bear.

Right now, she remained sitting on the road, licking her paw and casually looking about her, with a constant flicking of her tail.

Lakhan Singh held up his watch to my face and began tapping the surface. We had less than twenty minutes to reach the park exit. I wasn't even sure how far we were from the gate.

We had still not seen her in motion and the jeep could hardly bypass her. A few more minutes ticked by as the driver–guide duo's anxiety began to turn into panic.

Mallika looked too comfortable to allow us a timely exit or any dramatic footage.

Even Jaya wondered how much longer she could film the same pose, the same yawn and the same flicking of the tail.

It was Mallika who finally gave us a way out. In a second her head was up and she had assumed the position of a stalker. This movement happened in a flash, as her eyes or ears caught something in the distance down the road. I could see her ears move, cocking in the direction she was looking. I'd read that tigers could rotate their ears like a radar dish, to catch the slightest of sounds.

She remained frozen like this for a moment.

Then I noticed she made herself as small as that fine feline form could. Jaya had caught it all on film.

The next moment, she moved away, her belly brushing the ground, into the grasses and out of sight. She was gone.

What had she heard? Before I could answer the question in my head, Lakhan Singh made the most of the opportunity and raced down the track.

We had driven scarcely 100 metres when we came across a group of men, proceeding towards us down the track. These were not members of the forest department on patrol but apparently pilgrims on their way to a shrine in the forest that locals referred to as Behraon Ji ka Mandir. That's what Lakhan Singh told us.

I was taken aback. They could have been poachers too, so I started to film them on my mobile phone, the investigative reporter in me hoping to confront the park officials with this intrusion.

Faiz quietly suggested I put my phone away. My question to him on how people could be walking inside a tiger reserve went unanswered as we sped towards the exit gate. He simply shrugged.

I was surprised by what seemed to be a lackadaisical attitude to park management.

Mallika had been disturbed, in the middle of the park, and those men on foot did not realize their folly. Or the possible danger they were facing.

'They could have been killed!' I exclaimed to Faiz, louder than I had intended.

'Madam, Mallika does not eat junk food,' submitted Faiz weakly, in a bid to make light of the matter.

'Our tigers do not prey on humans and know when to move out when they need to,' he rejoined more seriously. 'The forest department discourages pilgrims from coming to the temple, but it's a delicate issue. If they are too forceful, then politics takes over, with the local leaders ready to protest it.'

I mulled over his response but then decided to brush it all aside. What mattered was that we had finally managed a sighting!

We had secured a *darshan* or audience with Mallika after so many hours spent in the jungle. It was deeply satisfying.

Given her legendary status, and the fact that her sightings were becoming more and more rare, a 'darshan' was how many of the park regulars referred to her sighting. A gift that only the blessed received.

Jaya and I had desperately sought this darshan for the last few days, as the feature piece that I had planned centred on her.

We had scoured the park, filming its rich ecosystem, a habitat as endangered as the denizens it protected. Our camera had caught kingfishers diving into deep waters looking for fish, and wild boar shuffling around in their search for nutrition underground. We had recorded the alarm calls of myriad species, from anxious spotted deer to gargantuan sambar. And sometimes we had stopped to simply observe the frolicking of langurs atop the copious jungle canopy.

We had interviewed various locals about the park and the legend of Mallika, as well as the Chambalgarh Forest Ranger on the conservation aspect.

But Mallika had remained elusive. It had been stressful as well because time was running out, and we were on a shoestring budget.

While my channel NNTV, or Nation News Television, gave space to environment and wildlife stories, there was pressure to manage really good reports within the limited resources available.

I had wanted to use the example of Mallika for the report I was doing on the relationship between conservation and tourism. I was trying to show that tourism, if done well, would actually help India's wildlife conservation in the long run.

It was pegged to the claim that Mallika's fame and charisma had brought crores of rupees to the tiger reserve through tourism, which was then pumped back into conservation. People around the country and the world had read about her, seen her pictures and would visit Chambalgarh in the hope of catching a glimpse of her or her progeny.

For many years, Indian wildlife conservation had a tenuous relationship with tourism. Tourism was seen as 'not good for wildlife', and making money off of wildlife was viewed as ignoble or exploitative.

Many wildlife parks had seen resorts mushrooming around them, that caused controversies of their own. Not all followed best practices, and there were extreme cases of even hosting loud parties and weddings right next to the wildlife reserve. Or dumping waste in the forest, and sometimes baiting wild animals, all of it illegal.

In my report I was making a case for the benefits of wildlife tourism, but also ensuring regulations so areas outside the park were not overly exploited.

Over the years, things had already changed for the better. There were more rules for tourism and for the resorts, while money earned from the park was to be used for conservation. It also helped the local economy with a constant demand for food and other supplies as well as employment opportunities.

Another favourable aspect of tourism was that it meant more eyes on the park to check if anything was amiss. It meant constant surveillance.

A recent survey had revealed there were barely any tigers left in two national parks in Bihar and Odisha.

These parks were rarely visited by tourists, as connectivity to them was bad, and there were hardly any resorts near them. Because of this no one had realized the tigers were disappearing, and the recent findings were a shock. There were even allegations of corruption, that some members of the local forest department had allowed poachers a free run.

This is why I was using Mallika's story to emphasize how, if used well, tourism could work for conservation as well as generate income for the area.

I felt elated as we raced out of the park, Lakhan driving as fast as the rules in the park allowed him. I would be able to do my report the way I had planned it.

Besides that, spotting a tiger in the jungle was always a matter of excitement. I looked at Jaya with a grin, and she gave me a thumbs-up.

In my head I was already working out how I could use the shots we had managed of Mallika in my script, how I would play up her crouching action and her quick disappearance into the tall grass.

But then, as we drove out of the park, I decided to pause my mental planning and just enjoy the last drive. The clean, crisp air and the beautiful views and vistas were to be appreciated, not ignored, especially when one craved them back in the city.

We drove from forested plains through a ravine where the temperature suddenly dropped by a few degrees. Massive creepers grew on either side, up the rocky surfaces where there were several small nooks and crannies. There was even a cave that was said to be a favoured birthing spot for leopards.

The jeep climbed up the rocky incline to the grassy plateau and then back down to the lake, which we circled to finally reach the gate.

As expected, we were fifteen minutes late. I accompanied Faiz to the forest guardroom to explain the reason for our delay. Fortunately I had a video of Mallika on my phone, showing her sprawled across the road in front of us.

Their attitude towards us changed the minute we mentioned we had seen her—from brusque and irritable to excited.

'You're lucky you got a darshan. Tourists haven't seen her for many days now,' one of the guards said to me.

I then showed them the footage of how she went into alert mode and then disappeared into the grass, and later of the pilgrims we met on the road.

The guards looked as irritated as I had been.

'Ma'am, we are helpless against these pilgrims who go in from time to time. There is too much local pressure from village groups and their representatives. We stop them when we see them, but they enter from other areas. We've held meetings, and it's come in the local papers as well,' said the senior guard, somewhat exasperated.

'We worry we will be blamed if anything happens to any of them. And it will create problems for the animals,' said another.

Seeing this, I didn't push the matter further, with them at least. They noted Mallika's details in a logbook kept to record tiger sightings in the park, and we were on our way.

'Madam ji, now you'll be able to do your programme like you wanted, won't you?' asked Lakhan Singh cheerily and, if I might add, cheekily.

'Yes, yes, Lakhan, it was just perfect!' I replied, all the earlier irritation now forgotten.

Over the last three days, both Lakhan Singh and Faiz had had a ringside view of our stress and dismay. Being on a shoot like this was exhilarating but also filled with tension.

Back at the forest lodge, Jaya and I indulged in a breakfast of champions! Nothing like the fresh forest air to work up an appetite, and then when you've had a tiger sighting, a big breakfast spread feels even more deserved.

A 'big breakfast' by the lodge standards meant aloo parathas, scrambled eggs and milky coffee. The Tiger-Eye Lodge wasn't exactly the lap of luxury but it was the best the office budget could provide.

In fact, we considered ourselves lucky to have got the budget cleared in the first place, since stories focused on wildlife and conservation weren't exactly what most news channels liked to spend on. That was the reason I loved working at NNTV. It allowed me to do the stories I really cared about, on issues that mattered.

Not to say I was constantly travelling from one wildlife park to another. NNTV was headquartered in Delhi, and that's where I worked and lived.

Day in, day out I put in the hours on my beat, covering regular city-related stories, like sanitation, health, pollution and education, and whatever else my editor would suggest.

Some days it meant standing for hours doing live reports about potholes or protests, student exams or water shortages but then, every once in a while, a plum assignment like this came along. Not that my city stories weren't rewarding and important, but my absolute passion was wildlife.

I had loved animals and wildlife since I was a child. As I grew older, I started reading books and articles related to wildlife—from Jim Corbett and Kenneth Anderson's tales of man-eaters and Indian forests to Gerald Durrell's hilarious adventures while starting a zoo to Salim Ali's account of how he went from killing a sparrow as a ten-year-old to a lifetime of passionately documenting the birds of India.

Growing up, I visited several wildlife parks on family holidays and school excursions, which only nurtured my interest further.

It was the reason I joined television news, to cover issues related to wildlife and environment. I hoped to make wildlife documentaries some day, but for now I was happy being a reporter and learning as much as I could.

The owner of Tiger-Eye Lodge came over to chat with us. An elderly man who had lived near Chambalgarh his whole life, he had become interested in our shoot and would speak to us daily about our safaris. He knew all about the stress and worry we had been experiencing over the last few days.

'I believe you finally saw her,' Suraj Lal said, sitting down at our table.

'We did! After all the effort we put in, on the last day, during the last hour of our safari, she appeared!' I replied excitedly. I showed him the footage I'd taken on my phone.

'She's looking well,' he said after a moment, putting on his glasses and studying the footage closely. 'Haven't seen recent pictures of her for a while now. She was displaced from her territory by one of her daughters, Laila. She's as fierce as her mother, so Mallika dare not venture near her. The forest department keeps a keen eye on Mallika though, even slipping her a goat now and then, when she's gone too many days without hunting.' We nodded as he had told us this story before.

'We were just discussing that earlier today,' Jaya said. 'The pros and cons of tiger feeding.'

'They'll never admit it on record of course, and especially not to you, the media,' he chuckled. 'But we have these regular visitors to the park who sponsor the goat for Mallika. They consider it an offering.'

'It's quite amazing to hear about the kind of legendary status she enjoys,' I said. 'It's not something everyone can understand, and I've heard some even question the special treatment she gets.'

'Well, there are all types. Mallika is a special being, a *shakthi*, and you are lucky to have seen her! Good things will come to you!' he said with a twinkle in his eye. Now that was certainly interesting given my superstition about 'signs from the universe' earlier in the day.

'All the best for your journey home,' he said as he got up to check on his other guests.

'I certainly hope he's right, about the luck part,' said Jaya, watching him walk across and greet another table.

I decided not to say anything further and let Jaya think things out by herself.

After breakfast, we went back to our room. I skimmed through the footage we'd managed to record over the last few days, and then made notes and transcribed some of the interviews we'd filmed. This would help me write the script quickly and begin the edit as soon as we were back in office.

We were booked on the afternoon train back to Delhi, and I was hoping to complete the edit by the end of the week.

I had to stop after about two hours of note-making and footage-viewing, otherwise we'd miss our train. Jaya packed up the equipment while I threw my things into my duffel. Check out took another fifteen minutes and we were on our way.

Away from the park, Samast Nagar, the closest township, was your typical small mofussil Indian town. It got loads of foreign tourists every year, but they arrived at the railway station or drove in from Jaipur and were quickly tucked into a luxury resort or hotel near the park, away from the town.

They weren't required to engage much with the town at all and vice versa. I had always felt the authorities could have made more of an effort to make the town more inviting, more tourist-friendly. It just required a little bit of planning, imagination and, most importantly, willingness, which, sadly, was lacking.

The town railway station, however, was very pretty. It was typically small-town, but they had painted lovely forest scenes and tiger murals on the walls.

'I wish they would make more of an effort with the town like they do with the railway station, don't you think?' I said to Jaya after we were finally seated in the train.

'Hmmm,' she nodded absent-mindedly, looking out the window.

'I just mean they could easily have a crafts bazaar or a street with nice local eateries, make the town more inviting so tourists would spend some of their money here as well,' I droned on. I realized I wasn't getting a response from Jaya.

'What's up? Tired?' I asked, as I scrolled through office mail on my phone.

'No. Actually, I was thinking about the issue we were discussing before Mallika appeared.'

Oh, about her 'arranged marriage'. I put away the phone.

I had decided not to push it any more than I already had, so I'd deliberately steered clear of any mention of it since the morning. After a point, being well meaning could slide into being obnoxious, and then strain a relationship.

I waited for her to talk.

'You were right. As much as I try to imagine a good scenario emerging from meeting this guy, this Mr Railway Engineer, it's not going to work for me. I didn't study mass communication and work all these years in a news organization to just get married and leave it all. I always thought I'd have my own production house one day or work in the movies, and I can't give that up. It's just the burden of expectations that's so difficult to ignore. The guilt.'

I could understand that. It happens so often in families, where the parents somehow live their lives through their children and the choices they make. It creates unfair pressure and obstacles on just living your best life!

'You know, I get it. The expectations of your family, of your parents, are not an easy thing to ignore. But I'm glad you realize you have to look out for yourself as well.'

'Oh well, may as well bite the bullet when I see them next week. I also have the example of a cousin who was similarly pressured to marry two years ago. It ended in tears. I can always bring up that cautionary tale. The tribe will survive without my sacrifice,' she smiled at me. I smiled back and gave her hand a squeeze. I didn't want to say anything to make her feel worse. It would pass.

She looked out of the window for a while.

I was relieved that she was thinking clearly. I had been seriously worried she was going to give it all up, just like that.

'In fact, we probably saw Mallika today thanks to my special prayers. I offered prayers to one of our forest *bonga*s as we entered the park. It's one of our deities. After all, we worship trees and sacred groves, and after my prayer, I just felt we would have a sighting,' Jaya said, after we had been sitting in contemplative silence for a few minutes.

'Well, thank your bonga on my behalf. What a relief we had such a great sighting!'

I sat back and looked out of the window. I was relieved Jaya had sorted out things for herself. It was a tricky situation, no doubt.

Thankfully, I wasn't facing any such pressure from home. Not overtly anyway. The odd mention here and there, which was unavoidable for single Indian women over twenty-five. Luckily, my elder sister, a go-getter investment banker, was happily married in London and had one child. That helped keep the pressure off me, as my parents were obsessed with their grandson and had a busy social life of their own. I was free to explore my passion for news journalism and wildlife. If anything, it was Didi who put constant pressure on me about marriage, about 'finding the right guy', etcetera, etcetera, but she I could handle.

2

A few months later, I was at my desk in the office, figuring out how to make a story on an NGO helping to provide drinking water to an urban slum sound riveting. I had filmed it and was happy with the shoot. The interviews were great, I had several heartfelt sound bites of the slum residents, and now I just had to script it in an interesting way. That was the challenging aspect of reporting such issues. There were so many problems that needed highlighting and many organizations were doing great work. But these stories weren't sexy—they weren't what people wanted to see. Even within the office I had to lobby for certain stories that I felt were really needed, the ones that deserved to be highlighted and, if given that coverage, could make a difference, but didn't really get much interest from my editors. There had to be a hook, one interesting family or a child or a woman, to tell their story and reel in the interest.

Just then I got a call from Leena, the Big Boss's assistant, that I had been summoned for a meeting in his office. That was surprising.

I wasn't very high in the pecking order, as far as hierarchy on the news desk went. But still, I was a senior reporter and happy with that for now.

So I wondered why I was suddenly being called into the Big Boss's room. Not that I hadn't been there before for meetings but usually with some notice and along with other colleagues.

Entering the office, the first person I spotted was Reena Talwar, our entertainment editor. I felt a little surprised on seeing her. We usually didn't attend the same meetings given our beats were at opposite ends of the spectrum. Then there was Lata Menon, the chief news editor, and the Big Boss.

'Aah, yes, yes, come in, Sunaina,' said Boss affably. 'We have an exciting proposal for you.'

I glanced at the fourth person in the room and saw it was Daleep Varma, a well-known PR personality and one of those typical Delhi types one hears of, who knows everyone who matters and can get things done. A squat, rotund man, with a booming voice, he was also something of a TV talking head, which meant he could talk on just about anything. His parties were sometimes featured in newspaper supplements, and magazines, compounding him as a 'SOMEONE'. He was basically famous for knowing famous people. A very Delhi thing.

When I had settled into one of the chairs in the room, suitably intrigued, Big Boss began.

'Sunaina, this is Daleep. He's brought us an interesting proposal that I'm sure you'll like because it involves staying and filming at a tiger park for a long duration. And that's what you're always trying to do anyway, isn't it? Escape to the forests?' he said with a smile.

I grinned back. I couldn't help it, although I felt a little self-conscious as the whole room was looking at me. But a proposal to film in a tiger park for a long duration? I was hooked!

'Daleep, why don't you explain?' said Lata.

'All right then,' said Daleep, sitting up straighter in his chair. 'Well, Sunaina, I'm sure you know of the actor Vikram Khanna?'

It was a rhetorical question because, of course, I knew who Vikram Khanna was. You'd have to be living under a rock not to.

He was a star kid. He'd been in a few movies, and two or three had even done well. Both his mother and father were big stars back in the 1980s and 1990s, and he was on track to possibly surpass them. But there had been some scandal surrounding him recently. I couldn't quite remember the specifics. I think it had been something to do with drugs.

'He's very keen to do something with your channel, a campaign to promote tiger conservation. You know the numbers are dwindling, and since it's our national animal, he wants to help create awareness. To this end, he's willing to go to a tiger park to film, talk about the issues involved and all that. I think it'll be great! What better than a superstar getting involved with such a good cause? Am I right? So that's what it is, in a nutshell. Now we need to plan it out.'

Wow. This sounded great! I had sent a proposal for a tiger conservation campaign a year ago. I'd been told if a sponsor showed interest, then maybe it would happen. A little later I'd asked one of the sales team people about it but had not got much of a response and had left it at that. So this was very exciting!

But then Daleep went on to describe what he imagined the coverage would be like.

'We can plan something big,' he said, leaning towards me and gesticulating with his hands.

'He can take a safari. You can film him looking at the tigers, you know, maybe one of them snarls even, it becomes a tense situation, maybe the forest guards step in. They might even need to point a rifle at the tiger, to emphasize the danger.' Daleep stood up as he described this imagined encounter between the actor and a tiger, pointing an imaginary gun.

'We can show Vikram talking about tigers and conservation with a tiger sitting in the background. He talks about tigers, talks about the country. India *ki shaan*, tiger. Or tiger tiger, let's keep it burning bright, you know, that kind of thing.' Now he was nodding excitedly at his own proposal, becoming more animated.

'Maybe we can do a concert around the campfire in the evening. I know some bands that can fly in for that. But it has to be amazing, something that grabs the eyeballs. Even gets him some international attention, you know what I mean? Everyone loves how Leonardo cares for the environment and climate change and all that, am I right? It did wonders for Leo, really increased his stature around the world.'

I didn't quite know how to respond to all that he'd just said. While the campaign sounded great, a concert next to the park was out of the question. And we definitely couldn't create drama while in the park for the wildlife campaign. Forest guards pointing rifles at a tiger? That was ridiculous. I looked around at everyone else in the room.

My face must have looked as incredulous as I felt because Boss decided to jump in.

'Look, Daleep. Leave the details to the experts on what to do and how to do it. They'll make a plan about what's possible and what's not. I know from Sunaina there are many restrictions around the tiger reserve, and we'll obviously have to play it by the rules. There can't be any negative publicity. But having said that, it's great to know a young film star is interested in promoting conservation and becoming an ambassador for tigers, isn't it, Sunaina?' he looked at me pointedly.

Collecting myself, I nodded. 'It's really commendable, and I'm sure it would bring a lot of attention to the issue. What are the timelines we're looking at?'

'Well, Vikram is in between films for three weeks from 1 October onwards, so that's the period we were looking at. We think Chambalgarh National Park would be perfect as tiger sightings there are said to be the easiest. Also, I have many contacts in the state government, so it would be easy to get permissions. Though any state government would be happy to host a shoot like this, am I right? After all, it would be a big draw, wouldn't it? It would make the park even more famous. Once the planning is done from the office, your team should get there as soon as possible to recce and figure out the shoot schedule.'

October. That was a good time in the park, which opened mid-September, after being shut for the monsoon. Jaya and I had been there for a shoot in June, just before it closed.

I saw Reena was nodding in agreement with Daleep.

'That's great. October in the park is a wonderful time. We'll start planning the details immediately,' I said.

'Reena will be handling all the online content around the shoot because we want it to be across platforms, you know, to build it up and create a big buzz,' said Lata. 'You'll be taking lots of pictures and videos during the filming, which can be shared across Twitter, Instagram and YouTube. We need to think of a catchy hashtag for the campaign.'

Ugh. I hated this part of any campaign. The social media aspect. There was so much pressure to make a big splash online, but I always felt it was very tricky and created some amount of stress. Though these days you couldn't do without it. Hopefully, with a big star, it would just happen organically.

We discussed a few more aspects of the campaign. Daleep already had a corporate sponsor who was ready to spend big on the campaign. Those details needed to be worked out, but that would be over email and handled by the marketing team.

'All right then,' said Daleep after half an hour, 'I'll leave you to it. Send me the shoot plan in a day or two and I'll send you back inputs. Remember, we've got to make this big! It's got to get everyone talking!'

With that, Big Boss got up to see Daleep off, as he always did with all visitors.

The minute they left the room I turned to Reena and Lata. 'Wow, this is quite something! I'm excited! But I'm sensing there's a backstory? How is a Bollywood star suddenly all set to slum it on a wildlife shoot and dedicate so much time to conservation and tigers?'

'It's so obvious, *yaar*,' said Reena, looking at me with a touch of disdain. 'He's trying to go for an image change after that drug scandal last year. It's so clear. Do you know how many clients he lost because of that? Besides tainting the Khanna name.'

Now I remembered. There was some major scandal over a year ago, something to do with a drug peddler and WhatsApp messages. I was in London at the time, visiting my sister, so I didn't follow it too closely. I thought it was a storm in a teacup that would blow over soon and didn't bother with the details.

'What was it exactly? I know there were some messages from him asking for drugs, right? I was on leave during that time, and didn't follow all the details.'

'Yes! But I always thought calling it a "DRUGS SCANDAL" was misleading. It was just weed. Or hash? Basically not hard drugs. There was this photographer who was also a dealer who got caught by the cops in Delhi in a sting operation. Small-time thing, except on his phone they found a chat involving the Maharashtra health minister's son. So someone in the government decided to go after him to embarrass the opposition party. It became biggish political news, but then during the investigation it emerged there was another WhatsApp chat on the phone from two years ago, involving Vikram Khanna and Zeba Khan. Zeba had asked *"maal hain?"* in the chat, which probe agencies immediately leaked to the media. Next thing you know, they were summoned for questioning. So that added a sexy, glamorous angle to the whole scandal and it just blew up.'

Yikes! I was glad I wasn't there during this time. Sometimes the kind of issues that become top news are so appalling, makes one despair about the profession.

As if she read my thoughts, Reena continued, 'Ugh, it was so ugly the way some of our fellow news channels went after them, almost like they had an agenda. Especially News Today and India Now. Obviously we didn't do any of that, though we did cover their questioning. But in a measured way.'

Zeba Khan was an upcoming actress with two hit films to her name. Suddenly I recalled Didi closely following the scandal in London because of the Bollywood connection, not so much for the politics.

'Now I remember. There was a car chase by the media when they had to come in for questioning. Reporters followed Vikram Khanna from the airport to the office. It was embarrassing. I was in London at the time and my brother-in-law had asked about it, whether this was a common feature, mainstream media acting like paparazzi. Are Zeba and he seeing each other?'

'Well, it's not public, whatever it is. You know these Bollywood types.' She arched her eyebrows. I clearly didn't know but it was a rhetorical question.

'Nothing even came of the drugs case. It also emerged that the peddler dealt in marijuana and hash. Nothing hard,' she continued. 'The whole thing just died down eventually. Lasted a few news cycles but was damaging enough, as you can imagine. They both lost endorsements.'

'But aren't drugs quite common in Bollywood? And weed is consumed all over the country. It's even legal in so many countries now. Why is it such a big deal that he lost endorsements over it?' I asked, genuinely puzzled.

'Arré! Don't be ridiculous!' Reena snapped. 'Even if everyone's doing it, you can't get caught like this. Also, they were really vilified by the media as well as on social media. "Entitled brats", "products of nepotism" doing drugs, setting a bad example for young people and all that. No brand wants to be associated with so much negativity. At least not for a while. He lost a Bournvita deal, a government "girl child" campaign, and who knows what else. Anyway, now he's clearly trying to resurrect his image with an environmental campaign involving tigers. Who doesn't love the national animal? Trust Daleep to come up with such a brilliant strategy,' Reena said, half scoffing, half in awe of Daleep's PR prowess.

'Though I don't think it's very nice, is it? He's jumping on the "Save Our Tigers" bandwagon to salvage his reputation! Who knows if he really cares about the issue? He just wants to be a desi DiCaprio, but without the commitment.' I was now feeling a little irritated thinking about it.

Lata, who had been quietly listening to us jabbering on, now spoke up.

'Listen to me, Sunaina. How many proposals have you sent us for wildlife and conservation reports over the last few years? At least a dozen? How many have been cleared by us? So far three, which involved travel, otherwise through stringer footage, isn't it? So why are you complaining? This is an opportunity that's fallen into your lap, thanks to this superstar. Daleep has already got a sponsor for the shoot, so I'd recommend you get to work and be grateful.'

When she put it like that, it made total sense. Why look a gift horse in the mouth? What was I even complaining about? I should be grateful for the drug-scandal-hit movie star who wants to resurrect his image with a tiger campaign.

Looking at her phone, Lata said, 'Okay, Boss and I have another meeting, so go on, you two, and come up with a brilliant plan for the shoot.'

Reena and I left the office and headed for the newsroom. We found an empty desk and I sat down, logging on to the computer so we could plan the shoot.

'Obviously you'll have to plan the shoots since I know jack all about safaris, tigers and whatnot. I'll handle all the social media stuff and some interviews post safaris, around the campfire,' said Reena while typing furiously on her phone as she leaned against the desk.

I opened my office mail account and started listing ideas in a mail to her and Lata.

'We can plan a few half-hour shows out of this. One about the history of tiger conservation in the country, then one, like a travelogue, about a safari. We can do another one with the forest department. Maybe get

Vikram Khanna to film with the guards on patrol, etc. That's if he's willing,' I said.

Then I stopped and looked at Reena. 'We'll need a whole team. That's another aspect we'll have to look in to.'

'Hmm, a whole production team, and I'll need to get a few people to help with social media. I'll take someone from the website also. How are you with social media?' she asked.

How was I with social media? Now that was a long and unhappy story.

I had joined Facebook a while ago though I wasn't big on updates like the rest of my friends. But after college, I split with my boyfriend at the time (as one often does after college is over). He, not so shockingly, turned out to be a bit of a psycho. Something I'd sensed during our relationship, given how controlling he was, and this had led to the aforementioned break-up.

But then he started stalking me on Facebook, sending nasty messages to my friends, and that drove me pretty much off the platform. I made my account super private and only kept a handful of friends and relatives on it. I also had to explain the embarrassing situation to each of the friends he had contacted and make them block him. It was mortifying.

I had joined Twitter in college to follow the news. And then when I joined NNTV, I used it to amplify the stories and issues I was reporting on. But then, a year ago, I was reporting on the displacement of slum dwellers to make way for a government project. The way it was done was absolutely brutal, with dozens of families left homeless overnight, their houses destroyed. I tweeted my story and my opinion.

Later I realized that someone in charge must have been very sensitive to the online criticism, because suddenly I found myself being trolled. It didn't help matters that I got into an online scrap with a well-known journalist from another channel that supported the government move. He tweeted about how it was left-leaning people and *jhola-wala* journalists (implying me) who held India back from seeking its full potential by constantly blocking development. I was relentlessly trolled and it drove me off that platform as well. I made my account private for a while and tweeted only now and then.

I had an Instagram account for fun stuff, but hardly posted on it. It was more to look at exotic places, and animal and food pictures.

But I wasn't going to tell Reena all this, so I simply said, 'I'm afraid I'm not very good at social media. I can try and help, though I'm not very active.'

'In this day and age?' she looked up from her phone with a surprised expression. 'You're a journalist with NNTV and you're good-looking. Why would you not be active on social media?'

A compliment from Reena? I was flattered. I knew, when it came to looks, I wasn't at the back of the bus, but I didn't consider myself a stunner either. Maybe growing up in the shadow of a more vivacious, pretty older sister, as well as having been more of a bookworm in an all-girls' school, had led to my humble opinion.

I became more aware of my looks in college, since I got quite a lot of attention from the opposite sex. In my first year of college, my friends taught me how to groom myself better, how to apply make-up and cut my long hair into a trendier shoulder-length style.

Even my family noticed the difference when I went back for the holidays that year. My mother and various aunts showered praise and remarks like, 'How much you've grown up!' 'How pretty you're looking.' That made me realize I must have looked really drab earlier.

When Didi saw me, she said, 'Finally! You didn't listen to me all these years but I'm glad you're wising up now. No harm in looking your best.' That felt secretly good even if I acted nonchalant.

Responding to Reena's compliment, I said, 'Thanks! Well, I am on all the platforms. I just don't use them as much. Maybe it's time for me to finally get active, especially since we're doing a high-profile campaign.'

Reena just shook her head, looking at me with a pitying expression.

But not one to waste time, she quickly moved on to the other issue at hand.

'We'll have to decide on a team ASAP and call a meeting. I'm going to ask for Debajyoti to be assigned as the producer. He's very good. I'll speak to Shweta and see who else she can suggest for a project like this. I want young, energetic producers. I'm sensing the shoot will require a lot of running around. We should aim at sending in the shoot plan by Friday so Daleep can go through it.'

Shweta Chaudhury was the head of production. She would decide and delegate our team. I'd worked with Debajyoti Roy, a senior producer. He was quite competent, experienced and had great ideas, so it would be good to get him.

We talked a bit more and then Reena went off to her room.

Clearly working with Reena was going to be a little challenging, but if she stuck to her areas of interest and expertise and I to mine, I was sure we would manage smoothly enough.

I went to the camera section to look for Jaya.

'Guess what?' I said, when I found her sitting on the couch playing games on her phone.

'We're going back to the jungle!'

3

And so it was, a few months later, after many meetings, discussions and a whole lot of coordination, that our team found itself on the railway platform of the Nizamuddin station at 7 a.m. I still hadn't actually spoken to Vikram Khanna but had had many interactions via video conference with his team. He was in Ladakh on a shoot, we were told.

His personal management team was led by a no-nonsense, impressive woman named Natasha. A total boss lady.

At the start of our interaction, she and I were on completely different wavelengths, given that she managed a film star, and her life consisted of all things Bollywood and glamour. I, on the other hand, was an environment and city reporter, and my life was a lot more practical and mundane. It was Reena who helped smooth over the rough bits during our interactions. Our priorities were different since my focus was more on the reportage and highlighting environmental issues and hers was on showcasing her star.

I had given ideas about the various shows we could do. A half hour based on the national park and tiger conservation, another one based on 'a day in the life of a forest guard', where Vikram would showcase what went into protecting the national park and another involving a safari 'competition', which still had to be fleshed out.

During one of our video conferences to discuss the programming, Natasha had actually asked if Vikram could fire a gun.

'Absolutely not!' I had said, aghast at the suggestion.

I then explained how India's forest guards don't usually have weapons, unless they're in Kaziranga in Assam, and even if they did, there's no way a visitor could use the gun.

Though, after the initial shock of her suggestion, I did admit that they would have a tranquillizer gun and perhaps he could shoot the dart into a tree. That was something we could possibly explore.

Another time, she had wanted to know if we could do a sequence by the lake and have Vikram actually take a dip. I had to explain that nobody was allowed to get out of the jeep in the tiger reserve, and also there were crocodiles in the lake.

I had helpfully suggested that the resort we had finalized did have a pool, so we could 'show off his body there'.

Reena had glared at me when I'd said those actual words during the video call, but fortunately Natasha didn't seem to notice the sarcasm and instead thought it was a good idea.

Then there were discussions about clothes.

Again, the Mumbai crew was clueless about safari clothing etiquette. I had to tell them absolutely no reds, yellows and bright blues. ('But those are his best colours!' they had complained.) They weren't too happy when I first told them clothes would have to be olive, khaki, brown and cream.

'So dull,' one of the stylists said in disgust.

So we sent them a whole bunch of 'safari glamour' pictures and that perked them up.

'Never heard of it,' said the same girl, Safar, when I first suggested a look based on *Out of Africa*. Reena gave me a 'don't react' look, so I controlled myself.

I suggested they looked at brands like Barbour, Rufiji, Jeep, Patagonia and Columbia for the outdoors look. Some of those brands were available only internationally, but I was sure they had the resources to get them.

After seeing all the possibilities, the stylists were now totally excited about Vikram's 'safari glam look', and had sourced a perfect wardrobe for the star. They had created a Harrison Ford as Indiana Jones meets Robert Redford from *Out of Africa* look.

When it came to the issue of where to stay, some big-name hotels were discussed.

However, I had pushed for Baagh Baadi, a smaller property I had been dying to stay at but of course could never afford. It was an old hunting lodge or *shikargah* that belonged to one of the erstwhile 'royal' families of the area.

It was right next to the park and reputed to have the best safari jeeps, drivers and guides. The 'shikargah', meaning the main house, had eight luxury suites, and there were also ten luxury tents on the property. So it was big enough for our team and small enough that there wouldn't be any other guests. I had heard it was so close to the park that animals, including tigers, occasionally crossed the property.

But it was a whole other task to convince the Baagh Baadi management to block the property for our stay, as they had other bookings.

Debajyoti had to have several discussions with their management and even go there for a visit, but when we said we would take all the rooms and most of the tents, they agreed to shift their guests to other properties. Also the fact that they would be hosting a Bollywood star, as well as get location credit on the show when it aired, helped confirm our booking and bring down the rates.

'*Uff*, remind me again why we have to take the train and can't fly?' asked Reena, looking around the platform irritably through her oversized sunglasses. She looked almost comical and totally out of place standing on the grey and slightly dirty railway platform in her tight white jeans, floral shirt, tan-coloured wedges and Louis Vuitton tote. Her hair fell in soft waves around her face. With her high cheekbones and immaculate make-up, she looked more ready for brunch than a train journey.

'Because we would have had to do two to three hours by car anyway, and we have so much equipment. Easier to do a five-and-a-half-hour journey by train and get there directly,' I replied patiently.

Of course this had all been discussed earlier, but Reena was clearly a complainer. Also, it was evident we were used to very different kinds of shoots.

Reena usually met actors in five-star settings or in studios. She would go on movie junkets and fly everywhere. This shoot, the kind I was used to, was very downmarket for her. At least the travel part of it.

The train pulled up shortly and we piled in, equipment and all. The producers, camera people and assistants all scrambled to get in all the equipment and place it securely in the train.

The hours went by quickly as we discussed the shoot, speculated on how much of a problem the Mumbai team and the star were going to create and hoped for the best tiger sightings.

The start of a shoot was always fun, full of excitement, and this one was bound to be even more so since it was such a big project.

The news team consisted of Jaya and Danish Kidwai for camera with their assistants, Reena and I were the reporters, and Debajyoti Roy was the producer of the shoot, with a team of four production assistants. And then there was Manju Yadav from the online team for social media, which Reena would also help with. And two engineers to assist in the uplinking and managing equipment.

It was a good team. Jaya and Danish had studied camera and film at the same mass communication college in Delhi, so they had a great rapport. Danish was tall and lanky, with slightly longish dark brown hair. He was pleasant-looking and had a great sense of humour. Jaya had told me how they had become friends after sitting together in their first class, and he had later helped her settle in. In the initial days she had felt overwhelmed, coming from a smaller town like Patna. He was an out-and-out Delhi boy, with his family home in Old Delhi.

We had all worked with Debajyoti or Debu, as he was known. Debu was more compact, bearded, bespectacled and intense. Also, as one of the most senior producers at the channel, he had extensive experience in outdoor shoots.

Manju had been in the organization for over a year now. I didn't know her too well as she belonged to the web team, and we hadn't had an opportunity to interact with each other. She was in her early twenties, dusky, pretty with pink highlights in her shoulder-length hair and a nose ring.

We finally pulled up at the station a few hours later. There was much commotion as we got off the train, with frantic checking to make sure we got all the equipment before the train took off again.

There was a junior manager from Baagh Baadi on the platform to pick us up. Porters were hired and all our luggage was piled into the open jeeps and other vehicles that had come from the resort.

Again, it was a big effort to make sure everything was safely shifted to the vehicles. Poor Debajyoti was running up and down, counting and recounting the equipment that was being loaded into the vehicles. The assistants were also checking lists and tallying everything.

'Please take responsibility for your personal luggage!' he yelled at everyone.

'Debu, please take a chill pill,' said Danish as he lugged his camera and tripod to one of the jeeps. 'This hectic vibe is not good for anyone.'

Fifteen minutes later, we finally left the station, luggage, equipment, people and all!

It was another half-hour drive to the resort, in the open jeeps, with the wind in our hair.

'Why do we have to travel in an open jeep!' Reena complained from the front seat, as she tried to control her flying hair.

Jaya and I suppressed our giggles. She didn't know that we were only going to travel in open jeeps for the next few days. Also, the two closed cars and SUV that had come to receive us were stuffed with the equipment and luggage.

It was around 2 p.m. when we arrived at the resort, and we were all starving.

We first passed through massive gates at the entrance of the property. It was almost like a fort entrance, made of stone with big wooden doors that were studded with metal. It made you feel like you were entering another era.

From the gate, it was a short drive on a gravelly road surrounded by trees and bushes to the main building. I finally had a chance to look at it up close. It was even more stunning than the pictures. It was an eclectic construct that was part lodge, part palace. Some sections had clearly undergone renovation and were more modern than the stone-and-mortar ones that were from an earlier age.

Baagh Baadi was less opulent than palaces found in the towns, more practical.

'Baadi' referred to a house with a courtyard or a big central, open space. I had read in an article it was given the name by a family member from Cooch Behar.

It was a two-storey structure, with arched windows and large pillars. The original sandstone structure and facade had been maintained. Facing us was the outer courtyard with a short flight of stairs that led to a large veranda. I could see a ramp at one end of the stairs, probably to help with the luggage or a guest in a wheelchair.

A big wooden door led us into the building and into the inner courtyard. There were large comfy chairs on the veranda, potted plants and a huge hanging three-seater swing.

There was also beautiful foliage around the building, old trees, some flowering plants and an old peepal tree on the left side. I could see a dash of vermillion on its trunk and red threads tied around it.

In front of the building was a little pond with an ornate stone fountain.

Debajyoti walked into the lobby area to check us in. Reena plonked herself on a comfy chair on the veranda and started scrolling through her phone, while Manju started clicking pictures of the property as the others milled around. The production assistants supervised unloading the equipment. Some staff from Baagh Baadi greeted us with glasses of chilled juice and khus.

Jaya and I decided to take a look around the property as we waited for Debajyoti to wrap up.

This would be our home for the next few days, and I was very excited to see it all. There were various paths from the main lodge leading to different locations. One sign said 'pool', the other said 'tents' and then another said 'machan'. We decided to head to the machan to check it out. It was in the direction of the national park, so we wanted to see if it would make a good location for a shoot.

We walked down the dirt path that was marked in the direction of the machan. There was tall grass on either side. There were sit-outs with benches and tables at intervals. One was on an elevated mound under a copse of dhak trees that provided a very picturesque view. The dhak trees, very typical in Rajasthan, were perfectly adapted for the arid climate. Their vibrant orange-red flowers added a dash of colour to the landscape and also gave them their English name, flame of the forest.

As we walked, we took in the natural beauty of the area—the tall grass, the trees and the occasional glimpse of the grassland ahead. The silence was only broken by the sound of our steps and the occasional chirping of birds.

On arriving at the machan, we realized someone was already on top with a camera and tripod, taking pictures of the grassland that lay ahead of it. The panoramic view it offered must have been stunning. The tall grass and shrubs stretched out before us, and, in the distance, the forest began, with the hills beyond that. The sun was shining, casting a warm glow over the entire landscape. The sky was a brilliant blue, with only a few wispy clouds dotting it, adding a touch of softness to the clear, bright day. The air was warm, but not uncomfortably so, and a gentle breeze blew, rustling the grass and leaves of the trees.

We decided not to disturb the person and come back later. Just as we were leaving, we saw a majestic sambar emerge from the trees.

The sambar is one of Asia's largest deer species and this fellow was one of the tallest I'd seen. He had huge antlers, and, after standing still for a moment, he began crossing the grass.

It was a beautiful sight as he gracefully walked through the tall grass. His large, sturdy antlers seemed to tower above, glinting in the sunlight. His coat was a rich dark brown that somewhat blended into the natural surroundings.

As he moved, he held his head high and ears perked up, taking in the surroundings with a watchful eye.

We could hear whoever was on the machan steadily clicking away.

But just then came sounds of someone approaching noisily behind us and a squeal of, 'Ooh look! Wow!'

Unfortunately the shrill voice carried and the sambar heard it too. He reacted with a start and made a quick dash back to the forest, leaving a cloud of dust.

We swung around to see a very excited Manju, clicking pictures with her phone, totally oblivious of what she had done, and, at the same time, we heard loud, angry exclamations from the machan.

Two feet appeared on top of the wooden steps and then long, khaki-clad legs, and finally down came a very angry-looking man, holding his camera in his hand.

'What was that?' he asked angrily. 'Why would you do that? You frightened the animal away!' he glared at all of us, since he obviously didn't know who was responsible.

Manju let out an 'I'm sorry, I didn't realize . . .', which trailed off weakly.

'Do you people not know how to behave in a forest camp?' he asked with a scowl.

He was tall with a stubble and dark tousled hair, dressed in well-worn khakis and an olive shirt. He looked like someone who spent more time in the jungle than the city.

'Do not make noise when you see an animal, and at least have consideration for those of us who spend hours waiting for a good shot. Have you not been briefed by the management?' he asked, glaring at us.

We were all initially a little gobsmacked. While I knew what Manju had done was really inconsiderate, he had no business being so rude to us. I felt myself getting angry.

'Look here, we're sorry, it wasn't done deliberately,' I said, bristling at his tone.

Manju continued to look stunned at the telling-off.

'We've just arrived and are waiting to get checked in. It was a mistake. I'm sure you'll get another chance,' I said, gesturing to Manju and Jaya to start walking back to the main building.

'Oh really? Thanks for that. Yes, maybe if I wait another two hours and I'm lucky, I will. Anyway, please go to the main lodge and get a proper briefing before wandering around,' he said gruffly, then abruptly turned around and went back up the machan.

We quietly trudged back.

'Sheesh!' said Manju, finally finding her tongue. 'Thanks for standing up for me. That was really uncalled for!'

Now I glared at her as Jaya spoke first, 'Look, Manju, he was right, you know. Even I would have yelled at someone who disturbed a shot like that. There's a certain etiquette in the wild, and since this place is right next to the forest, I guess it applies here too. Just please don't yell every time you see an animal, especially when we're on safari.'

'Okay, sorry,' said Manju, looking a little shamefaced. 'I just got so excited. It was my first time seeing a deer like that.'

'It was a sambar, a majestic fellow,' I said as we reached the main building. 'It was an honest mistake, irritating I admit, but even then, that guy was really rude and obnoxious!'

Debajyoti was standing at the top of the stairs, on the veranda. 'Come on guys, they're waiting for all of us so they can give us a briefing. It's really important they said before you go around the property.'

'Yes, we know,' I said with an eye roll as we walked in.

We were briefed by Tarun Shekhawat, the manager of Baagh Baadi. He was a sharp-looking young man with a well-groomed moustache. He greeted us with a smile and firm handshake. He was dressed in a brown coat and khaki-coloured jodhpurs and had quite a friendly demeanour.

Not everyone could carry off jodhpur pants, tight-fitting on the calves, flared around the thighs and hips. It's said they were inspired by the more traditional churidar and created by a Jodhpur royal, Pratap Singh, who was fond of playing polo. It made riding horses more comfortable, and he even wore them during Queen

Victoria's diamond jubilee, thereby introducing them to British society.

Tarun Shekhawat could have been a brand ambassador for jodhpurs, he looked so elegant in them.

As soon as we were all gathered, he began to brief us on the property. He started with the history of the park, how it was established in 1978, how eight villages had to be moved out of the core parts of the forest to leave it undisturbed for the animals. No easy task but it was accomplished by the forest department, which was led by passionate officers at the time.

He said the resort abutted the park, as the land was in the possession of the family who had owned it before it became a national park. A sizeable part of their land too became part of the park.

Because of its proximity to the forest, animals often walked through the grounds, and we were to be careful, not make noise or disturb them in any way.

Also, we weren't to wander around the grounds after dark by ourselves, always in twos and threes or with one of the staff members. Torches were available in all the rooms and tents.

'Should we complain about that rude guest?' Manju whispered to me.

'Just forget it, let's get settled into our tents,' I replied, not wanting to make more of an episode out of it.

The Mumbai crew arrived a day later and we wanted to have a schedule in place.

Debajyoti asked a few more questions about filming on the property and the safari schedules, which Tarun answered patiently.

Then, turning to all of us, he said, 'Mr Roy I will answer all your questions, but for now you and your team must have lunch. I'm sure you all are very hungry.' He smiled at everyone.

'Thank you!' said Danish immediately, with folded hands. 'Debu, please let us eat, I'm famished!'

Everyone laughed and there were murmurs of agreement.

Tarun led us to the courtyard inside the lodge where lunch had been laid out.

It was picturesque with pretty tiled flooring and large potted plants and trees. Tables with chairs were scattered around, while to one side there was a long table for serving food.

There was another fountain at the centre of the courtyard, similar to the one in front of the lodge, just a little smaller.

Lunch consisted of salads, a choice of pasta or risotto and a variety of breads which were clearly baked there. Dessert was vanilla panna cotta and strawberry coulis, and carrot cake. It was absolutely yummy, fresh and delicious. A perfect light lunch for the day.

After the meal we settled into our rooms or, rather, tents since that's where the production team was staying. Jaya and I had been assigned one of the tents at one end of the property, making it a ten-minute walk from the main building.

But these were tents like nothing I'd ever stayed in before. It had a little sit-out in front with a small table and two chairs; the inside was roomy, with twin beds that had side tables and lamps. There was coir matting on the floor with carpets and rugs, that gave it a cosy feel. To one side, there was a wooden wardrobe, a writing table and a jacket stand.

There was a little table with tea and coffee, an electric kettle and cups. There was no room service and all meals were served in the dining area.

The attached bathroom was a solid built-up structure. It was large, with a shower and a bathtub. It had a very earthy feel, as it had sandstone tiling and there was a window to one side with tall grass and plants on the outside.

I loved everything about it! I was really going to enjoy my new home for the next few days!

4

At 7 p.m., after getting some rest, we all met up in the lounge area. It was cosy and doubled up as a library and bar with lots of books on wildlife, conservation, travel and India.

There were prints and lithographs on the walls from the colonial era, featuring wild animals, hunts and Indian rulers rubbing shoulders with British colonial officers.

The decor gave a sense of history and had a feel of 'days of the Raj'. The furniture was comfortable and inviting, with oversized sofas, cosy chairs and lamps placed all around.

At one end there was a large bar with a broad wooden counter, bedecked with all manner of alcohol bottles on shelves behind it.

It was such a nice space and I would have loved to just spend time here relaxing, reading books, having a drink. But it was unlikely I would have any free time over the next few days.

Debajyoti called everyone's attention and began charting out our shoot plan for the next few days.

Jeeps had been booked for safaris, and one group would have to film with the film star, while another would have to get footage of the park, long shots, animal shots, etc. We'd have to make lists of our shots every evening so we'd know what we had and what was still missing. Two of the production assistants were made in charge of that.

We had a programming plan, an idea of the shows we were doing, and shoots would have to be done keeping the plan in mind.

Reena looked bored and added a bit here and there about filming with Vikram Khanna and planning locations for her 'exclusive' interviews.

As we continued our discussions, I suddenly noticed Manju wagging her eyebrows at me.

'What?' I asked.

'Look there,' she whispered, indicating the bar area at one end.

Following her gaze, I saw the tall, angry man we'd encountered earlier that day. He was sitting, having a beer and talking to the manager, Tarun. He had changed out of his outdoor clothes into a button-down cream linen shirt and khaki jodhpurs.

'Should we say something?' asked Manju.

'Like what?' said Jaya, who had been listening and now joined in, having also spotted the 'angry man'.

'That we ruined a shot he had been waiting two to three hours for, and he told us off, rightly so?'

Jaya was such a joker sometimes. Manju made an exasperated expression.

'But he was really rude to us, even if we disturbed him,' I said grimly.

Before Manju could respond, Tarun and the tall man started walking towards us. Coming to a stop next to Debajyoti, Tarun addressed all of us.

'I'd like to introduce all of you to Devraj Singh Rathore, the owner of Baagh Baadi. This property used to be his family's hunting lodge back in the day, when such things were allowed. It remained a forgotten property for a few decades before he restored it and converted it to what you now see,' said a beaming Tarun.

Jaya and my eyes met in horror. Oh my God, he was the owner!

'I'd like to welcome you all to Baagh Baadi,' said Devraj, looking around the group, and for a moment his eyes rested on Manju, Jaya and me.

'I have to admit when Tarun said a group from Bollywood was coming for a shoot, I wasn't really convinced that it was the best fit for us. I was imagining a noisy group that would like to party, make noise, not be sensitive to the surroundings—things that we don't really encourage here at Baagh Baadi. But then when he added that Nation News TV was involved, how could I say no? It's a great channel and your boss is a friend of my father's. Also, I understand the filming will be on issues related to conservation, so that's good to know.'

'How nice,' Reena piped up as soon as he finished speaking, showing more enthusiasm than she had shown in the last one hour. 'We were just planning our shoot schedule, and I'm sure you can give us some inputs. It would be great to get your views on conservation, tourism and the park.'

Jaya and I exchanged quizzical looks. Since when was this part of the plan? I was also pleasantly surprised Reena had picked up on the gist of what our reportage was going to be about. She hadn't looked particularly interested in it during the planning stage.

Debajyoti shook hands with Devraj and began asking him various questions about the park and property. He also introduced him to the rest of us, calling out our names, and we all nodded in response.

Then as they conversed among themselves, Jaya turned to Manju. 'So! It was the owner whom you pissed off, Manju, but thankfully Reena seems to be making up for it.'

'Well, shouldn't he be nicer to his guests?' Manju whispered back. 'Isn't that like hospitality 1-0-1?'

'That's true,' I replied. 'He was rather rude given that we are guests here. Agreed, we were in the wrong, but how can you just blast guests on your property? He seems like one of those typical entitled types—bored, rich, has a family property so decided to indulge his wildlife hobby or something.'

'Though, Sunaina, wasn't it you who lobbied hard for this property? I remember you raving about it, and how it was the best place for the wildlife experience because of the effort they put in?' asked Jaya, with one eyebrow raised.

Uff. Jaya could be so on point sometimes.

'Yes, that's true.' I rolled my eyes. 'Clearly he's managed to hire the right people for the job here. Anyway, it still doesn't excuse the snooty behaviour,' I said stubbornly, making a face as she laughed at me.

'Hello,' said a firm, deep voice from behind us.

With a start, we turned to find the subject of our discussion standing next to us. How long had he been standing there? Had he heard us? We just stared at him, too stunned to speak.

'I'd like to apologize for earlier,' he said quietly, after a beat, looking from one to the other. 'I'd been up on the machan for several hours with no luck before the sambar appeared. I really wanted to capture him against the backdrop of the forests in the centre of our grassland, to use in our yearly calendar. So you can imagine my frustration at being disturbed. But I shouldn't have snapped, and for that I'm sorry.' He gave us a tight smile.

Gradually relaxing, we all smiled in return. Manju looked somewhat mollified.

'I'm sorry too. I should have been more careful. It was an honest mistake,' she said contritely.

We nodded and smiled. There was a pause then, as none of us knew what to say. Luckily he spoke up before it became an awkward silence.

'Well, all the best for your shoot. Do let me know if you need anything.' He gave us a nod and moved on.

'Okay, that was unexpected,' said Jaya once he had stepped away. 'Good of him to apologize, wasn't it?'

'Yes, but a little condescending, I thought,' I said a little peevishly. While one couldn't deny it was decent of him to have apologized, since he had been very rude, it was a very perfunctory apology, in my opinion. He didn't really mean it—it just had to be done.

Just then, Reena came tottering over in her dainty sandals. All of us were dressed casually, in jeans,

T-shirts, kurtas, but not Reena. She was wearing a green and cream striped wraparound cotton dress with white wedge sandals.

'You didn't tell me this property belonged to Devraj Singh Rathore!' she hissed at me, almost in accusation. 'What were you talking to him about?'

'Well, I'd read it was owned by a Rathore family from Jodhpur–Jaipur and that it was run with a lot of emphasis on the wildlife experience. Why? Who is he?' I asked, a little perplexed.

'You're all so clueless! Devraj Singh was really well known in the Delhi society circles. Used to be in advertising and public relations, occasionally played polo and I think he even walked the ramp during one of the fashion weeks. His maternal grandfather was an army general and the younger brother of one of the maharajas. So he's related to many of these Rajasthan royal families.'

'Erstwhile royal families,' I corrected her.

I knew I was being pedantic, but I found the whole 'Rajasthan royalty' culture a bit over the top and anachronistic.

I had a good friend, Devika, from college who lived in Udaipur and was married to a minor 'royal' there. Every time I visited, it took some time to get used to all the bowing and fawning by the staff and others.

The first time I saw an elderly man crouch down and touch her husband's feet, my eyes had popped. But she didn't even blink. It was so matter of fact. He had been visiting from his village, and had come to their house-cum-hotel to ask a small favour.

'It's just how it is over here,' she said by way of explanation later. 'It's not right or wrong. It's just the custom and it's going to take a while to change many of these little things. Though, having said that, there are a lot of other things, socially, that have changed for the better over the years.'

Another time at dinner, when a senior 'royal' had visited, she had whipped her chiffon sari *pallu* on to her head and nearly crouched to the ground with folded palms to greet him with a *khamagani*, the traditional Rajasthani greeting. I'd also observed how chiffon saris were the de facto uniform of all Rajput royal ladies. This was the case ever since the iconic Maharani Gayatri Devi introduced them to Rajasthan society pre-Independence.

Later, as she stood up from her crouching position, Devika turned and winked at me, reassuring me she was the same girl who could beat us all at tequila shots back in college. It was an exotic and different world.

After all, the royal heritage is deeply ingrained in the traditions of the state. It's the palaces, forts and the rich history and culture of the area that draw many visitors to the state and are a major contributor to the tourism industry. Rajasthan is home to so many former princely states, each with their own unique history and culture. They can't help it.

'Yes, yes, you know what I mean,' said Reena impatiently to my comment about the 'erstwhile royal'.

'He suddenly disappeared from the social circuit a few years ago and I hadn't heard anything about him for a while. And now suddenly here he is. I wonder what the story is. Why did he just leave the Delhi scene, and now lives tucked away here in this jungle? Strange.' She was lost in thought for a moment.

'Well, the coverage I saw of this place doesn't talk about him, only mentions the family in general,' I replied.

'Surprising that they don't use him to promote the place. Anyway, Manju, you must get a few pictures of him as well when you start doing the social media features,' she said, looking at him as he chatted with Danish and others.

'Okay, sure,' said Manju, looking surprised.

'Believe me, he'll add to the whole social media thrust. It will definitely get traction among the Delhi–Mumbai society types, if you know what I mean.' She flipped her hair and walked away.

'Being "tucked away" in a jungle like this is my idea of an amazing life,' whispered Jaya to me. 'Must be because of people like Reena he left in the first place,' she chuckled.

'Yeah, I guess it's easy to take a break from city life if you have this ancestral property waiting for you to experiment with,' I said. Perhaps a little enviously, I admit.

We all looked towards Devraj Singh Rathore with renewed interest. He was chatting with Debajyoti again, and Tarun had also joined them.

'More drama for this already fraught-with-drama shoot, and the Mumbai crew hasn't even arrived yet!' I said.

I was a little nervous about the shoot because so much depended on Vikram Khanna and his team. It wasn't like any shoot I'd ever done before where it was just Jaya and me, and most things were in my control.

'Yes, I can't wait'! said Manju. 'I've had such a crush on Vikram for years! What fun to actually meet him and work with him.'

'Well, before Mr Vikram Khanna gets here, I'd like to get a sunrise shot tomorrow from the machan,' said Jaya. 'Later, we'll probably be going to the park every morning, so who knows when we'll get a chance?'

The rest of the evening passed pleasantly enough with the rest of the team. Dinner was Indian cuisine. 'Jungly maas' or spicy mutton curry, a Rajasthan speciality accompanied with ker sangri, another state speciality I loved. A bean-and-berry combination, it was a spicy and crunchy subzi made of ker berry and sangri beans. My friend Devika always made sure it was served every day whenever I visited her in Udaipur.

And then there were piping hot rotis, lachhas and naans straight from the tandoor. As always, when faced with food I loved and rarely got, I ended up overeating.

'Argh!' I complained to Jaya on the way back to our tent. 'I hate eating so much before an early start!'

'I don't know where you put it away!' said Jaya, looking at me and shaking her head. The fact that I ate so much and didn't put on weight irritated her a lot. Not that I was skinny, but years of athletics and sports at school had given me a good metabolism and lean physique.

'But we're in the jungle, it will all burn up fast. It's the fresh air!' I said optimistically.

Even so, I made her walk around a bit to help digest the enormous meal before we finally settled into bed.

5

The next day Jaya and I were up at 5 a.m. These early-morning shoots were something we were quite used to when out of Delhi, and we were both very efficient about it. We could get ready in record time. Having a kettle and coffee in the tent definitely helped!

Jaya would get ready first and I'd get an extra ten minutes to lie in bed.

It was still dark when we trudged to the machan.

We set up the camera on the tripod and were recording a time-lapse shot as the sun began to rise a little before 6 a.m. This meant fixing a still frame and then letting it record for a long duration. Later, during the editing, we would compress the half-hour shot of the sun gradually rising into a few seconds. It was always a nice shot to use in the final edit.

An early morning in a forest is one of the most serene and meditative experiences. The first rays of the sun hit the trees and birds begin their chirping, signalling the start of a new day.

The chill of the night slowly dissipates as the warmth of the sun envelops the forest. For a few minutes everything looks golden, almost ethereal. It's a bonus when there are some fat clouds in the sky and the rays burst out from the sides.

It's good for the soul to catch a sunrise in the forest once in a while.

We got a great time-lapse video of the sun rising over the hills with the grassland in the foreground. Jaya kept adjusting the exposure on the camera as it got brighter. There was a small herd of cheetals, or spotted deer, to one side of the grassland, and two sambars as well. Once the sun was up and our sunrise shot done, we began filming them.

We heard footsteps coming up the steps of the machan and turned to see Devraj's head appear.

'Oh, good morning. I didn't expect to find anyone here,' he said, as he climbed up the steps to the platform, camera in one hand and tripod in the other. We returned his 'good morning' as he proceeded to set up.

I was a little irritated at the interruption, though Jaya didn't seem to mind.

'Any sightings of the young stag yet?' he asked, referring to the sambar we'd seen the previous day.

'No, he didn't emerge,' replied Jaya. 'But there are some cheetal and sambar females.'

'I see your friend from yesterday isn't here,' he remarked, looking through his lens as he started clicking pictures.

An unwarranted comment. I rolled my eyes at Jaya who just shrugged. We remained on the machan for another half hour or so, taking shots till it was much brighter. The herd of cheetal had moved on.

Devraj ordered coffee for all of us from the kitchen as we waited some more.

'Look there,' he said, pointing to the sky as he peered through his camera lens. I followed his gaze and could make out a bird flying in the distance, its silhouette against the bright blue sky. 'It's a crested serpent eagle,' he said as Jaya also fixed her lens on the bird.

The bird cruised for a while above the grassland, surveying the ground below. Suddenly it dove down, its wings folded back as it stooped towards its target. But whatever it had wanted to catch managed to escape and it took to the sky again, its wings spread wide as it soared away.

We watched as the bird became a small dot on the horizon before disappearing from sight.

'It was probably after a snake or a rodent,' said Devraj, as he locked his tripod and sat back on a chair.

'That was a nice dive. I managed to film it,' said Jaya, looking pleased.

The attendant arrived just then with a tray of steaming coffee, the aroma wafting through the air as he carefully laid it out on the table.

Jaya and I took a break as well. It was a nice morning, the warm sun, a gentle breeze carrying the smells of the moonjh grass, making the moment all the more pleasant. Alongside the coffee, there was a spread of three different types of cookies and vanilla muffins, all arranged on a platter. The cookies were clearly home-made and the vanilla muffins looked fluffy and moist. As I eyed them my stomach rumbled, and I realized I was feeling quite hungry. The freshly brewed coffee smelled divine as it was poured out, the rich aroma of the beans filling the machan.

'What's the best sighting you've had from here?' asked Jaya as we took our first sips.

He looked thoughtful for a moment and then replied. 'I've actually seen a tiger chase a wild boar right here. And he managed to get him as well. Then he dragged off the body into those trees on the left.'

'Oh, amazing!' said Jaya in awe, looking towards the grassland, almost willing a tiger to appear.

'Did you manage to capture it on camera?'

For us television people, seeing something spectacular was great, but if you didn't manage to capture it on camera, well then, what was the point? We were a visual medium, after all.

'Sadly I was having coffee just like this when it happened. I did film the boar being dragged off later, but I missed the chase,' he said with a laugh as Jaya choked on her coffee, quickly looking back out at the grassland.

'Damn. That must have been painful. That would have been a spectacular shot to get! What I wouldn't give to see that,' I said wistfully. I genuinely felt sad that someone had missed filming a scene like that!

'Yes, it was.' He smiled back at me. 'But what made it even worse was I had another photographer from Kenya visiting at the time. He was at his camera but didn't film it. When I asked him why, he said he'd get it the "next time". This time he just wanted to watch, and I'm quoting him here, "the drama and the beauty" of the Indian jungle.'

'Oh my God. Why?' said Jaya, sounding pained at the thought.

'He was used to filming in the Maasai Mara, where something or the other is happening every other moment. A lion is hunting the wildebeest here or a cheetah chasing a gazelle there.

I then had to explain to him that in Indian forests these sightings are not so common. And especially for it to happen right on our property was very rare.' Devraj shook his head wistfully at the memory.

We were silent for some time. Jaya was probably thinking of the Kenyan photographer and the missed opportunity. I was thinking of the Maasai Mara. On my bucket list. One day.

'So what has your group got planned for today? Debajyoti said you may go for an afternoon safari?' said Devraj, breaking our reverie.

'Yes, we'd better get going. We'll need to discuss it with him, won't we, Sunaina? Danish may go for that, and I'll stay here and scout locations before the Mumbai team arrives,' Jaya said.

Nodding, I finished up my coffee so we could get going.

'Of course, the actor. Who can forget? He's the real hero of this story, isn't he? The animals are all the supporting cast,' Devraj said with a wry smile as he too moved to pick up his camera and stand up.

Just when I thought he wasn't so bad, he had to get my hackles up!

'No, not really,' I replied, bristling. 'It's special programming. We're using an actor to put the conservation story in focus. Thanks to his popularity, we can put the spotlight on issues that need attention. It's basically a win-win.'

'Yes, the changed narrative around him would be the win, isn't it?' Devraj said with a knowing look, and before I could react he went down the machan ladder.

I suppose for someone who used to be in advertising and PR, it was easy to put things together. A Bollywood star using a wholesome campaign to leave negative associations behind.

I turned to Jaya who was laughing at me.

'Look who's suddenly all gung-ho about filming with a movie star after grumbling earlier.'

I laughed too. 'It's okay between us, I'm not going to complain to an outsider.'

We were heading back to the tent when we saw Manju approaching us.

'Stop, guys! Smile!' she said and clicked a picture.

'I'm getting warmed up for our social media push. What should I caption this picture? Where were you?'

'Well, we were at the machan filming the sunrise,' said Jaya.

'Ooh, that sounds nice. Okay, I'll go with that in the description. Our film team, up at the crack of dawn to film the sun rising over the forest.' She gestured with her hand, indicating the headline.

'Sounds sensational,' I replied with a smile.

'What's the programme today?' she asked.

'Well, I'm planning to go to the park for the afternoon safari,' I said.

'Oh, I want to come too. I could get some great shots and get familiarized with the park. I've never been on safari, you know.'

'I think that's a good idea,' said Jaya. 'You should definitely get familiarized before the serious filming begins. And Manju, please remember. No squealing on safari. Ever!'

'Ha ha!' Manju replied sarcastically, scrunching up her face.

Jaya returned to the tent, while Manju and I went looking for Debajyoti to firm up the plan for the day.

We found him sitting for breakfast in the lounge and, after discussing the logistics for the shoot, we returned to our tent.

The hours passed quickly between breakfast and lunch, and soon it was time for the safari.

Danish, Debajyoti, Manju and I were waiting at the veranda for the jeep to pull up when Devraj Singh walked up with his camera.

He greeted everyone and then started dialling on his phone. I heard him talking to someone, summoning them to the porch.

I looked questioningly at Debajyoti, wondering how he had got included in our plan. He whispered that Devraj had offered to take us in his jeep. It was convenient, as he had a safari booked already and it saved us the hassle. Also, he knew the park and staff very well.

It wasn't ideal but made sense. Except now we would have to tolerate him for the next few hours.

The jeep pulled up and we all clambered in. Devraj sat next to the driver while the rest of us were in the back.

As we began driving out of the resort, Devraj turned around and introduced the driver to us. 'I'd like you all to meet Prem Singh who has done countless safaris with me and is one of the best safari drivers you would ever find, especially for filming. He knows all the right spots and has a great sense of where to stop, how to angle the jeep to get the best view. But I'll warn you, he and I are both allergic to crowds, so if we find a sighting gets overly crowded, we tend to move on from there.'

Prem Singh greeted all of us with a traditional 'khamagani'.

As I returned the greeting, I found myself irritated with Devraj's 'crowded sighting' comment. Only someone who had the luxury of many sightings could be so picky. As a filming crew, getting footage of the tiger was our priority, it didn't matter if there was a crowd or not. I resolved to speak to Debajyoti about this.

It took us fifteen minutes to reach the park gate. Another five minutes for the formalities at the gate and finally we entered the tiger reserve. Driving into a park was always such a treat for me.

Just a half-kilometre in, a little stream ran alongside the road. The stream's flow ebbed and intensified with the seasons. After the monsoon, it transformed into a powerful and lively force, gushing and bubbling through the forest, creating a symphony of sound. In the hot summer months, it became a mere trickle.

At this time, it wasn't in full spate, but merry enough, gurgling through the jungle.

On the opposite side of the stream, there was a steep hill face, with craggy rocks, trees and shrubs. One could imagine the animals watching us, even though we couldn't see them.

It was lovely to feel the wind in my hair and take deep breaths of jungle air. It felt fresh and reassuring when compared to the decidedly polluted air back home.

'I really hope we see a tiger,' said Manju excitedly.

'I know, so do I,' I replied. 'But even so, we should also just appreciate being in the jungle, watch out for all the other animals, the different birds, rather than being totally focused on the tiger. People tend to miss out on these little things, with the overemphasis on tiger spotting.'

'I agree,' said Devraj from the front. 'There is so much more to Chambalgarh than the tigers, but I can understand how you feel, Manju, if you've never seen one. Try and enjoy the safari to the fullest, and let's keep our fingers crossed.' He gave her a reassuring smile, and I could see she was pleased. That was rather nice of him, I thought grudgingly.

With that, we drove steadily on, pausing briefly at the first lake, and then up the hills towards what was called the 'silent valley'. We wanted to put as much distance between us and any other jeeps on the afternoon drive.

For several years now, rules in the park had changed to ensure there wasn't crowding, especially after the media had highlighted ugly pictures showing lines of jeeps surrounding a single tiger. Now the park had been divided into ten zones and in each zone only ten jeeps were allowed at a time. While that did help with the crowding situation, it still meant there were more than four to five jeeps at a good sighting.

We spent an hour driving around zone two, which was the area we were in. We stopped by all the major water holes and vantage points to scout locations for our shoot over the next few days. Danish filmed at each location and Manju clicked away.

We were filming some of the scenery near Kamal Jheel when we heard a distinct cheetal alarm call. It was a sharp, shrill cry that the deer let out when they saw or sensed a tiger. Different from a rutting call which one also occasionally heard from them, especially during the breeding season. A tiger was on the move!

'Let's go!' I said excitedly to Debajyoti, giving him a nudge.

'Where?' he asked, looking around.

'Did you not hear the alarm call?' I asked.

'The what?' he said, looking more confused as I gave him an exasperated look.

Devraj looked back, amused at our exchange.

'An alarm call is a sound a cheetal, sambar or monkey makes when they see a tiger. Even peacocks, occasionally,' he said by way of explanation. 'It's to warn others that the tiger is on the move, and we just heard one from that direction, so let's go check it out.'

'Oh, that's interesting,' Debajyoti said, nodding. He then turned to me with a peeved expression. 'You could have just explained it, Sunaina, instead of making faces. Also, we should get that "call" sound on camera'.

I looked at him in exasperation again, 'But you told me you'd been on a safari!'

'Arré baba, that was Kaziranga. You only see rhinos and elephants there. Very rarely a tiger, at least I wasn't lucky enough. And there were no alarm calls. Tigers aren't seen so much in the areas open to tourists there.'

Kaziranga was one of the most gorgeous national parks in the state of Assam, known more for the one-horned rhino found there. I'd visited once when I was in school. The forest there was very different to the ones in Rajasthan, more swampy and dense. The park would get flooded annually by the Brahmaputra.

We now set off in the direction of the call, hoping to hear more so we would get a better sense of where the tiger was.

And we weren't disappointed.

A little later we heard a monkey alarm call, a sharp and distinct bark, unlike the typical whooping calls that monkeys make. It was a clear indication of the presence of a predator in the area.

'*Hukum*, I think the tiger is moving towards the grassland because the first call was from the thicket on the right and now the second from near the lower road,' said Prem Singh. After conferring briefly, Prem Singh and Devraj decided the best bet would be to take the road towards the grassland and wait near a bend.

We waited there for fifteen minutes or so, but there were no more alarm calls.

'What happened?' asked Debajyoti.

'Sometimes the animal settles down somewhere so the calls stop,' I whispered back. 'Let's wait and see.'

Devraj looked back at us and nodded in agreement. After some time, Prem Singh, who had been peering through his binoculars, whispered something to Devraj, who also then looked through them.

He then leaned back to us and indicated to our left. We all peered at the foliage but couldn't make out anything.

'Two o'clock, under the tree. If you look closely, you'll see the tops of the ears through the grass. It's sitting down. That's why there's silence.'

When on safari, providing accurate directions for animal spotting is crucial. Devraj's instruction to look towards 'two o'clock' to the left meant that I should imagine a straight line perpendicular to the left, with twelve being the starting point, like on a clock face. Then I should look slightly to the right of that, to the imagined 'two' position on the imagined clock face.

He passed me the binoculars and I looked exactly where he had indicated, and, sure enough, I spotted those distinct tiger ears above the grass.

Tigers have white spots on the back of their ears, which are called 'ocelli' or 'eye spots'. The spots are circular and have a black border around them. It's thought they act as false eyes to warn anyone attacking from behind (though who would attack a tiger? It's at the top of the food chain). Another explanation I've read is that they are used for communication or signalling to another tiger, even warning them.

This tiger was sitting down, half of its body behind the tree, and seemed to be looking around, so one could see its ears.

We had three pairs of binoculars among us, and they were passed around so everyone could get a look.

Danish tried to zoom in and get a decent shot on camera.

Manju was very excited given it was her first time on safari and seeing a tiger.

'Now what?' she whispered to me.

'Now we wait some more,' I whispered back.

Patience is a virtue, especially in the forest, as safaris often involve endless waiting.

But it wasn't a long wait, thankfully. After a short while the tiger slowly rose to its feet, stretched and then ambled towards the road, crossing a little ahead of our jeep. It cast a fleeting glance back in our direction, but hardly gave us a second thought.

Many of the tigers in the park are accustomed to seeing jeeps and do not view them as a threat. That is why it is important to remain seated in the jeep when observing a tiger, to maintain the jeep's harmless shape and avoid startling the animal.

'It's Laila,' said Prem Singh.

Laila was the tigress Mallika's daughter and one of her fiercest ones.

She was the one who had displaced her mother from her favoured territory. Old Suraj Lal from Tiger-Eye Lodge had told us about her during our last visit.

As Laila walked farther along the road, we started up the jeep and began following her.

While Danish was hard at work filming, I, for once, just sat back and enjoyed the moment. There was something so magical about watching a tiger take a stroll in the forest. The burnished orange fur, with thick black stripes and the white underbelly, against the backdrop of an Indian jungle. Its sheer beauty and grace are why the tiger has been a subject of fascination for poets and authors.

From William Blake's iconic 'Tyger Tyger, burning bright, In the forests of the night' to Rudyard Kipling's famous *The Jungle Book*.

In the Mahabharata, there is a passage that says, 'Do not cut down the forests with its tigers. The forests are protected by the tigers, and the tigers protected by the forests.' Lines relevant even today.

Laila was a fine specimen as she walked along regally. I had read a tiger's gait was 'like a camel's', as they lift both limbs on the same side when walking. Though when a tiger walks it looks so powerful and graceful at the same time, far from camel-like.

She sprayed a tree as we clicked. Tigers spray parts of their territory with urine and secretions to mark it as theirs, so other tigers that come sniffing around would be aware. It's a way of mapping the area that comes under their control.

I was explaining this to Manju who wanted to know what she was doing, when Devraj spoke up.

'Well, for a tigress it could also be because they are about to go into oestrus, so they do it to lure in any willing males.'

'Oestrus? What's that?' asked Manju.

'It's when they're in heat, ready to mate,' I replied.

'Oh, OHHH,' said Manju, as realization dawned. 'Well, I did manage to get a picture of it. So she's leaving a message for a male? Rather forward, I say.'

'Hah! It's like Tiger Tinder,' I whispered, with a wink.

We giggled as silently as we could. I saw Devraj, though facing the front, break into a smile.

'Good you got a picture,' I said.

'"Tiger Tinder" can be the descriptor on the picture,' she whispered back.

'You know, since we're on the subject, I read tigresses sometimes fake-mate with a tiger,' I said as Laila continued sauntering on the road ahead.

'What? Like faking it? But why?' She seemed incredulous.

'They do it to protect their cubs. They mate with tigers so they leave her alone after that, and she can keep her cubs safe,' I whispered back.

'Wow, psychological games and the maternal instinct!' she said. 'That's quite something!'

Now Devraj turned around and joined our conversation. 'You know, Laila's mother, Mallika, lost a cub like that. She was so fierce even at that young age that she thought she could take on a male. After her first litter, she refused to mate with this other dominant male who was crossing her territory in the ravines. She was staying there after giving birth, hiding her three cubs, but then he killed one. She never made that mistake again.'

That gave us something to think about. In the jungle the male tiger is king, no matter how fierce or strong the female is. Mallika learnt it the hard way.

We were silent as we watched Laila settle under a tree off the road and start grooming herself. There were more alarm calls, and this time we managed to record them.

We spent another fifteen minutes uninterrupted, and then the inevitable happened. Another jeep arrived and, within another ten minutes, three or four more. By then, we were also ready to leave as we had to get back to the resort for the Mumbai arrivals.

We were all feeling rather elated as we left the park.

Manju, of course, was thrilled to bits. 'I got such amazing pictures! She was so gorgeous! Are sightings usually like this or were we lucky?' she gushed.

'Very lucky,' I said, smiling. 'Maybe it was your good karma that led to such a fantastic sighting on your first safari.'

It probably wasn't and had more to do with Prem Singh's tracking skills, but I just added it to make her feel special.

I could see Devraj in front holding back a smile, and our eyes met for a second in the rear-view mirror. Despite everything I thought of him after the circumstances of our first meeting, I realized we clearly had a shared love of the wild and more specifically tigers. So maybe he wasn't such a 'bad' person, I conceded to myself.

Debajyoti too was quite affected by our sighting, though not so effusive, and Danish was busy viewing his footage and showing it to all of us.

He had a whole variety of shots, from the ears above the grass to her standing up and then walking and spraying.

I gave him my 'professional take' on the shots.

'Jaya is going to be so jealous!' he said with a big grin. 'She's always telling me about her wildlife shoots, supposedly to discuss camera angles and techniques, though what she's really doing is low-key boasting. Wait till I show her these.'

We all laughed at his glee.

After a while, Devraj turned around and spoke to me. 'So I take it you're the wildlife expert here?'

'Yes, I guess I'm the most experienced compared to this lot. I'm the environment reporter for the channel. In fact, I was here just a few months ago for a special programme on tourism and conservation,' I said.

'Ah, that's interesting. I must check it out,' he said. 'Is it online?'

'Yes, it is. I'll send you the link. Would be nice to know what you think of it.'

'Sure,' he nodded and turned back.

I addressed Prem Singh now.

'Thank you, Prem Singh ji, that was a fantastic sighting. You really had a great sense of where the tiger would emerge. That was amazing!'

'Hukum,' Prem Singh smiled in my direction as he kept driving along the forest roads.

'I enjoy it so much more when you can track the tiger movement through the calls. Somehow it's more satisfying,' I said to the others.

'I agree,' said Devraj. 'It's more of a challenge, and yes, more satisfying than finding a bunch of jeeps around a tiger, isn't it?'

I nodded in agreement. So did Manju, who had just had her first tiger experience.

We reached the park gate, where a few forest guards on duty approached our jeep.

'Hukum.'

'Hukum.'

'Hukum *jai jai*.'

They all greeted Devraj. Greeting them back, he told them about the tiger we had spotted and where in the park it was. They said they would note it down in the register, and after a five-minute exchange we were off.

'Why do they say "hukum"?' Manju whispered loudly to me as we were moving swiftly and the wind was blowing in our ears.

'It's a type of greeting, particularly to someone in a higher position,' I replied, shouting to be heard over the wind. 'You know, Rajasthan is very traditional. It has remnants of feudal practices as well,' I added, trying to give her some context of the culture.

'It's just a respectful way to address someone,' said Devraj, turning around.

Oops, I hadn't realized he was listening to us.

'Yes, we are a traditional culture here, but it's the equivalent of saying "sir" or "sahib". I call people "hukum" as well. In different states you have various forms of greetings and addressing people.'

'Yes, that's true,' I said, nodding in agreement, feeling a little contrite. I wondered if I had offended him. Oh well.

Debajyoti was on the phone and told us that the Mumbai crew had just landed at a nearby air strip and was going to leave for the resort shortly. They had chartered a small plane from Mumbai as it was easier for them to manage.

We rushed back to the resort to freshen up before their arrival.

Jaya came down the steps at the main porch as we were getting out of the jeep.

'We had a fab sighting!' I told her excitedly.

'Yeah, Jaya!' said Danish. 'Wait till you see my footage!'

'As good as our Mallika sighting?' she asked, with an eyebrow raised.

'Nah, nothing can touch that,' I smiled. 'Though it was her daughter we saw today.'

'Oh, you've seen our local legend Mallika?' asked Devraj who was still sitting in the jeep.

'Yes, we did, and she helped me make a very important personal decision by granting the darshan,' said Jaya, with a wink in my direction.

'Do I dare ask?' he said, smiling.

'We're not that close,' Jaya replied with a grin, which led to a chuckle from Devraj.

'Well, there is time yet for us to become friends. You are here for a few days,' he said, flashing a smile at Jaya. And then at me. He then drove off with Prem Singh to the patch of land behind the building. Where they parked vehicles, I imagined.

We quickly wrapped up things and headed back to our tent.

I had a shower, and, as I got ready, Jaya filled me in on her afternoon while I told her about our safari.

Scrolling through her phone, she exclaimed, 'Oh! Check out Manju's posts! She's going on a Twitter–Instagram spree with your shoot today. Oh, nice picture of the tiger grooming. Another nice one of you looking through the binoculars. And that must be the back of Devraj's head.' She gave me a running commentary on the pictures. 'How was Manju? No loud exclamations in the park, I hope?'

'No, thankfully. She's a quick learner,' I laughed. 'And lucky as well! That was a great sighting for her first safari.'

Suddenly Jaya jumped up from the bed where she was lounging.

'Hey, let's go! They're here!'

'Was there a message on the WhatsApp group?' I asked, looking down at the phone on my table.

Debajyoti had helpfully created a WhatsApp group for coordination, so everyone could be on the same page.

'No! Manju just tweeted a picture of them arriving, let's go!'

6

When we got to the lodge, we saw everyone had gathered in the lounge. We could hear them all chattering away as we approached. An alert had been sent out on the WhatsApp group, summoning everyone.

Debajyoti was doing the introductions, and, as we arrived, he said, 'And this is Sunaina. She's our reporter, as you know, and passionate about wildlife. And Jaya, the other camera person in the team and equally passionate about wildlife.'

I finally met the formidable Natasha face to face. She was taller than I'd expected, but not as heavy as I'd thought. She was attractive, with sharp, angular features and beautiful long, flowing black hair, which added to her overall presence.

To my surprise, she gave me a big hug.

'It's so great to finally meet you!' she said enthusiastically. 'You are so lovely! The video call did not do you justice! I'm so looking forward to this shoot! I have to say, your passion for wildlife during our conversations rubbed off on me. I've been reading up on it, and I'm a lot better informed since we interacted.'

Well, that was unexpected, given the run-ins we'd had during those conference calls.

I smiled brightly and told her how excited we were about the campaign.

She met Jaya warmly as well.

'This is so different for us, and what a lovely property this is, whatever little I've seen of it so far,' she said, looking around. 'I will need a proper tour of this whole place, but we can always do that later!'

She introduced us to Maya Gupta and Safar Shaikh who were in charge of styling and social media. Maya was thin and petite with a pixie cut, while Safar was tall and curvy with long hair with blue highlights. Zaid Siddiqui, who was Natasha's deputy and number two in the team, was a stylish young man, with close cropped hair and one of those carefully styled short beards. He had two assistants, Charu Sawhney and George John. There were two more assistants, Zara Sethna and Sheelu Kumar, who were part of the styling team. There was also a two-person make-up and hair team.

I'd met most of them earlier on video and it was nice to meet them in person.

They had a plethora of questions and gushed about the lodge. We talked broadly about the shoot plan and they sought clarifications on various details.

Debajyoti and Reena discussed the lodging arrangements with Zaid, so he could efficiently coordinate the accommodation for the entire team.

We were chatting, when Natasha looked over my shoulder and said, 'Here he is! Here's our boy!'

I turned around, and there was Vikram Khanna walking up, smiling broadly, flanked by two bodyguards.

Looking at him, I couldn't help but acknowledge the fact that he was even more striking in person than he appeared on the silver screen. He was tall, lean and incredibly handsome, exuding a boyish charm. His tousled hair had just the right amount of nonchalance with style. He had a strong jawline, a hint of five o'clock shadow and bright, sparkling eyes that were complemented by a warm and inviting smile. Dressed in a simple pair of jeans and white shirt, he radiated a wholesome and positive energy.

He walked up to us and introduced himself.

'Hi, I'm Vikram Khanna.'

Now, there was something very charming and personable about that. Obviously we all knew who he was and he knew we knew, but he didn't presume it, and it came off as endearing.

We introduced ourselves.

'I see you already had a good sighting today. Natasha caught me up on your social media posts. I'm really very excited about this shoot! I've never actually seen a tiger in the wild,' he said with a broad smile.

'Oh, really? Never?' asked Reena, giving him her most dazzling smile. It looked like she had fifty teeth, I thought unkindly. It was an old college joke among my friends which we used when someone smiled too widely to impress.

'Only in a zoo and once in Thailand, at the monastery, but that's when I didn't know better. I read later the animals there may have been drugged. Glad that it was eventually exposed,' he replied.

We all smiled and nodded.

I was not quite sure what I was expecting from a movie star. I suppose somebody really filmi, the clichéd Bollywood hero, arrogant and brash, head in the clouds. But definitely not this, a very friendly, seemingly down to earth guy. Albeit a very good-looking guy, and someone with two bodyguards hovering around him. Also, the fact that he was aware of the controversy around the Thailand temple tigers impressed me.

As we all continued to gawk at Vikram, clearly bowled over by his affable charm and good looks, Natasha decided to take charge.

'Debajyoti, whom you just met, is the producer of the shoot.' Debajyoti stepped up and enthusiastically shook hands again. 'He can explain the plan over the next few days. I believe we have a safari tomorrow at the crack of dawn. It will be good to just ease into the whole thing. Vikram can get a little familiar with the safari experience. And we can work from there. I understand from our many video conversations that a big part of a wildlife shoot is up to chance and luck.'

Snapping out of his superstar-induced daze, Debajyoti got a hold of himself and addressed everyone, welcoming the Mumbai group. He spoke about how exciting the project was, what a great opportunity it was for everyone and how he hoped we'd all have a fantastic shoot, and that the campaign would be impactful.

Then Vikram decided to address everyone as well. Which was very nice of him. After all, he was the star of the shoot.

'I'd like to just thank you all. This is something very new for me and I'm excited. My team and I will be needing your help and guidance over the next few days since this is way out of our comfort or familiar zone.' He flashed his 100-watt smile and everyone laughed and clapped.

'Having said that, it's great to be in this very different environment, and I'm looking forward to the next few days being an adventure and learning experience. And, of course, seeing some tigers!'

Everyone clapped some more and cheered. It was just that kind of moment, the way he had spoken, his very positive attitude and the fact that he seemed genuinely excited.

I spotted Devraj at the back of the room, near the bar, with a drink. He was quietly watching our gathering and rolling his eyes, ever so slightly, when everyone started clapping.

I suppose, from his perspective, all this looked very contrived, though it really wasn't.

A little later, I was in conversation with Safar regarding the weather since she wanted to know, to help her plan outfits, when I found Vikram next to me.

'So tell me about the plan tomorrow,' he asked. 'It's a really early start, isn't it?'

'Yes, our plan is to depart by 6 a.m. As the saying goes, "the early bird catches the worm",' I replied with a forced smile, trying to appear very cool.

Eesh. I couldn't help but internally berate myself for using such a lame, clichéd adage.

Despite my inner self-criticism, I continued the conversation unfazed.

'But seriously, we leave early so we can drive deep into the park while the animals are on the move. As the day gets warmer, they all settle down and the movement stops till evening. So chances of catching some action are best in the early hours.'

'Okay, that makes sense. Hope we do catch sight of something tomorrow! I hear we're also not allowed to get down from the jeep?'

'Oh no, not at all. There are very strict rules inside the park, for your safety as well as to limit any interference with the animals. So we can only get down at one of the forest *chowki*s in the park or when accompanied by the forest guards. But, otherwise, that's an absolute no-no.'

'So I guess no "man versus wild" stuff on this shoot?' he said with a laugh. 'No picking up animal poop and wondering what it is or fishing in the lake?'

I laughed too, but oh my God! I hope that wasn't what he had in mind. Walking through the jungle and figuring out survival techniques Bear Grylls style. That was a whole different type of show.

'No, none of that. Though we have planned for you to accompany the forest guards on a patrol, so that should be interesting.'

'He'll be wearing olive and khaki for the first shoot,' said Maya, the other stylist, joining us. 'Since you're going to be in shots together, I thought you should know. I'd recommend cream and olive.'

'Okay, right,' I nodded, as if it was the most obvious thing to discuss, though coordinating what I'd wear with superstar Vikram Khanna hadn't even crossed my mind.

'Well, my wardrobe is mainly olives, khaki, browns, etc., so it shouldn't be a problem.'

'Ugh, such dull colours,' she said grimacing. 'Won't do you any favours,' she said running her eyes over me.

Again, I was at a loss for words. I just looked at her blankly.

'So what are the chances of seeing a tiger?' Vikram said, breaking the awkward silence.

'Very good!' I was glad for the change in subject from sartorial to something more up my street. 'The sightings have been pretty incredible the last couple of months, so fingers crossed.'

'Fingers crossed for what?' said Reena, coming over.

'That we see a tiger tomorrow,' Vikram said.

'Ooh yes. Sunaina, are we really leaving at 6 a.m.? Can't we delay it to 7:30 or something?'

I could have killed her. How could she bring that up as if it were negotiable? We didn't want to give the Mumbai team any choice in the matter. We had already been through all this during the planning meeting. If we didn't leave early we'd get limited filming time, as once the sun was overhead filming would not be possible as the light would be too harsh. Also, as I'd just explained, if you got in early, it gave you more time to scout around and the chances of seeing a tiger were greater.

'No, Reena. That's not possible,' I said evenly with a tight smile, trying hard to hide my irritation. 'Remember Debajyoti had said the safari timings were non-negotiable? It'll help us get the most out of the shoot.'

'Sooo early. I'm just not used to it, this safari life,' she said, sighing at Vikram. 'And how hot does it get? Thankfully I've got a range of hats.'

'Yeah, so do I,' said Vikram with a bright smile. 'My team went a little berserk with the hats. From Indiana Jones to Crocodile Dundee, I have a variety.'

'Now that was fun. Choosing various hats,' said Maya with a rare smile. 'We also had to make sure the hats don't look brand-new, so some of us wore them around the office for a while. Hilarious! Sunaina, do you plan to wear a hat tomorrow?' She then turned to me.

I had never been so glad for the Akubra hat my sister had gifted me after a visit to Australia. It looked posh and would hold up in the face of Maya's scrutiny. I had that and then another canvas hat bought from the hawkers at the park gate.

'Yes, an olive one that I usually wear. And then I have a tan canvas one.'

'Hmm, okay,' Maya replied. I couldn't tell if her tone was approving or not.

Before I could think any more of it, Reena called out loudly.

'Hi, Devraj! Do join us,' she said, again flashing her fifty-tooth smile.

Devraj, who was chatting with Debajyoti nearby, turned around and saw all of us looking at him. Once again he was wearing jodhpurs, crisp white ones, with a dark blue shirt.

He walked up to us with a smile.

'Do meet Vikram. Vikram, this is Devraj, the owner of this lovely property,' said Reena brightly.

'Khamagani,' said Devraj in the traditional style. 'Welcome to Baagh Baadi. We hope you will enjoy your stay with us.'

'Thank you, you have a beautiful place here,' said Vikram. 'I was just telling the team that this is my first time on a safari in India and I'm really very excited. Of course you must be going on safari every day, so it must be amusing to see a novice like me.'

'Not at all, many guests at Baagh Baadi have been first-timers, and we are very happy to be a part of that very exciting experience and to be associated with the memory. Seeing a tiger is special every single time. It's really a gift.'

'Nice, I like how you phrased that. I may steal it to use during the shoot. I have to have all these conversations with Sunaina during the shoot, and need to sound as knowledgeable as I can.'

'Oh, don't worry about that. I'm sure you'll be great,' gushed Reena.

'So this was a hunting lodge earlier? I read about this resort. This building we're in?' Vikram asked.

'It used to be in my grandfather's time. This was built by a maternal grand uncle. A little unusual to have such a large shikargah in the jungle, but he was said to be eccentric. It was a drought year, so it was also to help the locals earn a little money by helping in the construction. *Shikaar* was a popular sport then. The times were different and wildlife was in abundance. We do have a trophy room where I have hidden all the stuffed animal heads and even a whole tiger. We have permits for them all as they have been in the family for decades. But since times have changed and our focus is on conservation, I don't want them being displayed for guests. In case you're interested, I could show you sometime. Most of them have an interesting story to go along,' said Devraj.

Well, that was interesting. Most palaces and such family establishments in Rajasthan usually took pride in displaying the animal trophies, as you could get permits for old ones, so it wasn't illegal. That Devraj had chosen not to display them was a fresh and welcome approach. Sensitive even.

'Sure, that would be interesting to see!' said Vikram with enthusiasm. 'Don't worry, Sunaina, no filming there.' He winked at me and I just had to smile.

'I saw a picture of a vintage red Rolls-Royce on one of the walls and was very intrigued. I'm a bit of a vintage car buff so was wondering about it,' he asked.

'Oh, that.' Devraj smiled and shook his head. Pointing to a photograph hung near the bar, he said, 'The Tiger Car. It was one of the most ridiculous things if you think about it now. In the 1920s, one of our ancestors, not direct but related, a raja, had a red Rolls-Royce Phantom fitted with a hand-cranked machine gun to shoot tigers. It even had a Lantaka cannon mounted in the rear for elephants. That was taking the hunting obsession a bit too far.'

'Whoa, that's crazy,' said Vikram, quite taken aback by the story.

So was I, as I now looked at the picture with more interest. I imagined the raja driving around in this car in the forest, shooting at animals in his way. And from the back of the car as well!

'Needless to say, he was responsible for killing hundreds of tigers. Pains me to say it even,' said Devraj sombrely.

After we had some time to take in this news and ogle at the picture some more, Vikram asked about sightings.

'Is this a good time to see tigers? Is there a special season for tiger sightings?' he asked Devraj.

I smiled at the question, as it sounded very sweet but naive. A tiger season? But then was surprised when Devraj answered in the affirmative.

'The best season for tiger spotting is actually in the summer months. Most of the waterbodies dry up, and in the few that remain, one can always find a tiger. They like to sit in the water to cool off. But it's not the best season for tourists in the park as it's unbearably hot for us as well. The park then shuts during the monsoon season.'

'All right, well, even if it's not the season, I do hope we get to see tigers!' said Vikram with some feeling.

We all smiled at his enthusiasm. After a little more chit-chat, Devraj wished us goodnight and left.

Since it was an early start the next day, we soon moved on for dinner. The inner courtyard had been decorated with candles, lanterns and some pretty floral arrangements.

And dinner was a sumptuous affair to welcome the Mumbaikers to Rajasthan.

There was laal maas or 'red meat', which is mutton cooked in a fiery red curry, a Rajasthani favourite. In earlier times it would be cooked with venison or wild boar but now it's cooked with Rajasthani mutton, said to be the best in India. There was papad ki subzi, or papad cooked in a yogurt gravy, a recipe that originated from the drier parts of Rajasthan. Also Rajasthani kadi, a thick gravy with onion pakodas or fritters and an assortment of rotis from the tandoor and salads.

'So?' asked Jaya, after we had piled our plates and were finally seated. She nodded towards Vikram's table. 'Not so bad, eh? Not exactly the conceited Ken doll we had him pinned as.'

I nodded in agreement.

'I have to admit, maybe we were too judgemental, especially given that drug story background. Really, what's it to us as long as we have our chance to go on safaris, see tigers and have a cracker of a campaign.'

This was such a great opportunity for Jaya and me to do what we loved best. Film wildlife and drive around jungles. And, for once, there were producers and budgets, and everything was taken care of. I just had to sit back and enjoy myself, unlike other news shoots when everything was my responsibility.

Manju was busy taking candid pictures of the group.

'Not with my mouth full!' complained Jaya as she took a few of us. Manju moved on to Vikram's table.

'This food is awesome!' he declared as she took a picture of him with his laden plate.

'I hope my dietician, Sabreen, doesn't see this. I've gone over the daily calorie intake for sure but I can't stop eating this meat curry. They don't make curry like this in Mumbai! It's spicy yet full of flavour.'

'You're allowed to have cheat days,' Natasha laughed at his gluttonous display. But as he reached for another naan from the server she stopped him, 'You've cheated enough for tonight, I think!'

Everyone sitting nearby laughed at his crestfallen expression.

'That's some pressure,' I whispered to Jaya.

'Yikes, calorie count? I wouldn't know where to begin,' she replied. 'But that's showbiz. No pain, no gain,' she shrugged.

After dinner Manju got everyone in for a group shot, describing us as 'Team Tiger'. I was standing in the second row with Jaya and Danish. The group snap was clearly divided into Team Delhi and Team Mumbai.

As I was thinking this, Vikram spoke up, 'C'mon everyone, we should mix it up! Don't be shy! We're going to be spending the next couple of days together now. Let's be one big family!'

That made everyone laugh and relax. Another five minutes were spent regrouping for the picture. We all moved around and Vikram came and stood next to me. While Debajyoti went next to Natasha, Jaya went and stood with Maya and Safar. Finally, we got a few pictures that satisfied Manju.

'#TeamTiger and #SaveOurTigers! Those are the hashtags, people!' she announced. 'Please use that when you tweet or post on Instagram! We need to make this big!'

7

It was 6 a.m. the next morning and we were gathered at the porch, loading equipment on to the jeep. People were excited and groggy at the same time.

Vikram and his team arrived at 6.15, and, by 6.20, when there was no sign of Reena, an irritated Debajyoti said we'd just have to leave.

Vikram, Jaya and I were in one jeep with a guide, and Debajyoti, Danish, Safar and the forest guard were in the other. And Zaid, Manju and one of the bodyguards, Ravi, were in a third jeep. Natasha had decided to sleep in.

As we set off, our guide, Imran, turned around and introduced himself. He was visibly excited to be guiding a big movie star. This would give him a lot of fodder in the days to come, since guides thrive on stories to regale their guests. Vikram, Imran and I had cordless mikes on so that we could record conversations and reactions we may want to use later.

Imran launched into an introduction to the park. How it was set up in the 1970s after the then prime minister, Indira Gandhi, pushed for the creation of tiger reserves throughout the country. He spoke about how she had launched Project Tiger, India's first tiger conservation programme in 1973, to increase the dwindling numbers. How India had had over 50,000 tigers in the 1900s, and then just a few thousand in the 1960s. 'It is thanks to her vision that even as a developing country, we have so many sanctuaries and tiger reserves today,' said Imran.

Before it was declared a sanctuary, Chambalgarh used to be a hunting ground for royal families for years. Imran explained how there was a fort inside the north side of the park that had its own bloody history of battles and strife. He mentioned how Baagh Baadi was also originally a hunting lodge. 'Yes, Devraj told us about that yesterday. So, tell me, was it his family that hunted here?' asked Vikram.

Imran explained several royal families hunted in these forests back in the day. Then he launched into a long account of how Devraj's maternal grandfather was the son of a raja, whose principality was near Jaipur, and his paternal side was from another such principality near Jodhpur. He said there were no male descendants on his mother's side, so the lodge and other properties all came to him and his sister.

By this time we had reached the park gate and quickly went through the formalities. We stopped just after entering the gate, where it wasn't crowded. Two of the forest guards came up to meet Vikram who shook hands and even posed for a photo with them, much to their delight. Manju and Safar also clicked pictures of the exchange.

And then we were off on safari!

Imran explained to Vikram how it had taken quite an effort to create this park decades ago. There had been around eight villages inside it earlier, in the core area, but 'at that time you didn't have human rights activists and NGOs', said Imran, and so many villagers were turned out of their homes overnight and made to leave the park.

'It was a sad aspect of India's conservation story,' I said.

It did sound terrible now to think about it. India owes its sanctuaries and national parks to the unwilling and unrecognized sacrifice of so many villagers and tribals. With this in mind, I thought I should clarify that things were very different now.

'That is how it happened then but now they have a decent package for villages to move out of national parks. At least on paper. Activists and organizations still have to ensure that the families get all benefits due to them,' I said. 'Now the government pays Rs 10 lakh for every adult, and, frankly, many voluntarily move out of the forest to a better, more connected area where they have access to schools and hospitals. I've interviewed such families in other parts, like near Corbett Park in Uttarakhand where the Van Gujjar community took the deal and moved out. There were some challenges obviously but it did happen.'

Vikram nodded, but I wondered if I was plying him with too much information at the start. Must be such a change from whatever it was he was used to in his Bollywood world. Too much trivia may put him off!

Almost as if he read my mind, Vikram said he had read up a bit about tiger conservation in the country and issues around it, so he did know about Project Tiger and the man–animal conflict.

'Natasha gave me a bunch of reports and articles to read about tiger conservation and wildlife. If I'm getting involved in an issue, I like to know everything about it. While I had some idea, reading about it was quite fascinating. But I didn't think about poor people being chased out of their homes. Somehow that's always the case, isn't it? In fact, I am reading a script right now that centres around these villagers who will be displaced because of a dam on their river, how their sacred grove will be flooded. It's about their fight to save their land and way of life. I don't know if I'll do it because it seems a bit grim.'

Again, I was both surprised and impressed. He had done his homework, something I hadn't expected. We chatted some more about development versus displacement in India. He was very aware of many of the issues.

'Should we now run through a couple of questions and discussion points before we start filming?' Vikram asked.

'Yes, of course,' I replied, slightly embarrassed since I should have been the one to bring up the shoot. 'That would help give us a sense of flow.'

Debajyoti pulled up alongside. 'We're going to be filming you guys from afar. We'll stop at the top of the hill overlooking what they call "silent valley". That's where we can film an interaction, chat, etc.'

It was a beautiful morning and the view from the hill would be stunning.

Going up, we spotted a group of cheetal with a few fawns, and Vikram was thrilled. It was rather sweet, and I could see Jaya grinning.

We spent the next hour filming the views, as well as Vikram and I discussing the park and tiger conservation. Again, I was surprised by Vikram's keen interest and genuine enthusiasm for it all. I knew he was an actor but surely he wasn't that good that he could feign interest if he didn't genuinely care.

'Alarm call!' said Imran suddenly.

That's all it took for the mood to change dramatically. Everyone was suddenly charged and excited. We took off in the direction of the alarm call, as I explained to Vikram what an alarm call was.

'So this means a tiger is definitely nearby?' he asked.

'Well, it could be a leopard. Sometimes that happens as well.'

'Ooh, I hope not, I really hope it's a tiger,' he said with a big grin.

Imran and the driver decided on a route that seemed the most likely direction. After a short while we heard a clearer call. We rounded a bend and came to a halt, listening intently for further sounds. To our right, a steep ravine plunged down, and then rolling hills rose in the distance beyond.

'It seems the movement is towards the Pari Hills. If it starts climbing the hill, then it means the chances of seeing it are slim. It could then be gone in that direction for a few hours, and there are no roads there,' said Imran.

'Only 20 per cent of the park is open to tourists. There are so many tigers that live in this entire area, that we never even see.'

We drove a little farther and then stopped under a big peepal tree to wait it out. The sun was very strong as it was a cloudless day and it was getting quite warm.

We waited fifteen minutes but there were no other sounds indicating the presence of a tiger. Just the usual forest noises. Maybe it had sat down somewhere.

The forest guard, Ram Tiwari, got out of his jeep and came up to ours. 'Medum ji, it seems the tiger is gone, but we can wait some more if you want.'

'It may have sat down somewhere cool,' I said. 'That's why there are no more calls.'

'Oh damn. That's a big disappointment,' said Vikram, looking quite crestfallen. 'I was hoping to be one of those lucky people you hear about who have great sightings right on their first drive.'

We started up the jeep. I signalled to the others that we'd be moving on. There were disappointed faces all around.

Danish indicated he wanted to take a shot of the view, the ravine and hills.

As we waited, Ram Tiwari said he'd ask on his wireless if there had been any other sightings. Forest guards carry walkie-talkies into the park, which is very helpful since there's no cell phone connectivity through most of the drive.

As he was talking, we sat around looking fairly glum. Especially Vikram.

Jaya got Vikram to speak of his disappointment on his first drive. It was a nice element to add to the show because it's a very real experience many have. He also spoke about how much he enjoyed the drive, seeing other animals and the forest.

I watched Ram Tiwari hopefully, trying to overhear if there had been any other sightings during the morning drive. If another group had a sighting, we still had a little time to head there and check it out. It was getting quite warm now, and we would have to move soon. Ram Tiwari spoke with two of the forest jeeps that were patrolling the park, but it didn't seem like anyone had had a sighting that morning.

As I watched on, Ram Tiwari absent-mindedly swatted away a bee that had flown too close to him.

I glanced down at my phone to check the time and realized we had only forty-five minutes left in the park. Then, as I looked back up at Ram Tiwari, a sense of alarm washed over me. He was now surrounded by many more bees. There were at least half a dozen of them buzzing around him. And to my dismay, I realized that the bees were also beginning to buzz around us. My eyes followed the buzzing insects up to a large beehive, nestled in the branches above us, hidden by leaves. It was clear we needed to vacate the area immediately before the situation got worse.

'Guys, we've got to move NOW! We've disturbed a beehive!' I yelled.

Everyone was relaxing or chatting in their jeeps, some were taking pictures of the forest, others were clicking selfies, but on hearing me, they all now froze for a split second, registering what I had just said. And then a rush of activity immediately set in. Everyone got into their seats and the drivers started up the vehicles.

As Ram Tiwari ran to his jeep, there was a scream.

I looked over to Debajyoti's jeep, where Safar was holding her head and yelling. Oh no! She had been stung by a bee! They were in a panic as she was screaming in pain.

'Debajyoti, just move now! Don't stop!' I yelled to him. I realized someone else was yelling my name.

It was Ravi, Vikram's guard from the other jeep.

'Sunaina ji! Protect Vikram sir!' he yelled agitatedly as his jeep drove out first. Ravi had been reluctant about parting with Vikram when the jeeps were assigned in the morning. I had scoffed at him at the time and said don't worry, nothing would happen to Vikram, and anyway, our jeeps would be next to each other the whole time.

We couldn't have had him in our jeep as he would have crowded it and ruined the shots.

Now, looking at the slightly dazed Vikram sitting next to me, I realized it was my responsibility to make sure nothing happened to him. Crap! If our star got stung, this shoot would be over even before it started. Bees were buzzing all around us. Imran was crouched down in the front seat and the driver started to pull out.

'Get down!' yelled Jaya as she ducked in the back.

As we started moving, I took out the scarf I always kept with me on safaris and pulled Vikram down, on to the floor of the jeep, covering both of us with it. We held it tightly over our heads and torsos.

'Don't worry!' I told him, as we crouched down, doing my best to make it seem like this was no big deal. 'We'll leave them behind. Nothing will happen.'

It took a minute or so for the buzzing around us to finally stop, though it seemed like much longer.

I peeked out to see our jeep had pulled up at one of the little forest chowkis inside the park. I could hear other jeeps pulling up.

Manju called out from the jeep next to us, 'Guys, you can come out now.'

Vikram also looked out cautiously from under the scarf.

'Smile! You're safe!' said Manju. 'Let me take a picture of you guys.'

She clicked a picture of us peering out, holding up the scarf around us, and then we sat back in our seats.

'Well, that was something,' said Jaya. She was filming us too.

'Quite unexpected! That beehive was hidden up in the branches.'

Ravi quickly hopped out of his jeep and got in with us so he could be closer to Vikram and protect him from anything else we may encounter.

'That was a crazy experience!' exclaimed Vikram, still looking dazed. 'Here I thought we're going to have a close encounter with a tiger, but instead we had a swarm of killer bees chasing us!'

'Well, to be fair, they were just bees, not killer bees,' I tried to reason. 'And we were the ones who disturbed them. It was hot, and our engine fumes must have led to their sudden swarming. We put the engines on and off a few times.'

Jaya nodded as she kept filming Vikram's reaction.

'And poor Safar got bitten!' he exclaimed, standing up to get out of the jeep.

'That's stung, actually, not bitten,' I said weakly, trying to add my two bits again, but he wasn't listening.

He jumped out to the other jeep where everyone was fussing around poor Safar. She was holding a scarf to one side of her face. Jaya and I followed as well. I was feeling bad for her but a bee sting would be okay soon. We needed to get out of the park and get her some medication.

'Safar, darling, how are you feeling? I'm so sorry you had to go through this, baba! Show me,' said Vikram, standing next to her jeep as everyone gathered around the weeping Safar.

She slowly removed her scarf from her face and everyone instinctively recoiled. The right side of her face had puffed up and her eye was swollen shut. Even her lips seemed swollen.

'Am I hideous?' she wailed, covering her face again. 'It's burning.'

'Don't worry, don't cry,' Debajyoti told her, as he got ice out of the icebox. 'We're going back to the resort. We'll call a doctor and it will be fine. It looks bad but it will settle soon. Let's go everyone.'

He wrapped the ice in a handkerchief and gave it to Safar to hold against her face. Vikram fussed over her some more, but it was clear he was really shocked seeing the state of her face after the sting.

'Let's go to our jeep,' I told him. 'Debajyoti's right, it will be fine in a bit. I was stung as a child. It swells up instantly but will settle down soon. We'll call the doctor to help with meds. That will make it completely fine. Don't worry!' I was trying to calm everyone down so we could get moving.

The driver of the third jeep had also been stung on his arm but his wasn't so bad. Danish offered to drive but he waved him off.

Ram Tiwari, who had gone to make a report to the staff at the chowki, returned, and we all jumped into our jeeps to exit the park.

The drive out was quiet as everyone seemed a little shaken by the experience. I could see Debajyoti comforting Safar as best he could.

I thought about our morning in the park. What a first day, first shoot it had been.

Though, thankfully, it wasn't a write-off or anything. We did manage some decent footage of Vikram on safari, our conversations about the park and conservation, his disappointment at not seeing the tiger, which was a very common reaction. That would be a nice touch in the final edit.

All these thoughts were whirling through my mind when I realized Vikram was talking to me.

'Has this ever happened to you before? On a shoot? Your reaction was really quick. I didn't even realize what was happening and then Safar screamed.'

'No, never! I have to say this was a completely bizarre, one-off experience,' I said, trying to emphasize what a rarity it was before it spooked him.

'It was only because I was looking at Ram Tiwari that I realized he was surrounded by bees and then that we were too! Anyway, the good thing is we are out of it.'

'But poor Safar. Hope she's not in a lot of pain,' said Vikram.

'She will be fine later. Don't worry,' I said, glancing at the other jeep.

'Yes, poor girl. This is all so different for us. Safar's from South Mumbai. Your typical SoBo girl. She's well-travelled but not so much in India. This is all so alien at one level, if you know what I mean,' he said.

I wasn't quite sure what he meant.

'You mean she's never been on safaris or to jungles?' I asked.

'Yes. SoBo means South Bombay. It's a Mumbai thing. In fact, she was saying earlier how she'd never been to rural India. Or rural anywhere. She's only been to big cities all over the world,' he explained like it was the most natural thing. I guess in his circles it was.

'Thank God, sir, nothing happened to you,' piped up Ravi from the back, to my irritation. Why bring that up!

'Yeah, really!' Can you imagine if my face had swollen like that! Natasha would have freaked out! This shoot would have been over!' he exclaimed, as if considering the possibility.

It was the last direction I wanted his thoughts to wander!

'Which is why it's great that it didn't. Also, like I said, Safar will be fine by tomorrow. Don't worry,' I said, trying to play it down again. But he was right. If he had got stung, it would have been a whole different story! Small mercies. I glanced back at Jaya, making eyes at her, indicating she should also add something here to back me up.

She immediately spoke up. 'This was by far the most bizarre experience ever!' she exclaimed, a tad too forcefully. 'I've never heard of something like this happening! But Safar will be fine soon. I'm sure the swelling is subsiding already!'

By now, we were just a few minutes away from the resort. I could see Debajyoti on the phone with someone, so he must have called up ahead.

As soon as we arrived, the manager, Himanshu, Natasha, Maya and Reena came rushing out. There was another gentleman with them. They had been waiting for us.

Debajyoti jumped off and met the man who was standing by, whom I realized must be the doctor. Safar was helped out of the jeep.

'Oh my God, this is terrible!' shrieked Natasha when she saw Safar.

'Is it hurting badly?' asked Maya, as Reena looked on with a horrified expression.

It was pretty shocking when you looked at Safar. Her face had swollen up even more. Her right eye was now grotesque, stretched out and huge. Debajyoti and Zaid quickly took her inside, along with the doctor, followed by Maya and Natasha. Vikram also jumped out of the jeep and went in after them.

'Damn,' said Jaya when they had all gone in. 'I didn't expect it to get that bad. Poor thing. I just thought it was a little sting. I've been stung as a child.'

'Yeah, me too, it was painful but you get over it. What a morning! Hope she gets better soon!'

'The Mumbai team is pretty shook up. This was too much of the wild side for them. It was really a random thing to happen, and that too on day one!' Jaya shook her head. We started taking our stuff out of the jeep.

'What awesome pics, man!' We turned to see Manju sitting on the steps, scanning pictures on her camera. 'Really nice ones of you, Sunaina. And so much drama with the bees! Jaya, you must have got it too, right?'

Jaya nodded. 'You know I was rolling my camera, as Vikram was talking about his experience in the park when Sunaina suddenly yelled out about the bees, and I even got Safar screaming.'

'Dude, so was I!' said Danish, who was in the other jeep, offloading equipment. 'I even got a shot of the forest guard running back to the jeep.'

'This could actually give you an exciting five minutes in one of the episodes! Full-blown drama! I have stills of Vikram and you under the scarf,' said Manju.

'Hmm, she's right, you know,' I said to Jaya, who nodded.

'Then we'll need more footage for the entire sequence. Let me see if I can get a few discreet shots of Safar with the doctor, and everyone waiting around. We'll need that in the edit if we're to use this,' she said.

I nodded, but guiltily wondered how we'd so casually slid into a reality show mode. Though Jaya was right. Visually, we needed to get everything now and then decide which shots to use during the edit later.

Entering the lounge, we saw Safar lying on the sofa with Maya next to her as the doctor spoke to Natasha, Vikram and Zaid who were nodding seriously.

As least intrusively as possible Jaya took a couple of shots.

When the doctor was leaving, we asked him for a short sound bite. He said he had been visiting another place nearby when he got the call, which explained how he managed to arrive so quickly.

'I've given her a shot and medicines to bring down the swelling and help with the pain. She should be fine by tomorrow. You see, these jungle bees can be deadly. Thankfully she got stung only once. If you get stung by a couple, the poison is so strong you can even die or at least require hospitalization,' he said quite calmly. I hope he didn't say this to the rest of them!

It was a sobering thought. I felt grateful no one else was stung, and that Safar was stung only once. I even felt a little guilty for my earlier nonchalance, when I had thought it wasn't such a big deal.

We spent the rest of the day in the resort.

The afternoon safari was cancelled, though Danish took a jeep out to get some shots. Debajyoti was very worried about what the morning's events meant for the rest of our shoot. The Mumbai crew seemed very upset.

Natasha had fretted over Vikram and even expressed relief that the injured party was Safar and not him. It sounded heartless, but on one level I could understand where she was coming from. Vikram was the sun around whom their galaxy was centred.

That evening we went ahead with the campfire according to our shoot plan. It had been planned not just for fun, which campfires are, but also for us to get a few shots of the team unwinding post safari. To record a few comments from the various members.

A very relieved Debajyoti had informed us on our WhatsApp group that Safar was much better and the mood had lifted among the Mumbaikars. That was a relief. It was just as the doctor had predicted.

A fairly upbeat Vikram met us as we arrived at the campfire. 'Hello!' he said cheerily to us. 'What a crazy first safari we had! It was stressful at the time, but I have to say, thinking of it now, it was all very exciting. Fortunately, as you had predicted, Safar has almost recovered now. Let's hope tomorrow's better!'

I felt a huge sense of relief to find him in such a positive mood and talking about the next safari. I could see this had lifted everyone else's mood as well. It was also nice to see he had taken the morning's episode in his stride, as a learning experience, not as a reason to rethink stepping out of his comfort zone.

Manju showed Vikram and Natasha some of the pictures she had taken and got their go-ahead for the ones she could post.

Debajyoti was excitedly discussing plans for the next day's shoot, now that the cloud had lifted.

Devraj made an appearance and started chatting with Natasha, Reena and Vikram, who very animatedly started describing the events of the morning. Looking over to where I was chatting with Danish and Maya, he waved, asking me to join them.

'Sunaina was really amazing through it all. She was the first to realize we were in trouble and then her reaction was so fast! She covered me with a chunni she had with her. I can still hear that buzzing of the bees!' he said with a grin.

'Thanks!' I said, smiling at his account. 'I was the first to realize only because I was watching Ram

Tiwari so closely, still hoping to hear something about a tiger sighting. That's when I saw he was swatting away too many bees. It was just a few seconds between that realization and Safar's scream. Then it was full-blown panic for a few moments as the bees swarmed around us.'

'A few moments! It felt really long to me! I was a little confused initially, about what was happening, and then there was pandemonium!' exclaimed Vikram. 'Especially after Safar screamed!'

'I'm relieved I overslept and missed the safari,' said Reena, turning towards Vikram and fluttering her eyelashes. 'I'm very allergic to insect bites, and the way the doctor described the risks from the jungle bees, I would have needed to be hospitalized!'

Again, I wanted to strangle her. Here we all were trying our best to play it down and she was making it sound dangerous. And trust her to try and insert herself in the story. I looked away to suppress my eye roll and realized Devraj had caught my expression as he was smiling conspiratorially.

'Well, I'm glad you all are safe. No point worrying about what didn't happen,' said Devraj. Then, turning to Vikram, he said, 'You've had quite an eventful and, dare I say, dramatic first safari. Very different from the usual. Did you know bees were considered messengers of the gods in ancient Rome and Greece? The Greeks even had a god of beekeeping. In Chinese culture, bees are associated with good luck and prosperity. So, I must say, your shoot has started on an auspicious note. If one believes in those kind of things.'

Now that gave Vikram something to chew on and he was very excited to talk more about bees. I was so relieved at the direction Devraj had taken the conversation I could have given him a hug.

'About tomorrow, I will speak to my friends in the forest department and try to figure out the tiger movement,' said Devraj after a few minutes. 'Sometimes they can be very helpful and may have information about which area we should visit, where tiger-spotting possibilities are the highest.'

'Ooh,' gushed Reena, 'then I'd better not miss it tomorrow.'

The rest of the evening was fairly pleasant. Debajyoti strummed his guitar as we sat around the fire. Jaya and Danish got shots of the gathering. Reena did a little interview with Vikram about his first safari, where he again launched into a description of the 'attack of the bees', as everyone was referring to it.

It was soon time for dinner and everyone was quite hungry!

Since we were sitting around the campfire, the dinner was finger food from the tandoor. There was an array of succulent kebabs, burra and seekhs. The vegetarians were not left out and there were tandoori potatoes, paneer, broccoli, cauliflower, dahi kebabs as well as stuffed naans. The cheese naans were especially fabulous, and I decided they were my favourite. We wrapped up dinner soon and called it a night. Hopefully, the next day we'd have more luck on safari.

8

The next morning we were at the jeeps again.

We were loading up our equipment when Reena tottered up in her tan boots, tight olive-green pants and a fitted khaki shirt. She was also wearing a slightly largish, stylish hat.

'Manju, take a picture, please,' she called out as she posed on the side of the jeep. 'The hashtag will be "safari glam".'

Manju took a few fun pictures and we all laughed as Reena struck different poses.

While it was easy to make fun of Reena's frivolousness, there was also a carefree and fun quality about her that I grudgingly admired. I tended to take work so seriously most of the time and get caught up in the various issues that concerned me. I made a mental note to stop being so judgemental. To each his own, whatever makes you happy.

'Come on, Sunaina. We're the two reporters on the campaign. Let's get a picture together,' she called out, now sitting on the bonnet of the jeep. It was as if she had heard my little self-sermon.

Oh, what the hell, I thought to myself and stood beside her in my brown cargo pants and olive-green camo T-shirt. I put my hat on as Manju took another picture.

'A photo session without me?' called out Vikram as he walked up with Natasha. Dressed in an olive green shirt and khaki pants, he looked bright and cheerful. His hair was carefully styled, and he held his hat in his hands.

Reena giggled in delight and Vikram happily joined us, striking a pose next to the jeep.

He then put his arms around us and made a 'V' sign. Manju was also thrilled to have Vikram join the photo session and clicked away.

'Good morning, are we ready to leave now?' called out a slightly stern voice.

It was Devraj, standing next to the second jeep with a bemused expression. Somehow, the realization that he had watched our little photo session made me cringe.

I was also surprised he was coming along with us.

'Good morning!' Debajyoti replied. 'Thanks so much for agreeing to take us today. Hope you were able to get some helpful information from your forest department friends.'

'Hey, man! Hope it's going to be our lucky day!' said Vikram, enthusiastically greeting him.

'Well, we're going into zone five today. Yesterday evening the forest department team spotted a kill in the ravine there,' said Devraj. 'We expect the tiger would be somewhere nearby.'

On that exciting note, we all got into the vehicles. The production assistants came up with wireless mikes for us to put on. One was given to Devraj as well. Debajyoti assigned Jaya, Vikram and me to one jeep, with Devraj sitting in the front with Prem Singh.

Natasha, Reena and Debajyoti were in the second jeep with one of the bodyguards, and the rest were in the third jeep with Ram Tiwari, who would join us at the gate.

Soon we were deep in the park, near the ravine we had been told about. We stopped the jeeps near a culvert. Devraj turned around and said softly that the kill was behind some grass on the right side. While we couldn't see it, there was a very strong smell of decaying meat.

'Ew,' said Vikram, scrunching up his nose. 'That smells foul.'

We drove around the area, up one road, down another. But remained nearby. With no luck, we came back to the culvert and decided to continue waiting there. Half an hour went by as we whispered and fidgeted in the jeep.

The day grew increasingly oppressive as the heat intensified and the smell of decaying meat from the kill became more and more overpowering. A small cheetal had been killed, according to the information Devraj had got from the forest department. Suddenly, there was a commotion from the other jeep. We all turned to see Reena leaning over the side, her face contorted in disgust as she retched violently. Debajyoti was simultaneously

helping her and shushing her. The sound of her gagging
and retching filled the air.

We all watched her, like a horror show that one
couldn't look away from.

Suddenly, her beautiful hat that she had been trying
to hold on to, went tumbling on to the ground, where it
then rolled a little away from the jeep.

Just then, Prem Singh whispered urgently. 'Hukum,
look there,' he said pointing to a grassy mound a little
distance away. It had two or three big boulders on it.

As we all looked at the mound, there was a little
movement behind it. And then up rose a curious tiger
face.

The whole time we had been sitting in this spot, the
tiger had been sleeping behind the mound. And now,
perhaps because of Reena's loud retching, it had woken up.

It slowly stood up, its tail twitching.

'Oh my God, there it is!' said Vikram excitedly.

I could hear Reena saying something about her hat,
but she was immediately shushed by Debajyoti and
Natasha.

As we all watched, the tiger gracefully stretched out
its body in that classic feline posture, with its front paws
extended, torso lowered and hindquarters raised up,
displaying its power and grace.

Jaya filmed Vikram's reactions, while Danish
captured the tiger's movements.

After the leisurely stretch, the tiger padded across to
a tall tree. It stood there for a moment, its nose twitching
as it took in the various scents of the forest. Then, with
fluid movements, it stood on its hind legs and embraced

the tree trunk. While it looked like it was hugging the tree, it used its sharp claws to leave deep scratches on the bark. Finally, it turned around and marked the tree with its own pungent scent.

This was such an incredible sighting! I had never seen a tiger mark a tree before!

'It's Zalim,' said Devraj, looking at Prem Singh for confirmation.

'Hukum,' he replied, in agreement.

'The tiger has a name?' asked Vikram.

'Well, technically, now they're not supposed to, just a number, like T-15 or T-20, but then invariably some guide, driver or regular visitor gives them a nickname that sticks and then everyone uses it.'

'Oh, that's cool. I'd love to name a tiger,' said Vikram.

'Hukum gave him that name,' said Prem Singh, looking towards Devraj.

'Oh, really? How did you come up with it?' I asked.

'Well, he was very aggressive as a young cub, troubling his sisters. We've been watching him since then. I said Zalim was an appropriate name for him during one of the drives. There were a few jeeps around and others commented as well. And somehow, after that, all the guides started calling him that,' said Devraj.

'Why is he scratching the tree?' Vikram asked.

Before I could answer, Devraj said, 'It's to mark his territory so other male tigers don't venture here. Also, you can see how high he reached up to mark the tree. That will give any other male an idea of how big he is, and he will quietly leave the area if he knows what's good for him.'

'Whoa. That's some real alpha male stuff,' Vikram said in admiration.

Meanwhile, Zalim had settled down under a tree. After a little while, he lay down flat.

'Look at his stomach, it's so full and heavy. He's not going anywhere. He must have fed for a few hours and then passed out near that mound till we disturbed him. He has probably woken up because of the heat,' said Devraj. 'Though the forest department had said it was a tigress who made the kill.'

'He must have taken it as usual,' replied Prem Singh.

'What, he took someone else's kill?' asked Vikram.

'Yes, he's famous for that. He's very lazy, and when a female in his territory makes a kill, he usually locates it and takes over. The females try and eat as much as they can when they make the kill and feed their cubs, because they know they may not have it for long.'

'Wicked!' said Vikram, as we looked on at the resting Zalim. 'Makes the female do the work and takes the perks.'

'That's so interesting,' I replied. 'While there's a lot of information and studies about tiger behaviour, I guess it's also important to acknowledge that tigers can have different traits. Almost like different personalities.'

'Yes, that's quite right. There definitely needs to be more study on tiger behaviour, keeping in mind that some tigers differ from the broad generalizations,' said Devraj.

'How do you mean?' asked Vikram as he kept looking at the tiger sleeping nearby.

'Well, there are so many anecdotal accounts one hears about unusual behaviour, different from what we would usually expect. Like the sisters who hunt together in Bandhavgarh, Madhya Pradesh. Tigers usually never hunt in pairs once they are adults. Or a male tiger in Corbett who is still sighted with his mother even though he's four years old and she's had another litter. He refuses to move out on his own. It's quite interesting.'

'I did hear about the Bandhavgarh sisters! In fact, I'd even proposed to cover it for a story to my office, but they didn't think it was interesting,' I replied.

'I got a few pictures of them together when I visited Bandhavgarh six months ago. I can show you when we're back at the resort,' he said with a smile. 'We also have the example of Mallika here in Chambalgarh who has had a long-running feud with bears. It's said that because a bear killed one of her cubs, she is always out to get them. That means she is able to hold that memory for a long time. Or else just got programmed to detest bears.'

'There's also that book by John Vaillant about an Amur tiger in Russia that stalked and killed a hunter who injured him. Apparently it's a true story, and the tiger took revenge,' I said.

'Ah yes, *A True Story of Vengeance and Survival*. That's a great book,' said Devraj, nodding.

Our conversation might have gone on much longer if it wasn't for the two jeeps that pulled up just then, people excitedly pointing and clicking pictures of Zalim.

Then a third jeep arrived, and Devraj seemed inclined to move. But Danish was filming Vikram, and Jaya wanted more shots of the big cat from our perspective.

We waited for around fifteen minutes but then realized that the people in the other jeeps had stopped looking at Zalim, who wasn't moving anyway, and had started looking towards us and taking pictures. They had spotted Vikram and couldn't believe it.

'Hi, Vikram!' two girls from one of the jeeps called out.

'Hey,' he responded, waving back, leading to squeals from the girls and more photographs being clicked. The guide in their jeep shushed them.

'I think it's time we moved from here,' said Devraj irritably, clearly exasperated with all the excitement.

By now, quite a few people were leaning out of their jeeps, trying to get pictures and interact with Vikram.

As we left, Vikram waved bye to this fans who seemed to have forgotten all about the sleeping tiger.

It was a bit of a jolt to be reminded of his star power. Perhaps, because we'd all been together and he was fairly down to earth, one forgot that he was Bollywood's 'next big thing'.

Once we had moved away from the other jeeps, Vikram turned to us with a sheepish shake of his head.

'I have to be extra nice when interacting with people, otherwise they'll post on social media or Instagram how I was stand-offish and rude, and you have all these tabloid-type websites that love to write bitchy pieces about these things. They're always on the lookout.'

'You gotta do what you gotta do,' I replied with a smile.

Devraj simply nodded, expressionless. I thought that was rather cold as Vikram was clearly embarrassed.

We waited on the side of the road as Debajyoti wanted Danish's jeep ahead of us to take shots of us exiting the park.

We got out of the park soon enough, without another incident.

'Well, I finally saw my first tiger!' said Vikram happily. 'And that was a good sighting, right? We even saw him scratching the tree. That was quite something.'

'Good sighting?' That was an understatement!

'Vikram, that qualifies as a fabulous sighting! It was the first time I saw a tiger mark a tree,' I replied. 'I've only seen the markings on trees, never the actual act! That was definitely special!'

'Okay! Wow! I thought so, but still wanted to check with the experts. Thanks Devraj, that was amazing.' Devraj turned and gave him a slight smile and nod in reply.

We got back to the resort and were getting out of the jeeps when a very determined-looking Reena purposefully walked up to us and cornered Devraj. She asked him if it would be possible to get her hat back, as it had fallen off where we had seen the tiger, and at that time it wasn't possible to retrieve it as you couldn't get down from the jeep. 'At least that's what the guide said even though I kept asking him!' she said petulantly.

We were all amused, especially since Devraj seemed taken aback.

'Can't you use your contacts in the forest department?' she pleaded.

Looking at her with a mixture of confusion and amusement, he replied, 'I'm not sure if the forest department has a lost-and-found for designer hats, but I'll see what I can do.'

Not to be deterred by sarcasm, Reena went on about how it was a special hat she had bought in Italy and she wasn't going to lose it like this.

Again Devraj said he would try and do his best, but clearly he was befuddled by the request.

Finally, Vikram intervened. 'Reena! I'll get you another hat, I promise!' he said, giving her a hug. 'After all, the tiger woke up because of your puking!'

That made everyone laugh, and even Reena couldn't help but look a little mollified.

9

Later that day, at around noon, I lay in my tent after all the excitement of the morning.

We'd all had the post-safari traditional 'breakfast of champions'—eggs, sausages, pancakes, waffles and a variety of fruit—and I had decided to skip lunch.

Jaya was moving around, putting her camera batteries on charge and checking the footage from the morning. I had dozed off when Manju came rushing into the tent and woke me up. She looked very excited.

'Sunaina! I have something to show you! But first I want to ask, why are you not on Twitter or Instagram?'

'What happened?' I said sleepily. 'I am on Twitter but have a very low-key, protected account after I got trolled. Not worth the stress. I'm on Instagram but not too active, and Facebook, I'm very private because of a psycho ex-boyfriend but that's a long story. Why?'

'Well, right now Vikram's pictures in the park are getting a lot of traction! I'd posted them last night on

Instagram and Twitter, and I didn't really check this morning as we started off early. Then in the park the connectivity was not so good, so again I couldn't check. But when I went online a short while ago, there were so many reactions! Like OMG! So many hits and comments. It's crazy. I guess there is a different level of interest among the masses for these Bollywood guys. We never get so many hits for other stories!'

'Wow, that's amazing. Good! At least the campaign will get some attention because of Vikram. Come for the star, learn a little about tigers! Am I right?' I replied, happy that Manju was so happy.

'Yes! Exactly. Some of the accounts promoting and retweeting are also Vikram Khanna fan-club accounts, so they could be proxies run by Natasha. All stars have this kind of online support going on, you know, run by their teams. Helps amplify. Though a few of the fan clubs are genuine as well.'

'I wouldn't know,' I replied, still feeling sleepy. I glanced at my phone and saw there was a WhatsApp message from an unknown number. 'Hi Sunaina, this is Devraj', it read.

I perked up to read the rest of it when I realized Manju was still talking to me.

'Actually, that's not all I wanted to tell you. It's not just the campaign. You're getting a lot of attention as well. Many people are talking about you,' she said, looking at me excitedly.

For a minute I was confused.

'What does that even mean? Why are they interested in me? Show me!'

Jaya and I looked at Manju's phone. We had created a separate handle for the shoot, to post all the pictures and information, to create a buzz around the campaign. This would be occasionally retweeted by our main news handle.

There were many pictures of Vikram and our shoot that were getting attention and lots of comments and engagements.

But the picture that was generating a lot of interest was the picture of Vikram and me, peeping out from under the scarf after the 'attack of the bees' incident. Vikram's expression was of wide-eyed wonderment, clearly playing for the camera.

I, on the other hand, simply had a tight smile. But overall, it was a cute picture.

The caption read 'Relief after reaching safety, following an unexpected encounter with bees in the jungle #TeamTiger #SaveOurTigers #AllSafe #Environment #Safari #wildlife #JungleBees, etc. etc.', and tagged Vikram.

Now Vikram had posted it to his handle with a caption #MyHero & #SavedByTheBelle, which I had to admit was quite clever.

Since he was such a big star, this had sparked a quite a reaction on Instagram, with it being reposted on his fan pages and other handles. Many people were reacting to the photo with curiosity, wondering about the bees and about me. Some had obviously identified me as a reporter from the channel.

There were a variety of comments about Vikram, many of his fans gushing. Others wondered what had happened in the forest, how had I 'saved' him. There were questions about what Vikram was doing in a national park, what was 'Team Tiger'. There was some trolling, snide comments about his drug scandal and escaping to the forest, etc.

Then even speculation about Vikram and me!

'Who are you getting cosy with in the jungle?'

'What a cute picture, is this your new girlfriend?'

'Are reporters allowed to cosy up like this?'

'Perks of the job!' And on and on.

I felt my face go hot with embarrassment looking at some of the comments. This was mortifying!

After all, I was just a news reporter and this was just another shoot for me, admittedly a more high-profile one. But to be the subject of this kind of gossip wasn't something I'd anticipated. Especially when it was all untrue!

'Arré, don't worry,' said Jaya, looking at my ashen face. 'It's just stupid social media stuff. It will die down.'

'I hope so! How ridiculous! This is why I stay away from all this!' I said, a little shriller than I intended.

Then another thought struck me. People in the group would see this, and what if other people I knew saw it too? The thought of that was even more mortifying. Hopefully it would just fade away and amount to nothing.

'Manju, please tell me this will all die down! Please don't post any pictures of me now!'

'Yeah, of course it will. Don't worry!' she reassured me, even as she kept scrolling through her phone. 'These things are like that, but the good thing is the amount of attention the campaign is getting overall. And it's sparked interest about tigers! Just like you wanted.'

She looked up, grinning at me. I was taken aback!

'Is this a joke to you? People are talking rubbish, and you're only concerned about getting traction on social media!' I was getting agitated now. I needed some fresh air.

All thoughts of a siesta now gone, I stomped out of the tent towards the main building. My thoughts were all over the place. After walking a bit, I started thinking I might be overreacting. Or not. I wasn't sure.

I looked at my phone and read Devraj's message.

'Hi Sunaina, this is Devraj here. Hope you don't mind, I got your number from Debajyoti. Do send me the report you did featuring Mallika. Thanks.'

That was nice. He actually wanted to see my report! I had it saved in a folder on my phone and forwarded it to him. 'Let me know what you think.'

I also saved his number. Oddly, I hoped he would like my report.

I entered the lounge area and found Natasha sitting there. She was on her laptop and talking to someone on the phone at the same time. Maybe talking to her about the social media issue would help.

'May I join you?' I asked.

She motioned me to sit down as she continued talking on the phone. She spoke animatedly for another five minutes regarding the terms of a deal, as far as I could tell. Finally she finished.

'Hello, what's up?' she said, turning to me as her eyes kept darting back to her phone.

'I'm a little distressed. I don't know if you've seen it, but this picture of Vikram and me that Manju posted has got quite a reaction. Lots of comments, but some people are even speculating if there's something going on between Vikram and me. It's all very silly and embarrassing!'

'Yes, of course, I saw it. It's my job to know everything,' she said, smiling. 'But don't get distressed. These things always happen around a movie star. People are so interested in their life, you never know what suddenly sparks a reaction.'

'True, I can only imagine what it's like. But it's mortifying for me as a journalist.'

'Pshaw!' she said, almost scoffing. 'What does it matter? It will soon blow over. But it's also generated a lot of conversation about what Vikram is doing here, and there have been a lot of positive reactions. It's really good for his image. And being linked to a reporter is a nice change for him,' she laughed.

My jaw nearly hit the floor. I didn't know if she was serious, but this highly embarrassing episode for me was nothing more than some positive image-building for Natasha.

I had always been a very private person, unlike many of my friends and elder sister who shared a lot of their lives on social media. Given this somewhat private past, what was happening now was fairly stressful!

Or was I creating too much out of it in my head?

'Do you really think it will die down? I'm really not comfortable with all this,' I said weakly.

'Darling, don't worry. In two days no one will even remember. Just relax for now and concentrate on completing the shoot. Today was a very good day. It was the first time I saw a tiger. It was just amazing! What have you got planned for later today?'

'We have the shoot with the forest guards lined up in the afternoon.'

'Great! Then concentrate on that rather than all this. I'll give the afternoon drive a skip and have a nap,' she said, gathering her things.

Feeling slightly better, I went back to my tent where Jaya was snoozing. I tried to get some sleep, but didn't manage any. I checked out Instagram and saw there were even more comments. Yikes. I decided to leave it. It would die down, as everyone said.

Just then I got a message from Devraj.

'It was a really good report! You got great footage of Mallika. Impressed.'

Now that cheered me up. I sent him a 'Thank you!' and a smiley face and immediately regretted it. Devraj didn't seem like an emoticon kind of guy, and that was a slightly more casual vibe than I wanted to go for.

I was just thinking or rather overthinking it when I got a message back. It was a thumbs-up sign. Okay, whew.

It was nearly 3 p.m. now, and we were supposed to leave at 3:30 p.m. I got ready for the shoot and decided to go back to the dining area and have a coffee.

As I entered the dining area, I almost did an about-turn! Reena, Zaid, Maya and Safar were sitting together at a table. Probably the last people I wanted to see at this time.

'Oh, look who's here! Our social media sensation!' Reena called out.

'Please, Reena, it's so silly. And it will just blow over,' I said, taking a seat and acting very casual.

'Are you kidding me? It's great! I posted our pictures from this morning as well and they've had a big reaction as well! My hat looked so good in the pictures, so sad I lost it,' she sighed, looking sad and wistful for a moment. But then she perked up, 'You need to start dressing better, wearing some make-up now, if you're going to get so much attention.'

Trust Reena to be totally unaware of my obvious discomfort.

'Don't be silly. It's just one of those social media blips. It'll be over tomorrow. Natasha also feels it will die down,' I replied, trying to appear casual.

I saw Reena, Maya and Safar exchange looks at this remark. They obviously had talked about what was happening online and had 'thoughts'.

'Safar, how are you feeling? You look totally recovered,' I said quickly, trying to change the topic.

'I'm much better, thanks.' Her hand instinctively went to her right cheek. 'One moment I was looking through the binoculars for the tiger, the other minute I was swatting away buzzing bees, and then this excruciating pain near my ear!' she said, again touching the side of her face self-consciously.

Calling a waiter, I asked for a strong French press coffee.

Just then Debajyoti walked in. Relieved to see him, I asked, 'So we're set for the next shoot? The forest guards are ready? They're expecting us?'

We started talking about plans for the shoot. I could see Reena fidgeting as she clearly wanted to talk more about the campaign's online splash but fortunately didn't interrupt us.

We were still in a discussion when Devraj walked into the lounge.

Debajyoti waved to him and asked him to join us.

'Well, your shoot is suddenly getting a lot of attention,' he said, sitting down. 'I've had some of the local media and even media from Jaipur calling to ask about Vikram's stay. They're asking what NNTV is doing here and even about you, Sunaina.' He nodded towards me. I could feel my face go red. The fact that even Devraj knew about the little online hubbub was very embarrassing.

'I guess with the social media thrust, now everyone knows Vikram is here, and he's a huge star, so this was inevitable,' Debajyoti replied matter-of-factly.

'Of course,' said Reena with a toss of her hair. 'This is just the start. Now there will be huge interest in what he's doing here and our shoot.'

'Yes, well, I've increased security at the gate, and told them not to let anyone in without checking with either Himanshu or me. Just be careful when going to the park. You may find more people than you bargained for.'

'I'm sure. We'll just have to handle all that,' said Reena.

One of the staff members came up and said something to Devraj. He excused himself and walked out.

I looked at Debajyoti with a what-is-going-on expression, but he shrugged.

'I guess working with a movie star is bound to have its own issues. We knew this. We might not be used to it, but it is what it is,' he said.

'I'm telling you to dress up a bit now! Maya and I can help you,' said Reena again with a saucy smile.

'Yeah, babe,' Maya chirped in. 'We've got lots of accessories and stuff. We got some for you just in case too. Some extra hats and scarves, I'll send them across.'

'The make-up guy, Mickey, can do your hair and make-up as well ahead of the shoots. We can totally send him across to your tent,' Safar chirped up.

This was all getting a bit much. I thanked them and said I'll think about it. Then, saying I had to call Jaya, I stepped out to be by myself.

I sat out on the veranda and called Jaya, who said she was coming to the lodge.

I was sitting there, stewing in my thoughts, when Vikram walked out with his guards.

'Why are you sitting here by yourself? Isn't it time for the shoot?' he asked.

'Yes, it is. We're leaving in fifteen minutes. But there was something I wanted to clear up with you,' I said, thinking to myself I may as well take the bull by the horns. 'Have you seen these online comments about you and me? I just saw them and it's kind of disturbed me.'

'I did, my team told me. They have to tell me anything that's said about me online,' he nodded. 'But why are you disturbed?'

'Well, that photograph of you and me has got people speculating about us,' I said as delicately as I could.

'Oh that? Don't worry about it. These things happen and they blow over. People have nothing better to do.'

'All right. It's just weird and unusual for me. You must be used to all this attention and scrutiny.' I smiled.

'Oh yes. From a young age! What with my family and all. And then when I started acting. It's relentless and I can't let it get to me. I know it's strange for you, but really, don't worry about it. You, my dear, have just been added to a long list of ladies whom I have been linked with,' he chuckled. Then, seeing Debajyoti emerge from the lounge, he waved him over.

'Boss, are we all set to leave? Or can I get a coffee too?'

'Yeah sure, we'll get one to go,' he said, and they all walked inside.

The exchange with Vikram left me feeling a little ill. 'Long list of ladies!' Ugh. Well, it was better to not think about it. And, with this resolve, I got up to join the rest for the shoot.

In about five minutes everyone had gathered around in the veranda. Jaya had also arrived and, looking concerned, asked me if I was fine. I gave her a cheerful smile and shrug, as Debajyoti started outlining the plan. Vikram and I were going to accompany some forest guards on their patrol, take a look at their quarters in the park and later, when it got darker, film them keeping watch on a machan.

We all got into the jeeps and headed to the park. I was chatting with Jaya as we arrived at the park entrance. Sure enough, there was a larger than usual crowd outside the gate, and, as we came to a stop, we were surrounded by photographers.

'Vikram! Vikram!' they yelled as the subject of their attention waved to them.

'What are you doing here?' one of them with a mike asked.

'I'm learning about tigers and conservation, and enjoying myself in this beautiful park.'

'What have you been learning?' another asked.

'About the amazing sanctuaries we have in the country and the effort that goes into protecting them! The history of Chambalgarh Tiger reserve. And I have a lovely teacher as well,' he said with a flourish, indicating me.

What the WHAT! I had been trying to look inconspicuous in my corner of the jeep when I suddenly found myself being clicked along with Vikram.

'How long are you here, Vikram? Was it the first time you saw a tiger?'

'Yes, it was and it was magical. He got up and hugged a tree, put his marks on it! It was quite a sighting.' He acted it out, to the delight of the journalists.

Now the crowd was getting bigger and there was even some jostling, so two forest guards from the chowki came and started clearing the way as other jeeps were being blocked.

'Okay, let's go, people,' said Debajyoti, who had quickly completed the formalities at the gate, and thankfully we were off.

As we drove along the park entry road, I turned to Vikram.

'What was that?!' I asked, genuinely perplexed.

He grinned back at me. 'Well, it is true, right? Just wanted to show them I'm genuinely here to learn about all the conservation issues, and who better to learn from than a reporter who covers wildlife,' he replied smoothly.

I wasn't completely convinced by his banal take but we had reached our shoot location.

There was a group of four forest guards, including Ram Tiwari, waiting at a chowki near Kamal Jheel. We would spend the next hour accompanying them on patrol. They took us up a winding trail, with two guards ahead of us and two bringing up the rear.

Jaya and Danish filmed us from various angles. The area had been inspected by the guards before we arrived. Even so, as the guards led the way, their eyes kept scanning the foliage for any signs of movement. They pointed out different species of trees, plants and birds to us, sharing their knowledge of the park's ecology. They stopped now and then, holding their fingers to their lips as they listened intently and looked for any sign of movement, before gesturing to the group to follow.

After we had reached a clearing, we filmed Vikram and me walking and talking with the guards. Vikram was his charming self, plying them with questions.

Bachi Singh, the seniormost guard, answered him.

'Bachi ji, tell me something, you don't have guns as I can see' said Vikram. 'But what do you do when you come face to face with a tiger on patrol?'

'Well, sir ji, usually tigers avoid humans. They hear us approaching, get our smell and they move away from the area. We always walk in groups during patrol, and because we stand tall on two feet, they don't identify us as prey. They have a huge prey base here in the jungle to choose from, so they're not interested in us,' replied Bachi Singh.

'But you only have lathis? Have you ever come face to face with a tiger?'

'Yes, a few times. The first time, many years ago, I was walking with two other guards, and we turned a corner and 10 feet from us there was this tiger, sitting under a tree watching us. He was called Masti and was the dominant male in the area. I'll admit I was petrified on seeing him, but he just watched us very casually. I was younger then, and there was a senior guard leading us. After stopping for a moment, looking at the tiger, who kept looking at us, he told us to slowly back away. Not to turn around, but walk backwards slowly. He said this very calmly to us but kept looking at the tiger. So we did what he said, and, as soon as we were out of the tiger's line of sight, we turned and nearly ran back to the chowki! Later, I remembered we had been taught this in our training, to never turn your back if you can help it, but when you come face to face with a tiger for the first time, you forget everything!'

'Wow! That must have been really frightening! So you should keep facing the tiger? Why is that?' Vikram asked.

'Yes, it's better not to show your back, and for the tiger to see your eyes at all times. Then it knows you're watching it. If the animal exhibits any aggression, even then you should calmly walk back. But if you feel it's going to attack, only then you should make a loud noise and raise your arms to appear taller. They don't know how powerless we are against them, but this gives the impression we're big and fierce.'

'You mean like this?' Vikram said and proceeded to wave his arms above his head, as he jumped up and down. We all started laughing as Jaya and Danish filmed him.

'And in your mind, you must pray to all the gods and powers you believe in, that it works!' Bachi Singh added, laughing.

I laughed, watching his antics. 'It's very possible a tiger is watching you right now, wondering who this strange creature is.'

We continued walking through the grassy meadow with the guards pointing out the different plants in this habitat.

'You live in the forest for days together, away from your families? Must be very tough,' Vikram now asked. This was something I had told him about.

Bachi Singh spoke about his wife and two sons who lived in a nearby village. He got to see them every fortnight or so if he was lucky.

'It's a sacrifice, sir, but we knew it when we took the job. Also, we're very lucky to have this government job; otherwise, I would have been working in my village fields with my elder brothers,' he said. 'Or would have had to move to a city like Jaipur to get work. So I'm actually very fortunate.'

Vikram nodded along, but the difference in their stations in life struck me.

It was such a starkly different world Vikram was encountering here. I wondered how often he interacted with the 'other half', the majority of India that lived in the villages and towns.

Vikram was highly likely among the top 1 per cent of the country's wealthiest individuals, and certainly among the top 10 per cent. In India, the top 10 per cent are believed to possess more than 70 per cent of the country's total wealth, while the rest of the population falls significantly below this level.

We came to a stop near a man-made water hole. The forest guards explained how this water hole was filled by the department for the animals during the summer months when most waterbodies dried up. It was located strategically, easily accessible and in an area where animals crossed. There was enough vegetation around to provide shade and cover.

There was a camera trap placed near the water hole to capture pictures of the diverse wildlife. One of the guards took out the chip and put it in their camera, and showed us the wide variety of animals that came along this way at night. From a tiger to a porcupine!

It was a pretty location, so Debajyoti decided we could film the guards taking a break here and continue the conversation. For the next half hour, Vikram had a light-hearted chat with them. He even got Bachi Singh to sing one of his favourite Hindi film songs which turned out to be from a hit movie Vikram's father had acted in, back in the day. Vikram sang along as well. It was a delight and made for great television. I could see the smiles all around, as I sat on a log next to them and watched.

We then walked back to the chowki. Danish and Jaya remained hard at work, taking shots and close-ups of the group. It went a lot faster as we had already filmed a lot and didn't need to stop again and again.

Back at the chowki, we were set up for a tea break. We had planned to film this and use it in the show as well.

The drivers from the lodge had laid out tea, coffee and snacks on the bonnets of the jeeps. They had found a nice spot, where you had a beautiful view of the forest and the hills behind it. It was a nice spread—home-baked cookies, nankhatais, vanilla cake slices and namkeens. The coffee was just what I needed, and I was going to ask someone to pour me a cup, when Vikram said he wanted to have the tea the guards had offered him.

They were sitting on benches and chairs, next to the chowki, while one of them was making tea on a *chullah*. We had offered them tea but they didn't want our teabag tea. Instead, they preferred their boiled tea made on a smoky wood fire. Now I couldn't opt for the divine-smelling coffee as it would be bad form to not have the tea the guards were making. Especially since Vikram was going to have it, even though I hated milky boiled tea.

I could see Jaya smirking at me because this was a common peeve of ours. During a shoot, whenever we visited a house or a government office to do an interview or get a sound bite, we'd invariably be offered sweet, milky tea. We both disliked it but would have it as it was considered rude not to accept. And if we happened to visit two or three places in a single shoot, we'd have to have tea every time. Our code name for it was T-T—tea-torture.

I sat with Vikram next to the chullah and accepted a glass of the freshly boiled tea.

Vikram asked the guards about the challenges they faced in the job. Ram Tiwari said the most challenging thing for him was to work all day, do the patrols, etc., and then return to the chowki and cook. That he said was the most difficult thing, as everyone laughed.

Finally, Vikram asked about their most frightening experience in the forest. Bachi Singh told him another tale, about the time he had witnessed a fight between a tiger and bear. It was during the monsoon when the park was shut. He was patrolling in a jeep, when he turned a bend and found a tiger and bear facing off. It was Mallika of course, because of her lifelong hatred for bears. Most tigers avoid a confrontation with them.

Both animals were snarling at one another, and while it was fascinating to see, he and the driver tried to reverse, to be at a safe distance. But because of the heavy rain, the dirt roads were muddy and when they tried to reverse their back tyre got stuck. They had to then sit there quietly and witness the entire fight. He said Mallika and the bear went at each other a few times, but finally both retreated. It was the most ferocious thing he'd ever witnessed, and he was petrified through most of it. Only after both the animals were gone for over half an hour did they dare get out of the jeep and dig around the wheel that was stuck.

Another younger guard, Kesar Meena, told him about the time he had been mock chased by a tiger on his motorcycle in the park. He was so frightened that he accelerated too hard, and nearly fell down after the bike went over a rock on the road. The tiger had stopped the chase after his initial charge, but Kesar Meena felt if he'd fallen down, he would have been a goner.

'Which tiger was that?' I asked. 'Did you recognize it?'

'It was Zalim. This was just last year. He's a very mischievous tiger, madam. A real *badmash*! If he's in the mood, he looks for opportunities to chase you. He's done the same two or three times with pilgrims who go to the fort temple,' said Kesar Meena.

'We saw Zalim! I was told he got that name because he was boisterous,' said Vikram.

'Yes sir, he's also very unpredictable. We all watch out for him when we're in his territory. He's the only tiger that likes to regularly go out of the jungle and sit on the road. He goes to villages also sometimes because he's too lazy to hunt and kills livestock. Causes a lot of trouble for us with the villagers.'

'Okay, that's enough, Kesar,' said Bachi Singh, frowning at him.

Clearly, Bachi Singh didn't want any kind of negativity to be recorded. A tiger whom the guards feared was not good news. We stopped filming then as we had got enough material, and everyone relaxed and enjoyed their tea and snacks.

Leaning against the jeep, in which Ram Tiwari was sitting, I asked him about what Kesar had said about Zalim.

'Mischievous' was a very kind way to put it, but a tiger that liked to chase motorcycles and go to villages was not something to be taken lightly.

'Madam, now what can I say? Obviously I can't officially comment, but we've found his behaviour concerning over the last two years, since he became the dominant male of his territory. As Kesar said, he often goes outside the park into the adjoining villages. He even sits on the main road sometimes at night, causing small traffic jams. He once chased a motorcyclist who fell down, but then luckily there were people around, and a car honked and chased him away. The matter was hushed up. Last year, a woodcutter, who had entered the forest late at night, was killed in an attack. It wasn't confirmed if it was a tiger or leopard, and there was anger as it was in Zalim's territory. But then the man had illegally entered the park, so that point was highlighted by the forest department. The post-mortem report took a few days, and the family wanted the body back, even holding a protest, so we couldn't keep it as evidence. Then it was time for the local election, so media attention moved on. But we heard later the report indicated it was a tiger.'

Now this information was very interesting to me. Man–animal conflict was a huge issue in India, with many parts of the country experiencing these pressures of saving wildlife while ensuring the welfare of locals who lived around the national parks. It was something I'd been wanting to cover.

If wild animals destroy crops, kill livestock or, God forbid, a person, it causes serious issues for the forest department, as they need the support of the villagers for their conservation effort. The forest department has such a huge area to monitor and protect with very limited resources and manpower. Villagers often view wild animals as a menace and a threat to their lives and livelihoods. Monetary compensation is one way of handling this, but if something more is required, like removing the animal, it becomes trickier. There are several levels of clearance required, and any kind of adverse reporting makes it more challenging. Local reporting and national-level reporting are very different on these kinds of issues.

I made a mental note to myself to find out more, maybe for a future report.

The sun was about to set and it was time for us to go to the machan. Since we needed a much smaller group for that, only Vikram, Jaya, Debajyoti and I proceeded with Bachi Singh, Ram Tiwari and one of the bodyguards, Ravi.

The machan overlooked grassland with a small lake on one side. It was easily accessible for animals and a popular spot at night. Or so we were told. We filmed a sequence of us walking to the machan and climbing up the ladder a few times, to get all the different angles.

When we were on top and waiting, Vikram whispered to me, 'Are we absolutely safe here?'

'Yes, of course. Why wouldn't we be?' I whispered back.

'But these people don't even have guns. What if something were to happen? Now I can't stop thinking of a tiger fighting a bear, or a tiger who likes to chase people for fun!'

Somehow, a tiger fighting a bear sounded like an amazing sight to me. Really! What I wouldn't give to witness something like that. But I realized the idea of being in the middle of a forest full of tigers, leopards, bears and even crocodiles during the night without much protection, could seem very frightening to those who weren't used to it.

'Don't worry, these guards do it all the time and nothing ever happens. Those were just a few stray incidents that happened over many years,' I reassured him. 'Also being on a machan in the forest is so Jim Corbett! You know? The famous hunter–conservationist? In all his books he spends so many nights on machans. Though he was usually tracking man-eating leopards and tigers.'

'Thanks for mentioning man-eating tigers now!' he said, rolling his eyes. 'Very reassuring!'

I stifled a giggle.

After a beat, he said 'And no, I haven't read Jim Corbett but I will now. Maybe Devraj has a copy.'

'He definitely does, in his elaborate library bar,' I whispered back.

We fell silent for some time. It was a serene feeling, to be surrounded by the symphony of the jungle. Distant calls echoed through the air, accompanied by the haunting cry of a nightjar, the rustle of the grass beneath and the gentle rippling of the water nearby. The moon shone overhead, casting its silver light across the grassland.

Ram Tiwari shone a torch briefly over the grassland as Jaya filmed it. There was a herd of deer in one part of the grassland. Two eyes shone back from a tree nearby that made Vikram jump but it was only the nightjar we'd heard earlier, a common nocturnal bird. Then we saw a pair of eyes at the far side of the waterbody. It was a crocodile that slowly sank back into the depths. Then, towards the right of the machan, we saw a little shadowy movement. On closer scrutiny, we realized it was a jungle cat that had come to drink water.

We sat in silence again for nearly an hour. We scanned the water a few times and saw more deer and a sambar come to drink water.

There was rustling and movement in the grass near the machan. We all peered in the dark and could make out some largish shadow. Shining the torch briefly, Ram Tiwari said it could be a tiger, he thought he saw the fur but couldn't make out clearly. I could see Vikram's eyes widen in the moonlight. Even Ravi looked alert, as if anticipating danger.

We waited some more and then as the shadows emerged from the grass directly under the machan, Ram Tiwari directed the light downwards to reveal two striped hyenas walking to the water.

'They're hyenas!' I whispered to Vikram, who seemed relieved.

'Let's get a good shot of them!' said Debajyoti, as Jaya moved to the other side of the machan, towards the water.

We watched the hyenas move, their sloping backs giving them a distinct silhouette, their gait slightly hunched and hurried. After a brief moment at the water, they soon disappeared into the darkness.

We spent another half hour on the machan and then decided it was a wrap.

'I'm actually glad to be going back,' Vikram admitted as we loaded up the jeep. 'It's one thing to read the shoot proposal, an evening on the machan after sunset, but to actually be here after dark is quite another experience.'

We drove out slowly in the darkness towards the main gate. Jaya continued to hold on to her camera. 'Just in case,' she said.

'Always,' I replied. It was another fun ritual we had on shoot.

It was so different being in the jungle in the dark as the darkness added an eerie element, and I could understand why some might find it intimidating, even scary.

It was pitch-black save for the beams from our headlights. The darkness made it difficult to see far ahead, and I couldn't help but wonder what kind of creatures might be lurking in the shadows. Suddenly, our car came to an abrupt stop, causing us to nearly fall forward. In the middle of the road ahead was a massive black blob that was shuffling along.

'What is it?!' whispered Debajyoti.

'A sloth bear!' I answered. 'This is the time they like to move around.'

We watched as it moved slowly along, grunting, digging in the mud, stopping to sniff around.

'It looks really harmless,' whispered Vikram.

'Oh believe me, you don't want to get on the wrong side of that. They can be really fierce.'

After fifteen minutes, the bear shuffled off the road, but threw a parting glance in our direction.

Or so it seemed.

'They can't actually see very well,' I whispered to Vikram. 'But their sense of smell is very good.'

'Ravi, it must be smelling your cologne,' Vikram whispered to him. 'I told you not to wear such a strong one. It was in the list of dos and don'ts in the safari handbook given in the rooms.'

Ravi looked sorry and we laughed quietly.

'That is correct. Strong scents can attract insects or animals, or disrupt the balance in the surroundings,' I replied, impressed he'd read the handbook.

'In fact, it must have been Ravi's cologne that agitated the bees that day! Wait till I tell Safar!' he teased Ravi some more.

We were now headed for the gate.

'So that was an interesting finale to the day,' said Debajyoti.

'It really was!' I said. 'It was a bonus seeing a bear, though I don't think we managed any good shots of it. We'll have to check when we get back.'

'It's not all about the shots, you know,' Vikram quipped. 'Even the experience counts.'

That made me laugh. It sounded like something I must have said to him earlier.

Back at the resort, I was fairly exhausted after the long day, and following a quick dinner, decided to call it a night. Thankfully, the next day was not as hectic.

Everyone else was sitting around after dinner, some even enjoying a drink, when I decided to return to my tent. It had been quite an eventful day. I hadn't bothered to look at social media again as it would only stress me out.

I was leaving the dining area when I bumped into Devraj. He looked like he'd come straight from a shower. His hair was slightly damp, and he was dressed in a crisp white linen shirt and khakis.

'Off so soon?' he asked as I greeted him.

'Yes, completely exhausted. It was a long day.' I felt quite dishevelled compared to him. I self-consciously ran my hand through my hair to settle it.

'I enjoyed your report on tourism and conservation. I messaged you about it. It's important to have these conversations.'

I felt pleased at his praise.

'Yes, that was the idea. Put the spotlight on this aspect and hope it starts a discussion or changes attitudes.'

'Any interesting sightings during your evening drive?'

'We were filming with the forest guards this evening. That was fun. We also got to spend over an hour on the machan after dark. That was a special experience though Vikram seemed a little anxious. I told him it was very Jim Corbett, being up on a machan.'

'Hah! Did he know about the old Carpet Sahib? Or did you have to tell him what a Jim Corbett experience was?'

I laughed at that. Jim Corbett was called Carpet Sahib back in the early 1900s by the people of Kumaon. In the local language 'Car-payt' meant excellent marksman, and so the moniker Carpet Sahib.

'Well, he didn't know but he was willing to learn. In fact, he may ask you for a book.'

'I do have a well-thumbed copy of *Man-Eaters of Kumaon* in my office. That's my favourite.'

'Mine too!' I replied.

'Come, I'll walk you to your tent. You can't go alone.'

We started walking out of the lodge towards the tents.

'I actually wanted to ask you something. I heard some chatter about Zalim, how his behaviour has been aggressive and the guards are wary?'

I could see a slight shift in his easy demeanour.

'Well, they should have known better than to talk to the media about this,' he said.

Now it was my turn to bristle.

'It was just a conversation, not something I'm planning to report. It's an issue that interests me,' I said curtly. Just when I was beginning to think Devraj was quite nice, he went ahead and said something to irritate me.

'No no, I'm sorry. I didn't mean it like that.' He put up his hands and came to a stop. I stopped too.

'I just meant these matters are so sensitive and layered. There has been some chatter in the local media about Zalim's behaviour, towards the forest guards and in general, in the area. It creates some stress among the forest staff. I have discussed it with the director, and he's concerned as well. We've been building a file on him, and I know a conversation has been had with Jaipur on a possible solution.'

'All right, I was just wondering and thought to ask.' I was still annoyed by his 'media' jibe.

'Though I have to say I was irritated at first with the local media coverage. They made it very sensational and painted him in a bad light, something that could affect how tigers are perceived here. That's why the "media" comment. Not everyone tries to understand the issues.'

'Okay, I get it. Media can sometimes be all about the sensational headline.'

'Sometimes?' he asked with a smile and raised an eyebrow.

That made me laugh.

'There are theories in the forest department about why Zalim is the way he is. Some say it's because he was tranquilized twice, once as a sub-adult and then once more later on, and this is the reason why he is aggressive towards people. But who knows tiger psychology?' he said with a shrug.

'Why was he tranquilized twice?' I asked, surprised, my irritation forgotten.

'The first time was when they were transferring some tigers to another park. They meant to take this other male and they tranquilized Zalim by mistake. He was too young for the shift, and he spent many hours in a cage before they released him. Another time they felt he was unwell, behaving oddly. After observing him for a while, they realized he was severely constipated. We had a tiger scientist here in the park from the Wildlife Institute at the time. So, under his guidance and advice, for whatever reason, they decided to tranquilize and treat him. But as they were giving him an enema, he regained consciousness and ran off. He was groggy from the tranquillizer, so thankfully nothing happened to the team, except, to use a crude but apt phrase, they shat themselves,' he said, laughing.

The last bit was so absurd, I started to laugh too. We began walking to the tent again.

'Is that a lesson in tiger psychology?' I said, laughing. 'Why does Chambalgarh have an aggressive male tiger? The answer is an enema!'

Devraj laughed too.

'Decades ago, I believe, there was another male tiger who behaved like this, so who knows what the reason is? I've heard stories from Prem Singh and others. He would deliberately block the road, chase vehicles. He went on to kill five people and was finally shot by a hired hunter. Of course the forest department was very different then and conservation wasn't what it is now.'

We had reached my tent.

'That sounds frightening. Must have been terrible for the people living around the park. I'll read up on that,' I said, as I stifled a yawn. I was feeling drained now. It had been such a long day.

'Okay, better hit the sack then,' said Devraj, smiling. 'I'll show you those pictures of the Bandhavgarh sisters tomorrow. Goodnight.'

I thanked him for walking me back and wished him goodnight.

As I lay in bed, drifting off to sleep, I thought to myself, *Devraj isn't so bad after all.*

10

The next morning I got up leisurely, at 7 a.m. A change from the usual 5 a.m.

I was making my morning coffee when Manju came to our tent.

'Good morning! How are you feeling today?' she asked, a little too brightly.

'All fine,' I said. 'Managed a full eight hours of sleep, which is a luxury on a shoot.'

She sat on the side of my bed and seemed to be studying my face.

'Would you like a coffee?' I asked, looking at her. She nodded, but seemed somewhat pensive.

'Something wrong?' I asked. She was about to answer when my phone started ringing.

Looking at it, I saw it was my sister Sameera from London.

Picking up, I said, 'Hi, Di! What's up?'

I could hear some kind of screeching on the other end. I loved my sister, she was really amazing, super smart, a go-getter, life of the party and all that, but our personalities couldn't be more different. While I was calm, composed and serious on most occasions, she was the opposite.

Which basically meant she was very excitable and loud.

'Di, slow down. I can't understand what you're saying.'

She paused for a moment. Then she said very slowly, 'How can my younger sister be linked to the hottest Bollywood star and not say anything to me? This is crazy! Why do I have to read this on MsDiva.com?'

'Wait. What? I'm not linked to any star! What is MsDiva.com, and why are you even reading something like that?'

'That's not answering the question.'

'Di, I really don't know what you're talking about! There's really nothing. I'm on a shoot, I'd messaged you about the campaign. Yes, it's with Vikram Khanna, but it's totally professional. Please don't believe any old rubbish!'

'He didn't call you his "lovely teacher" quote, unquote? And you weren't both wrapped up together in some jeep in the park, and you saved him from some monster bees?'

Now I started feeling queasy.

'Yes, something like that happened, Didi, but that's a very twisted and sensational version of events!'

I could hear some clicking of a computer keyboard.

'Oh God. There's another piece on BollyVilla.com. What the hell, Sunaina! If you get linked to a hot movie star, I expect you to call and tell me first! Imagine my shock when, in my daily Bollywood updates, I got news about my own flesh and blood.'

'Di, I'm going to put the phone down and call you later. I haven't even read what you're talking about! If there was something to tell you, obviously I would have told you, but this is just ridiculous gossip!'

'Oh, now you've had it. Bunty Bua has just sent the piece on the family WhatsApp group,' she said.

'WHAT!' Bunty Bua was my nosiest aunt.

Trust Di to talk on the phone and check WhatsApp updates at the same time.

'Didi, just tell her what I told you please.'

Disconnecting the call, I turned around to Jaya and Manju who were both watching me closely.

'Sooooo,' started Manju cautiously, 'I was coming to warn you about more developments on the gossip-about-you-and-Vikram front, but I guess you just heard about it.'

'There's no me-and-Vikram. The least you could do was warn me!' I was truly exasperated now.

'It's exactly because of your shoot-the-messenger attitude that I didn't tell you immediately! I was working my way up to it when you got that call from your sister,' she then pulled out her iPad and opened the MsDiva.com site.

'Is Bollywood's heartthrob doing *mangal* in the jungle?' read the ridiculous headline.

It then went on to describe how Vikram was on a shoot in Chambalgarh National Park for a cause close to his heart, creating awareness about India's tigers and conservation issues, and that, during the course of the shoot, he'd become 'close' to Sunaina Joshi, the news reporter he was working with on the campaign.

How I 'saved' him when the team was 'attacked' by a swarm of bees. There was the now 'famous' or, in my view, 'infamous' picture of us.

And then his quote from yesterday morning where he told the media that I was his 'lovely teacher'. The whole piece was full of a lot of nudge-nudge, wink-wink, but nothing credible at all!

'Oh my God!' I said, putting my head in my hands. 'This is really ridiculous! Who reads this stuff, and, more importantly, who writes it? I'll never believe another celebrity gossip piece again! They just make up stuff from thin air!'

Jaya was rereading the piece.

'They've picked up lots of pictures from social media, with due credit. Even a picture from Reena's Instagram account,' she said. It was the picture of Vikram, Reena and I, posing in front of the jeep. He had his arms around our waists. I was laughing and Vikram was looking at me.

'This is so mortifying. Everyone was so relaxed about it, even Natasha claimed it was frivolous news!' I wailed.

Manju was looking at me nervously.

'But maybe Natasha is right. Fine, it's gone on for two days now but that's because he's still on this shoot. And look at it this way, at least even the gossip sites are writing about tigers and conservation.'

I looked at her incredulously.

'Manju, I feel like slapping you right now.' But both Jaya and Manju started giggling. And then I joined in as well. It was all so preposterous.

'Come on,' said Jaya, laughing. 'It's stupid but just ignore it. It's not every day you get linked to a movie star! That's something, isn't it?'

'But now I'll have that tag!' I started fretting again. 'The Internet never forgets! This was really not what I had in mind when we planned this campaign around a Bollywood star.'

After a few more minutes of venting, I finally felt a bit more collected, so I called up my sister and spoke to her so she could calm down. I'm glad I did because she also told me she had handled annoying Bunty Bua in the family group. Though one of my more catty cousins had also responded. I asked my sister to say I was away from connectivity, in the forest.

Around mid-morning, we had to go to the lodge for a production meeting called by Debajyoti. Everyone was sitting around in the lounge when Jaya and I got there. Looking up from her phone as we approached, Reena called out with a wicked smile, 'Oh, look who's here. Ms Diva herself!'

At some point, while walking to the lounge, I had decided to brazen it out. Yes, it was mortifying, but instead of letting people know that it was getting to me, I had decided that I'd adopt a blasé attitude. It would blow over.

Armed with this new outlook, I just smiled at Reena and wiggled my hands next to my face.

'Oh, look who's come around! Good you're not freaking out any more. I was just telling the team how this is a great thing for the campaign and we can really capitalize on it. Our handle has already got 80,000 followers since yesterday and it'll keep growing. The marketing guys will be very happy, I can tell you,' she gushed.

Okay, so this was getting into new, unanticipated territory. I had resolved not to overreact about the coverage, but was Reena actually planning to ramp it up?

Luckily, Debajyoti intervened just then before my cool facade slipped away.

'Reena, let's not encourage this. I don't think anybody wants that. It's a serious campaign, and I don't think it's fair to Sunaina,' he said, looking sternly at her.

I wanted to hug him in relief. Reena shrugged and rolled her eyes.

'People, let's discuss the shoot today. That's my priority. We're going to the park again today to get more shots of Vikram and hopefully see another tiger. Later in the evening Reena can interview Vikram. Where do you want to do that? Poolside?'

Reena, who was looking a little miffed, seemed a bit mollified at the prospect of her big interview.

'Yes, we haven't filmed there yet. And we can light up the area with those lamps they use. They can hang them around everywhere. It will be dusky by then,' said Reena.

We discussed the day's programme for the next half hour. The Mumbai group was taking it easy this morning as none of them had surfaced.

Manju clicked a few pictures. When I glared at her, she looked apologetic but said she had to upload a daily diary.

I spent the rest of the day in the tent. Debajyoti wanted me to write out a structure of the two half-hour shows so we could figure out what was missing and what remained to be done.

I avoided looking at Twitter and Instagram.

Earlier, in the lounge, Reena kept announcing all the hits and comments our accounts on Instagram and Twitter were getting. She was also pleased her own account was getting more attention.

It was very difficult to keep focused on work when there was so much else on my mind.

Social media is such a boon and bane at the same time. There's so much information one can disseminate instantly, as well as get instantly. But then there's also so much aggression and negativity. And when it came to personal promotion, many get a kick from the number of followers and likes, the random praise and compliments. They literally get a dopamine kick that sends a happy message to their brain, but soon it becomes a need.

In fact, 'influencers' have made a career of it, including some of my college friends, but the trade-off with the ugly aspects was too much for me to handle.

Trying to push all the disturbing thoughts to the back of my mind, I worked for the next few hours on scripting the shows.

'Let's go,' called Jaya, poking her head into the tent. She had gone to scout a location for the interview later in the evening.

Now it was time for the afternoon safari.

I quickly got ready and we walked across to the main building. Glancing at my phone, I saw I had a message from Devraj.

'Hello, didn't see you today. I need to tell you something regarding your shoot. I'll see you at the lodge.'

I wondered what it could be.

Almost everyone going for the shoot was assembled at the porch area except Vikram and whoever was accompanying him that day. Debajyoti was discussing the shoot plan when Devraj walked up to us purposefully with Himanshu in tow.

'There seems to be a bit of a problem at the gate today,' he said.

This must be what he was referring to in his message.

Everyone fell silent, wondering what had happened.

'See, your shoot has been getting a lot of attention in the media.' He glanced fleetingly at me again. Cringe. I wondered if he'd seen the articles! I felt my face redden at the thought.

'Well, publicity attracts all types. And now there's a protest against Vikram at the gate.'

'I heard my name!' said Vikram who had just walked up with Ravi, Natasha and Zaid. 'What's happening, folks?'

'It seems a group in Rajasthan is not happy about you being here. Or they simply want to use you to get some publicity for themselves. They're called the Bhawani Sena, and they're protesting against you at the park gate,' said Devraj.

'Me? But why?' said Vikram, looking extremely shocked.

'What's this about?!' said Natasha, instantly concerned.

'Are you playing Rana Sanga in a movie?' Devraj asked.

'Yes, I am. It's a battle film, very dramatic. But that's currently in pre-production! We haven't even started filming so why should anyone be offended?' he asked, puzzled.

'And did you say in some interview that Rana Sanga made two big mistakes, how many believe he called Babar to India, thinking he would help defeat Lodi and then leave, and the second was overconfidence? Ahead of the battle of Khanwa against Babar?'

'Yes, I did, but there's nothing new in what I said. Those things are known. I didn't make it up! You can't change the battle of Khanwa! He lost to Babar because of various factors, including overconfidence. You can't change history! And, like I said, it's early days. It will be a while before we begin filming!' he replied, aghast.

'Well, they're outraged because they feel you insulted the great Rajput icon, Rana Sanga. The local channels carried the interview. And, frankly, don't look for logic. This group just needs to find an excuse to protest. It's more of an extortion racket. Right now, there are no elections so they don't have much to do. Otherwise, they make up numbers at rallies or protest at the rally, depending on what they're paid for.' Devraj spread his hands in exasperation.

'How bad is this?' I asked. 'Are they blocking the gate?'

'The forest department is getting back to me on this. This must be them.' His phone was ringing and he moved away to take the call.

'So what is the situation? Can we go to the park?' asked a very worried Debajyoti.

'Well, currently they're claiming they have a right to protest,' said Himanshu. 'And they're creating a nuisance at the gate. This is the local unit of the Sena.'

'And here I thought they would be happy I was playing Rana Sanga. How can people be upset about what actually happened, when it's all recorded history?' Vikram said, turning towards Natasha.

'Well, you were the one who wanted to do a serious historical movie. You described it as a role with meat in it. I still think it's a great role. But somehow, these days, our history itself has got so contentious. You're right, you can't change history, but sadly enough, there are attempts being made to do just that. It's a post-truth world,' she replied with a shake of her head.

Getting off the phone, Devraj returned to the group.

'I've requested the forest department to send a closed jeep to come here and take you into the park. It will have some forest guards and hopefully you can go in without a problem. You go on ahead and then the rest of the group can go a little later. I'll accompany them. I know some of these people. I'll talk to them,' he said.

We all looked at him now, a little shocked at that piece of news.

'Oh God, you all are such city people,' he said, shaking his head. 'In Rajasthan, we all know and work with a wide range of people. In fact, the son of the Bhawani Sena's founder was with me in college. He's a very nice guy, not political at all. We played cricket together. And I also know some members of the local unit.'

After that, things moved quickly. Natasha was a little apprehensive, asking several questions about Vikram's safety with 'these thugs over there'. Devraj and Himanshu reassured her. Still, she had Zaid call Sohan, the second bodyguard, so he could also be with the team.

Devraj got a call to say the police were also at the gate, trying to ensure no one got blocked from entering.

The forest department vehicle arrived with Ram Tiwari in it and two other people. Devraj had a word with them as did Natasha, and they assured her there was nothing to worry about. Vikram got in with Ravi.

Around fifteen minutes after they had left, we left as well. It was Jaya, Danish, myself, Manju and Sohan along with Devraj in two separate jeeps. Arriving at the gate, we saw a group of around twenty to thirty people on one side holding posters and sloganeering.

'Vikram Khanna *hai hai*!' they yelled periodically, glaring at the passing jeeps. They didn't look too threatening and some members even looked bored.

We couldn't see the forest department jeep anywhere and hoped it had managed to get through.

On seeing us, the group suddenly got energized.

It must have been on spotting the cameras and we looked like a TV crew, because suddenly they surrounded our jeeps, yelling slogans, waving their banners. There were two local news teams that also swung into action, filming the protest, which in turn pepped them up further.

Jumping out of the jeep, Devraj caught the attention of one of the protesters and took him aside. The jeeps moved to one side of the road due to the chaos, so as not to block the road.

They continued to shout half-hearted slogans around the jeep, staring at us, while we sat quietly staring back at them. Danish and Jaya even filmed the protest. After all, you never know what you may land up using in the final cut.

It was a strange, precarious situation, like we were all waiting for something to happen but we didn't know what it was. They had realized Vikram was not among us but couldn't figure out what their next move was. The cops had also come up now and were telling the protesters to move on.

Finally, Devraj returned with the person he had taken aside. The man signalled to the group to move aside and let us pass.

Jaya and I exchanged glances. He really did have connections in this loutish group.

We entered the park gate and kept driving to the first chowki inside. This was where we had planned to connect with Vikram.

He was waiting by the jeep with Ravi and the forest guards, and waved as we arrived.

'It was quite a crowd at the gate, wasn't it? Luckily when we got there, they were busy giving interviews to the channels and didn't really look at our jeep,' he said to me with a grin after we had pulled up and he had got into our jeep.

'They did surround us for a bit, but then Devraj had a word with one of the leaders of the group and they let us pass. Also, they realized you weren't among us, so that helped,' I replied.

'Dude, when we get back, I really want to know how you know these guys and just who they are,' Vikram said, turning to Devraj who was at the front of the jeep.

One could make out from Devraj's expression that he wasn't very interested in having that conversation but before he could respond, Debajyoti called out, asking for everyone's attention.

After a brief discussion, we decided to drive out to a large plateau nearby. It had a waterbody and grassy plains. There were reports of some tiger movement in the area. Calls had been heard. Hopefully, we could have another tiger sighting.

So we headed out in that direction, filming the safari. After arriving at the small lake, we spent the next half hour filming sequences around there, more interactions between Vikram and the forest guards. Then there was a short interview with me about his experience on safari as well as what aspects of the park he liked the most.

A little later, I sat in the second jeep so Danish and Jaya could film Vikram with the guards.

Glancing at Devraj, I could see he was getting fairly impatient.

'I'm sorry you got sucked into our shoot today, but thank you for helping out. I really don't know how we would have dealt with this by ourselves,' I said, hoping to mollify him.

'You would have managed, I'm sure, though it could have cost you a packet,' he replied.

'What!' I exclaimed, and then lowered my voice. 'What do you mean? They would have demanded money?'

'Well, they wouldn't have called off the protest and would have delayed your shoot. When you would have got desperate, a middleman would have appeared, usually someone representing them, it could be a cop or a local sarpanch, and they would have told you to cough up a certain amount, or they wouldn't call off the protest. And after you paid up a lakh or so, the protest would have stopped. That's how it usually goes. They also get a little media coverage out of it, so net-net it works out well for them.'

'Ugh. So much for ideology and hurt sentiments. In the end, it's always all about the money and politics!' I said, shaking my head.

'Yes, though when this group started off, it was to represent Rajput interests and it gained major popularity over certain issues. But that was decades ago. Much has changed since then. There are also local factions. So it's become an employment generator for some. Since legitimate employment options are also limited these days,' he said with a wry smile.

'Our bad luck they decided to target us! Must be really hard up for things to do.'

'Well, your shoot has been getting a lot of attention. Himanshu has compiled all the coverage it got online, given you are all staying at our property. And it's quite a lot,' he said, looking ahead. 'It's low-hanging fruit for them.'

I could feel my face redden again at the thought of Devraj having read those ridiculous gossip pieces.

Suddenly, we heard a shrill piercing yelp of a cheetal. An alarm call!

Even Vikram recognized it this time, as he turned to us with an excited expression, pointing in the direction of the call.

We drove the jeeps next to one another so Vikram could get back into our jeep.

'It's coming from the right, over there, from that side,' I said, indicating the forested part that began a little distance away from the lake.

We waited some more.

'Let's move in that direction, we can position ourselves on the bend of the road,' said Devraj, indicating a part of the road that curved around the lake and then went off to the side of the forest.

The location provided a clear view of the forest and lake, with an elevated vantage point that would give us an optimal chance of spotting the big cat, were it to appear.

As we settled in to wait, another call caught our attention, raising our hopes of a sighting. The minutes ticked by, increasing our anticipation as we scanned the underbrush for any sign of a tiger.

Suddenly, a rustling in the bushes ahead caught our eye. We continued watching, and soon a face peered out, its black and orange stripes stark against the lush greenery. The white circles on its ears stood out, as it cautiously surveyed the area.

Yes! Finally there it was!

Vikram excitedly squeezed my hand as I grinned back at him. I looked to the other jeep and saw Jaya and Danish hard at work, capturing the moment.

Then the tiger's body emerged slowly, as if it were taking its time to fully appear. It paused for a moment, its flicking tail still in the underbrush, as the rest of it stood on the edge of the grassland and then gracefully padded out towards the lake.

I recognized her regal air and slightly frail physique.

'Is that Mallika?' I asked excitedly. Having seen her a few months ago, I could identify her. She was thinner, slightly smaller than some of the other tigers in the park.

Devraj, who now had his camera ready, looked back, giving me a wide smile and nodded.

'She's the very famous one, isn't she?' Vikram whispered. 'Yes, she is!' I replied.

Even though she looked old, there was something very grand about her. This was the area she had lorded over for years, but now she looked around a little warily, in case any of the younger lot were around to challenge her.

'Oh Mallika, you beauty,' I heard Devraj say softly as he continued clicking pictures on his camera.

We spent the next half hour enthralled as she walked to the water, had a drink, then settled on the side, under a tree, lying down after a while. A small herd of cheetal approached the lake a little distance away, to drink water. Sensing their presence Mallika perked up, fixating her gaze on the graceful creatures.

There was an aura of suspense and anticipation as we wondered what she would do next. She carefully observed the herd for a while, as if calculating her next move. Although she was no longer as nimble and powerful as she once was, she could consider the possibility of taking down a fawn, as there were several within the group.

The sight of the fawns was both adorable and conflicting. On the one hand they were tiny and playful, evoking memories of Bambi and innocent cuteness. On the other hand, they were potential easy prey for the hungry tiger. These were the harsh realities of the wild, where the laws of the jungle dictate survival and the circle of life prevails.

As the wind changed direction, one of the deer in the group suddenly became alert, gazing intently at its surroundings for two fleeting seconds before giving the now familiar short bark and dashing away. The rest of the herd followed suit, almost in unison.

Mallika had gone into an alert position, but then relaxed after the deer fled.

With a deliberate swipe of her tongue, she began grooming her paws, deep in thought as she pondered her next move.

Her ears pricked up and we all heard the rumble of an approaching vehicle. Two tourist jeeps had spotted us and were approaching.

'I want to get one long shot of Vikram looking at Mallika,' said Jaya from the other jeep. 'So keep looking and be a little animated.'

Their jeep reversed a little to give some distance so Jaya could get her shot.

'So I believe this is a really special tiger?' Vikram asked Devraj. 'Jaya said she's probably the oldest known tiger?'

'Yes, she is. She was the dominant tigress here for many, many years. She was undoubtedly the most formidable tiger, male or female, I have ever encountered.

She hated bears with a vengeance. Usually tigers try and avoid bears, but she's the only one who would deliberately target them. She broke one of her canines, they say, after a fight with a crocodile. Now she's a lot older, slower, obviously, so she finds it difficult to hunt.'

'So how does she manage then?' Vikram asked.

'She manages a little something here or there. Then the forest department feeds her from time to time. The odd goat is left out near the chowki when she has gone without food for many days. But don't ask them about it, it's not spoken of openly.'

'Whoa! Really?' said Vikram, looking surprised.

'I heard that the last time I was here,' I said, nodding. 'That's probably how she's been around as long as she has. But if you look at it from purely a conservation point of view, that's interfering in the wild, isn't it? You're not letting nature run its course?'

'Well, she's the most famous tigress in the country. People visit this park from all over to get a glimpse of her. She's part of the forest lore here. And now that she's in the twilight of her life, the forest department won't turn its back on her! She can't be allowed to just starve like any other tiger,' he said a little forcefully, with some emotion.

It was clearly a subject close to his heart, and an academic discussion on the merits and drawbacks of human interference versus letting nature run its course was not welcome.

I also liked how passionate he got when talking about Mallika. It wasn't often you came across people who felt so strongly about issues like wildlife and tigers. Respect.

He seemed to relax after a moment. Maybe he realized he'd been a little sharp.

Turning to me, he said, 'Lucky you. You've got to see her on two consecutive trips. That's a sign of good karma.'

I smiled back at him. It was nice of him to have added that. Did he also believe in signs from the fates? I would have to tell Jaya about this!

Just then, Vikram, who had been busy giving profile shots to Jaya and Danish, gestured to me to stand with him. As I stood up, he pulled me closer, pointed to Mallika and made some small talk for the benefit of the cameras. I got the full Vikram Khanna charm offensive and it was impressive. Even though he was 'acting', his dazzling smile and expressive eyes trained on me were quite something.

I saw Manju was taking pictures of us from the other jeep. I'd better remember to tell her to show me the pictures so I could veto them before she shared them online. I also realized Devraj was watching us closely, his eyes hooded, expressionless.

The two other jeeps full of people had pulled up nearby.

Devraj seemed to get tense for a moment. Maybe he was wondering if we'd have a repeat of the squealing when people realized it was Vikram in the next jeep. But he needn't have worried; these jeeps were full of serious photographers who only had eyes for the tiger. They had pulled out their big bazooka lenses and were clicking away.

'Are we done then?' said Devraj in a slightly clipped tone. I looked at the other jeep and waved at Debajyoti, asking if it was a wrap.

He conferred with Jaya and Danish and then indicated we could leave. We carefully reversed out without disturbing the photographers. Mallika was lying on her side now, though her tail was twitching.

We were soon on our way out of the park, feeling quite elated!

'That was a fantastic sighting, wasn't it! So glad we came to the park and didn't cancel like Natasha wanted. Thanks for that, man!' said Vikram, looking quite pleased.

'Yeah, sure,' replied Devraj. 'It's always great to see Mallika, so I should thank you. Her appearances have become more and more rare.'

He showed Vikram and me some of the shots he'd taken on his camera. The lighting was perfect and the shots had come out great. We oohed and aahed over the photos.

I was feeling quite satisfied. We'd had a fantastic shoot, I couldn't be happier. Great content for the show.

Since we had completed our shoot we were exiting the park at 5:30 p.m., which was earlier than usual. As we crossed the gate, we paused so Ram Tiwari could get off and go tell the forest guards about our sighting for their logbook.

What we didn't realize was that the Bhawani Sena men were still hanging around near the tea stalls opposite the gate.

One of them must have spotted Vikram because suddenly we were surrounded by a dozen of them, waving placards and banners, yelling. 'Vikram Khanna hai hai' and 'Nahi chalega, nahi chalega'.

Vikram and I were seated in the middle seat of the jeep, with Sohan in the back and Devraj and Prem Singh in the front.

There was absolute chaos for two to three minutes. The crowd around the jeep was most excited, now that they had found their target. Some were almost leaning in, and Sohan was getting agitated trying to protect Vikram.

Vikram, on the other hand, was trying to protect me, though no one from the crowd was interested in me, since their focus was on him and creating a scene worthy of making news.

As I looked around, I spotted Ravi, who had jumped out of the other jeep, making his way towards us. Meanwhile, Devraj had got out and was pushing back some of the crowd while shouting for the policemen. The cops had been sitting at the gate but were now running towards us.

Ravi managed to clamber on to the jeep while preventing others from doing the same. Sohan and Ravi were both blocking people and using their arms to prevent anyone from getting close to Vikram. Vikram and I were standing up now and he was holding me as I tried to look around to see if any help was coming.

The cops and Devraj were at the front of the jeep now, trying to push back the crowd and clear the way. The crowd had also grown significantly, given the number of people who are usually just hanging out around the park gate. There were jeeps with other tourists gawking at the spectacle. I could see that many had their phones out and were taking pictures.

Somehow, through their combined efforts, the cops and Devraj managed to clear the way in front of the jeep and Prem Singh quickly drove off.

'Oh my God, that was something!' said Vikram finally, when we'd managed to put some distance between us and the crowd.

Both Ravi and Sohan looked very agitated and kept looking back, like they were worried someone was following us.

'What about Devraj?' he asked me.

'I'm sure he'll come in the other jeep. Damn, we should have anticipated those people would still be around,' I said, a little shaken by the experience. 'Look at poor Sohan and Ravi. They're so on edge.'

'Yeah, they're probably bugged that they couldn't beat up anyone. And worried in case they shoved anyone too hard. They're under strict instructions from Natasha. Last time there was a situation outside a nightclub, when a drunk guy got very aggressive with me, and they had to push him back. Unfortunately, someone took a picture and it looked like they were manhandling the person. So Natasha told them not to use any force or be seen to be using force if they could help it. It just becomes another source of negative publicity and invariably the blame always comes on me,' he said with a shrug.

'That was quite an experience!' I shook my head. 'Thankfully nothing happened. Those men were really aggressive and everything was so chaotic for a few moments!'

Looking back again at Ravi and Sohan in the jeep, I added sheepishly, 'For all the times I've commented on you having bodyguards in the jungle, I have to say I've never been more grateful for Sohan and Ravi!'

Vikram, listening to me, simply nodded.

Then he seemed to register what I had just said and he looked very surprised.

'Wait, you made fun of me for having Sohan and Ravi?' he asked incredulously.

'Hah! That's hardly important now!' I said, laughing and feeling rather embarrassed.

'And I'm sorry for it! They were lifesavers!'

I turned around and gave them a thumbs-up. They gave me tight smiles in return.

By way of explanation I said, 'It's such a different world from mine, all the fans, the trolls, the entourage, the bodyguards and whatnot. That's all it was, and I know I shouldn't be so quick to judge.' I shook my head in self-admonishment.

Vikram laughed at this.

'Well, your world of tigers, forest guards and safaris is very different from mine too! And I only want to learn more.'

With that, we fell into a contemplative silence.

I looked down at my phone to see several messages from Devraj.

'Are you all right?'

'Let me know when you reach the resort.'

'I'm really sorry about what happened. Hope you're okay.'

Why should he be sorry, I thought.

'We're fine. Thanks for clearing the way for us,' I replied. After all, it was because of his efforts with the cops that we got out of there so quickly.

I was glad to see we had arrived at the resort gate. 'Finally, so relieved to get back behind these gates!' I sighed, as we drove in.

Soon enough we pulled up in front of the lodge.

Natasha and Zaid were waiting for us at the top of the steps.

'What happened? Are you all right?' she asked, hurrying towards us.

'Yes, yes, we're fine,' said Vikram smoothly. 'We had a great shoot in the park, managed to evade the mob. But we weren't so lucky on our way out. They surrounded us at the gate, but the police came and cleared the way. And we managed to make our escape. Devraj also helped deal with them. And Ravi and Sohan were reasonably well behaved.'

'Oh God. I was so worried! This whole time I had a bad feeling! *Shukar* hai, you're safe!' She fussed around him as he got off. Ravi and Sohan also got off and stood behind him, looking grim.

'Did someone call and tell you?' I asked, getting off the jeep. I was surprised she had already heard. Maybe Devraj or Debajyoti had called her.

'Yes, I got a call from Debajyoti! Also, it's all over social media!' she exclaimed.

'What, already?' Vikram responded.

Sohan and Ravi looked at each other. They didn't seem happy at all. Must be worried about how they looked in the visuals. Then it dawned on me that I should be worried too!

I took out my phone to check. I looked for Vikram on Twitter, and, sure enough, there were some pictures and videos of the scene. These were shared by tourists, maybe some journalists who were there. They had been picked up by some local news handles as well.

One picture was being widely shared, where Vikram and I were standing in the jeep, his one arm protectively around me and the other stretched out, the protesters all around us.

I looked wide-eyed and frightened, my hair cascading over one shoulder. I had loosened my hair momentarily when the jeep had stopped at the gate, meaning to tie it up again in a tighter ponytail, but then the chaos had broken out. Also, my 'wide-eyed' look was actually me looking to see what Devraj and the cops were doing.

But this picture made it all look far more dramatic than it had been. It had been confusing and chaotic, but the angle of the shot intensified the situation, making it seem like we were in real danger.

The picture also made it look more intimate than it had been. I looked like I was clutching Vikram as he held me close with one arm.

And this was the picture that was now going viral! I could see it was creating quite a reaction among Vikram's fans.

Many heart and fire emojis, comments about how Vikram was 'so hot', 'so brave', 'a real hero'. Speculation about what was happening. Outrage against the Bhawani Sena. No one was quite clear why they were protesting yet.

Looking at Vikram in dismay, I said, 'Your fans have gone bonkers over this picture!'

He was looking at photo on Zaid's phone and grinned.

'I look like I'm saving you from a frenzied mob, though you can see Ravi's back since he was the one blocking people. In the picture, though, he looks like a part of the crowd,' he said, highly amused.

'Well, you look great. I'm the one looking very "damsel in distress"! Eesh!' I replied, scrunching my face.

'Yeah, when Natasha and I saw the picture, we didn't know what to think! You look so frightened, Sunaina, and the crowd looks ready to pounce!' said Zaid. 'So glad you're all safe!'

This made me feel worse!

'Relax, it's all good. We came out of it safe and sound. Sohan here did not beat up anyone. And hopefully there won't be any further controversy,' Vikram laughed, punching Sohan in the arm. They had a laugh, with Sohan finally seeming to relax.

'I just hope this issue over Rana Sanga just settles down! And now I really need something to eat! This safari has given me an appetite!' said Vikram. He turned and went inside with Sohan and Ravi.

Natasha shook her head at me, laughing at my distressed face.

'Chill out, Sunaina. It's just fans doing what fans do, and since Vikram has so many young female fans, they're all really excited about this.' She held up her phone with the photo of us together.

'Yeah, look how viral it's going! And reactions have been so positive! Sympathetic,' said Zaid.

'Except there is no "this" though?' I replied wearily to what Natasha had said.

'Yes, but they don't know that. And this interest around the campaign and you is frankly doing Vikram good. Makes him seem less arrogant and more down to earth, though still a superstar. That, along with his effort for tiger conservation.'

With that, Natasha and Zaid also went inside the building, leaving me to stew on my own.

Again, I felt irritated at this total lack of consideration for what I might think about this situation. I was just a pawn in the PR game! But I realized it was pointless to argue. No one saw it from my end of things, and people didn't take my concerns seriously.

Also, these 'situations' just seemed to be happening, without any kind of engineering by anyone, so there was no one to blame on that front either. First, the incident with the bees and the picture taken there by Manju. Then this latest picture of Vikram and me on the jeep. At the time, when we were surrounded by the mob, it hadn't felt like an intimate gesture, him putting his arm around me. But in the photograph it did seem like that.

The other jeeps were pulling up now. I went down the porch to meet the team.

'Hey! You all right?' called Jaya, as she jumped from the jeep and ran towards me.

'Oh yeah, I'm absolutely fine,' I said, touched by her concern. 'When the police cleared the way, we just zoomed out of there.'

'Thank God it turned out fine!' said Debajyoti, jumping out of his jeep. 'But there was a scary moment when all of you were surrounded by those guys! It happened so fast! Ravi completely freaked out and dashed across to help you all. I was worried he was going to get into a fight with those men! He had to push a few aside to get to the jeep.'

'Yes, I saw. But they're very careful about how they behave, because they've got into trouble over it before. Beating people in their enthusiasm to protect Vikram.'

'Yeah, I can see that happening,' said Danish with a grin as he unloaded the equipment. 'It was action-packed and I filmed most of it! You looked fairly calm through it.'

'I'm glad you thought so. Though for a few seconds there, I have to admit I was totally frozen. When they say people's reaction to danger is fight or flight, they should include frozen as well! I was very glad for Ravi and Sohan.'

Devraj now came up to where we were standing. He looked very grim. Turning to him, I said, 'Thanks so much for everything, clearing the crowd so we could escape! Didn't realize they would still be outside when we exited.'

'Yes, I should have anticipated it. Don't know how I forgot about them. I should have asked ahead at the gate,' he replied, shaking his head, still looking grim.

'Though they were no longer at the gate, they were hanging out at some tea stall, so maybe they wouldn't have known,' I replied, realizing he was blaming himself.

'Hmm, but still, I should have been more alert. Sorry you had to go through that.'

'Oh, please don't apologize. No harm done. It was chaotic but it turned out alright in the end,' I smiled.

For a moment Devraj's expression softened and he smiled back.

'No, you're right!' said Debajyoti all of a sudden, and very vehemently. Everyone turned to look at him. 'I'm the producer. I should have made sure we were careful! It was my responsibility! If something would have happened, it would have been my fault!' he declared loudly, and a tad dramatically.

'Relax, Debu! It turned out all right and Vikram is perfectly fine. He's not upset, so don't get over emotional, please!' I tried to calm him.

'Dude, the footage is sick! And like Sunaina said, everyone's fine,' Danish drawled. 'We totally have to use the footage in one of the episodes. Chill out, Debu, no harm, no foul.'

'Hey guys!' Just then, Reena emerged from the building. Walking up to where we were standing, she said, 'You all had quite an adventure, didn't you! I saw the pictures. Thank God everyone's fine!'

'What pictures?' asked Jaya, as she put her camera down carefully on a table on the veranda.

'They're all over social media! Vikram's jeep got surrounded by a mob and how he protected Sunaina from those horrid goons!' she replied, excitedly pulling out her phone to show everyone.

'What?' asked Devraj sharply, his face hardening.

'See, this is the picture that's gone viral.' Much to my consternation, she showed the same 'hero-saves-damsel' picture to everyone.

'Dude!' said Danish, laughing at the picture. 'He really looks like your saviour there, Sunaina! Though it was Sohan and Ravi, and Devraj who did the heavy lifting.'

'That's a dramatic picture, all right,' said Jaya, trying to suppress a grin, since she could sense my irritation with it.

'Well, as long as everyone is fine and the campaign isn't getting flak,' said Debajyoti, relaxing a bit.

Devraj didn't say anything. But he looked quite irritated. Picking up his camera bag and stand, he stalked off. I felt slightly disturbed, like I wanted to explain to him what happened. But then he had been there, he knew what happened and how this picture was hardly reality. Also, I realized that I cared about what he thought, which took me by surprise.

'Sunaina, you've become quite a sensation thanks to this!' Reena went on, oblivious to everything else. 'You're getting so much attention. A couple of my Mumbai journalist friends want to know if you'll do an interview,' she said. But then seeing my expression she quickly added, 'But I told them that's not something you'd be interested in.'

'I should hope so, and please tell me you're not telling them anything. Not that there's anything to tell,' I said angrily.

'No no, what would I say? I told them we're doing this shoot for the tiger campaign and for Vikram it's a great experience, et cetera, et cetera. You know, the usual spiel. I said "no comment" on this link-up story.'

'Reena! Why "no comment"! That makes it seem like there is something to comment!' I remarked in exasperation.

'Yeah, exactly. I said there's nothing to say and I won't comment,' she replied smoothly. 'Chalo, I have to go prepare for my interview. See you at dinner,' and she waltzed off.

Shaking her head at Reena's departure, Jaya laughed. 'Come on, let's get back to the tent now. What a day!'

Back at the tent, I got a call from our news desk about the gate incident. They were carrying the footage and wanted to do a phone interview with me!

I was put through to the studio, and Vijay, the anchor, asked me a few questions about the protest and how we had been surrounded. I explained about the channel's campaign, Vikram's involvement. Then about the Bhawani Sena and the reason for their protest against Vikram. How it was to do with his upcoming role as Rana Sanga and the Sena had taken offence at his statements. It sounded ridiculous saying it out loud, and I had to work hard to keep my tone neutral. I added how we had eventually managed to leave safely.

Finishing up the call, I had a shower and waited as Jaya got ready. I checked my phone to see if there was a message from Devraj.

'Are you feeling fine now?' Jaya called out. 'Whatever you say, that was quite an experience at the gate. It looked pretty gnarly for a few minutes. Can't tell you how relieved I was when your jeep sped off.'

She was right, I had to admit. There were some scary moments. Thinking back to the peak of the chaos, for a few moments I had felt absolutely terrified.

My heart had been pounding, and I could feel the adrenaline pumping.

It's such a rare feeling, genuine deep fear, so when it happens, it shakes you up. The heightened awareness. The senses feeling sharper. The absolute alertness. I guess that's what makes some people adrenaline junkies. The rush.

'We were lucky it didn't get out of hand, like you said on the phone,' said Jaya, emerging from the bathroom.

'There have been all those mob attack episodes over the last few years, when they just get carried away. Luckily, this wasn't that. This was more for the publicity than any real anger.'

'Exactly. They just wanted their fifteen minutes of fame, rather than to do any harm,' I said. 'But it was quite frightening in the midst of it.'

'Some sites already have a piece on it,' said Jaya, scrolling through her phone. 'Reena shared some write-ups on the WhatsApp group. And these are the non-gossipy ones, so they're talking about Rana Sanga and why the Bhawani Sena is misguidedly protesting against Vikram.'

'At least history is being discussed,' I said with a laugh.

'Debajyoti has also messaged to check if you did the phone interview with the office.'

I picked up my phone and scrolled through the messages on the WhatsApp group. Besides the links Reena had sent, everyone wanted to know if I was fine, to which I responded in the affirmative.

Debajyoti messaged that we had to discuss the next day's programme over dinner so everyone should come to the lodge.

11

Jaya and I arrived at the main building a little after 8 p.m.

Most of the team had assembled and was sitting around in the dining area. Debajyoti was holding a meeting with all the producers as everyone else waited around.

Manju called us over to where she was sitting with Danish. She looked very excited, which gave me a sense of dread. Now what could have happened?

'Guess what? Zeba Khan is coming tomorrow!' she said excitedly. 'We're hoping she lets us shoot with her too!'

Now this was a very surprising development. Why would Zeba Khan suddenly arrive for a visit? This shoot had enough drama, and somehow this seemed likely to lead to more.

'That's interesting,' I said, a little carefully. 'Do we know why? You're right. If she shoots with us, that would be a bonus.'

'It might actually help take the heat off you, Sunaina,' said Jaya. 'If she comes here, then the gossip will shift to her, right?'

'I didn't think of it that way, but you're right. This could be a very good thing! How do we know she's coming? Did Natasha tell you?' I asked, feeling more positive about the news now.

'She announced it on Instagram. She commented on a post of Vikram's and said you're having so much fun, I'm coming too. And Maya told me she's coming tomorrow! It seems they have been discussing it for a while.'

'So we don't know for sure yet?' asked Jaya, sitting down. 'It would be such a bonus for us if she did. I'm sure this was planned. They must discuss these things before commenting in public.'

'We're waiting for the Mumbai team to tell us what the plan is. Probably Natasha will,' said Manju.

'Yeah,' said Danish. 'I'm excited! She's really hot!'

We all started laughing.

'Yes, objectifying the Bollywood star, so typical, Danish,' said Jaya.

'Hey, it's what she promotes! Have you seen her Insta feed? Her pictures are like hot, hotter, hottest! Don't expect me to be politically correct! She wants us to say it,' Danish said with a wink.

'Though I don't know how much it's going to take the heat off you, Sunaina,' said Manju, looking down at her phone.

'What do you mean?' I asked.

'People are now speculating that she's coming here because Vikram has been linked to you!' she said. 'Oh

God, people are so dramatic. It's a triangle, according to them!'

She started laughing as she scrolled on her phone, but then stopped after seeing my expression.

What fresh hell was this! And just as I was feeling relieved about Zeba Khan joining us and hopeful that this could change the narrative around Vikram and me.

I glared at Danish and Jaya who were laughing.

'Don't worry, Sunaina,' Manju said. 'I was talking to Zaid earlier and he was also telling me about the fan clubs stars have online. He admitted some are even in touch with him and Natasha. They're the ones who follow the stars so closely on social media and then hype things. So who knows how real this even is? I'm sure Zeba has her own fan clubs.'

Debajyoti had now walked over to us.

'Even so. You do realize this stuff could follow me, right? The Internet never forgets. The Mumbai team will go back to Bollywood and their glamorous lives. On the other hand, this could affect my career!' I said, getting quite agitated now.

'No one will take me seriously. What if Boss sees it? Oh my God, I didn't even think of that!' I covered my face with my hands.

'Well, actually, I did get a call from Lata asking if everything was fine, especially after what happened at the gate,' said Debajyoti. 'I told her we'd had some adventures but it was all right. I also told her this online stuff about you and Vikram was all rubbish, just because of a picture here and there. She seemed relieved.'

'What!' I squealed. 'She actually thought it was true?'

Now my embarrassment knew no bounds.

'No, I'm sure she didn't!' Debajyoti tried to reassure me. 'She's been in the media so long, so I'm sure she knows how these things happen. Don't worry about this following you. It will blow over. In fact, she said to call her in case you were stressed.'

That was nice of Lata. Maybe I would call her later to clear things. As for 'blowing over', that's what everyone had said from the start but it still hadn't.

'Hello, people! I have some exciting news!' We all turned to see Natasha and Zaid approaching our table.

'Come, sit,' said Debajyoti, jumping up. More chairs were pulled up and they both joined us.

'Soooo, guess what!?' she said dramatically, pausing for effect. We all remained attentive, looking at her in anticipation.

'Vikram's friend Zeba Khan is coming tomorrow!' She scanned our faces to see the impact of her announcement. We all reacted with varying degrees of enthusiasm and even some exclamations. (Manju was the loudest.)

Zaid clapped gleefully to add to the effect.

Satisfied, Natasha explained, 'She was quite intrigued by what Vikram was doing and the whole tiger campaign. So remember, one of the shoots we discussed was a tiger-spotting show, where you get marks for things? Well, we got her to agree to do it! So we can do it like a competition between Vikram and Zeba! What do you think?'

We all turned to look at Debajyoti to whom the question was directed.

'That's amazing!' he said with enthusiasm. 'That will make it such a good show. But I hope she doesn't expect any payment because our budgets are quite tight now.'

'No. No payment. She thought it would be fun to do it, and it's for a good cause,' Natasha replied. 'So what I was thinking was we could have Vikram and Sunaina in one jeep, and Zeba and Devraj in another. That could be our two teams? What do you think? Do you think Devraj would agree to it? I think he'd look good and the whole thing would have great chemistry, don't you think?'

'Yes, it would be good to get him. I'm sure he'd look good on camera. That's a great idea. Two balanced teams. He's been with us on a few drives. Hopefully he'd be open to doing a shoot with us,' nodded Debajyoti.

'Dude, I'm going to shoot with the Zeba team. I've said it now,' Danish drawled, raising his hand.

'Oh God, okay Danish, I get it!' said Debajyoti, as we all started laughing.

As they continued discussing the shoot, I thought about this whole situation. Did Zeba Khan know about me and the online, patently false gossip around Vikram and me? I had a sinking feeling she did. These stars all monitored social media and kept tabs on things.

I felt my phone beep. It was my sister messaging me. I'd silenced other messages as I had been getting quite a few from friends and acquaintances. I didn't have the bandwidth to deal with all of them.

'Hey! Are you all right? Now there's online gossip speculating about you and Zeba Khan vis-à-vis Vikram? Sounds juicy if I didn't know any better (laughing, winking emoji).'

Trust my sister to be updated with the latest gossip, and monitoring social media closely. I replied, 'Di, glad you know better! I'm also impressed you know all the latest nonsense online (eye roll emoji).'

She promptly replied, 'I have an alert for you now. Have to be on top of things. BTW I tried calling an hour ago after I saw those pictures from the park gate. Didn't get through. Hope all is fine? (big eyes, round mouth emoji).'

'Yes, Di, thanks (hug emoji).'

I also had a message from my Jodhpur friend, Devika.

'Babe! What the hell is happening! Call me when you get a chance, because all this stuff is so crazy (crazy face, tongue out emoji).'

Aww, Devika knew me well enough not to believe any of the nonsense she was reading.

I replied, 'I will when I have a chance. It's all bunkum! Everything is sooo exaggerated '

She promptly replied, 'I thought as much! But people I know here are also asking me, since they know I'm your friend. Lame (eye roll). Hope you're having a good time though! Can't wait to hear all about it! And about Devraj Singh! Remind me to tell you about him later! This shoot sounds like an adventure!'

I smiled at her message. That was a positive spin to it all. It was an adventure for sure! Except for the damn rumours! What did she have to tell me about Devraj? Obviously she knew him, all these families know one another.

The group was still discussing the shoot, so I decided to go for a walk to clear my head and scroll through social media without anyone seeing me do it. I wandered down the path that led to the pool. It was so beautiful at night, almost meditative.

Sitting on one of the lounge chairs, I reflected on how strange the situation was. From staying away from social media to being dragged right into this cesspool! I decided to look at pictures from the shoot that Manju had sent on the WhatsApp group. A palate cleanser for all the toxic social media news.

There were nice pictures of Mallika in various poses. Vikram looking through the binoculars. Vikram and I talking. Then one of Devraj smiling at us. Vikram and I were standing, our backs in the foreground, and Devraj was looking up at us, with a slight smile on his face. He was quite good-looking, I had to admit, in a rugged, careless way. Initially I had thought he was the arrogant, entitled 'type' that one often came across in north India. The type I went to great pains to avoid.

But over these last few days I had realized he wasn't like that. He was hard-working and aware, and he cared about things. In fact, I found myself enjoying our conversations and the time we spent together.

Then, despite my misgivings, I went on to Twitter and then Instagram, and scrolled through some of the comments on entertainment handles on the Vikram story and THE PICTURE.

Some were nice, others very rude and even disparaging. I scrolled more and more, and found myself going down a rabbit hole.

Ugh! It was all too much! STOP IT! I told myself. Just avoid it. That's probably the best way to deal with this. Just concentrate on the campaign, forget about the gossip! Having made this decision, I heaved a big sigh.

'Tough day?'

I nearly jumped out of my skin.

Peering in the direction of the voice, I realized it was Devraj seated at a table, on an elevated platform, adjacent to the pool. It was fairly dark, and I had been so engrossed in my own thoughts that I hadn't realized there was anyone else out here.

'Yes, it's been quite an eventful day, to say the least. I thought our Mallika sighting was going to be the big highlight of the day, but then there was all that drama that followed!'

'Yes. Dramatic is one way to put it.' He got up and came next to me. 'May I?'

'Yes, please sit. I can do with some company,' I nodded, indicating to the chair next to me.

'I've been in a foul mood since the evening myself,' he shook his head. 'I can't believe the nonsense that happened at the gate. I should have known better. This is my area. It was on my watch.'

'No no, you shouldn't blame yourself! Even Debajyoti was blaming himself. Hindsight is always 20/20. But luckily no harm was done. Except for the accompanying sensationalism,' I said wryly.

'Yes, I saw that picture that's become very popular,' he fixed his gaze on me.

I laughed. 'That's putting it mildly. Crazy thing about this social media. I was just sitting here thinking about how I've pretty much avoided it since the last couple of years, and now it's caught up with me in a big way.' I sighed again.

Then, looking at him, I said, 'I didn't realize you were following it online.'

'Hey, just because I live in the jungle doesn't mean I live under a rock,' he laughed. 'Also, many of my media friends have been asking about what's going on here. About you and Vikram. I told them I could not confirm or deny.'

'What! Please deny. There's nothing going on here! It's all a big social media concoction. I'm sure you know that?' I looked at him. I don't know why but it suddenly felt very important that he should know it wasn't true.

'Well, you can never be sure. I didn't want to presume either way,' he looked at me intently.

Our eyes locked for a few moments. But then, feeling my face heat up, I looked away. Thank God it was dark.

'People just looked at pictures online, put two and two together and came up with twenty! It's all quite ridiculous,' I said with a shake of my head.

'I can see how that happened. He is a big name and folks love this kind of stuff. I used to be involved with PR, brand building and events earlier, in what I like to think of as my "past life",' he smiled.

'In the first picture that generated interest, you were saving him from a bee attack, and in the second he was saving you from a mob. People must be so amazed at all the drama that goes on down here.'

We laughed. He was right. It had been quite eventful.

'So why are you so pensive? Isn't this good? It's created a big buzz, whatever the reality is. Media loves buzz.'

'*Et tu*? That's what everyone keeps saying and it's driving me nuts! Yes, it's good for the campaign, creating a lot of interest, but I don't like being dragged into salacious stuff like this! I really don't want my colleagues and other reporters I know seeing this nonsense.' I covered my face and shook my head. 'But here everyone thinks I'm overreacting. That it will just die down soon. Maybe I am. God knows.' I spread out my hands in an exasperated way.

He laughed. 'Well, maybe they're right? Don't worry about it too much. These things tend to blow over. In a few days no one will remember, they'd have moved on to the next thing.'

'Inshallah,' I said.

Just then his phone started beeping.

'Oh, it seems I'm being sought,' Devraj said, looking at his phone, which had lit up. 'I have a few missed calls from your producer. The connectivity is patchy here, comes and goes.'

We got up to return. I was feeling better after joking about the whole thing, that too strangely enough with Devraj of all people. Who would have thought he could be so comforting and sensitive?

We started walking back to the main building. Devraj, who was behind me, took out a flashlight to light up the path.

Debajyoti probably wanted to talk to him about the shoot tomorrow! Damn, I'd forgotten all about that!

I was looking down, lost in thought, when suddenly Devraj grabbed my arm to pull me back. Startled, I looked up at him to find he was staring at something to the right of the path.

As I peered at it I realized there was something in the tall grass, behind a large bush. I'd been looking at the path and hadn't noticed.

Feeling frightened for the second time that day, I quickly moved closer to Devraj, holding on to his arm. He switched off the torch.

'What is it?' I whispered, peering at the bushes. I could hear some grunts and a shuffling sound.

'I can't make out, but I know it's not a deer. I'm just worried it's a sloth bear. They cross here sometimes and we don't want to surprise it or run into it,' he whispered, putting his arm around me and taking a careful step back. 'We'll have to wait for it to move.'

We kept standing like that for a few moments.

After a beat, as the initial shock wore off, I suddenly became aware of how close we were, his arm around me, pulling me up close to him. The fear I had initially felt was replaced by an overwhelming sense of awareness, both of his touch and the heat radiating from his body.

As we remained in this position, our bodies stuck together, I could feel a hot flush grow inside me.

Bending down to whisper in my ear, Devraj said, 'Let's try and move towards the left.'

Feeling his hot breath on my ear and neck did not help matters. His face was close to mine and all I could do was look up at him and nod. My heart seemed to be beating right out of my chest, and now it wasn't only because of the possibly dangerous animal near us.

We shuffled towards the left.

I felt a bit dizzy with his nearness. The body was reacting in ways the mind had no control over.

For a second time in the day, I could feel my adrenaline pumping. It was like all my senses had jumped from five to ten. A sensory overdrive. I was acutely aware of his arm, protectively around me, and my body pressed against his.

We remained like that for what seemed like a very long time though it was probably just a few minutes.

Finally, there was some movement and a snort from the darkness on the right.

We saw a big shadow moving out from behind the bushes.

Now fear took over again, and I clutched Devraj's arm tighter as he moved to shield me.

The shadow now took shape and we saw it was a big wild boar. It grunted and shook its head. Then, after standing still for a moment, as if deciding what to do next, it moved towards the right, away from us, and then disappeared into the darkness and trees beyond.

I let out a shaky, nervous laugh.

'Okay, so just a wild boar. I guess we overreacted,' I said, aware of his arm still around me.

He smiled at me and gave my shoulder a squeeze and finally let go.

'Sometimes it's wiser to overreact. Also, if we'd startled the boar it could have charged at us. It's happened before on the property,' he said.

We started walking down the path towards the lodge.

I felt shaken and embarrassed by what had just happened. I was still tingling all over. Where had these feelings come from?!

'Thank God it didn't charge at us! What are you supposed to do when attacked by a boar? Is it true they only run straight, and you just have to step out of their path and they'll just keep on running straight? I've been told that, but maybe it's a myth.'

Now I was blabbering away to cover up my embarrassment. I felt kind of giddy.

'Oh God, we're so late!' I went on. 'Debajyoti must be wondering where we are. Actually, they must be wondering where you are. They wanted to talk to you. We have to plan tomorrow's shoot.'

It was like I couldn't stop talking.

Devraj, on the other hand, was silent. I felt a tension between us. I didn't dare look at his face, just kept up the chatter as we walked on.

We were near the main building now, given I was walking so briskly to shake off the feeling.

What the hell had just happened? Was it just me or had he felt it too? There was no denying it. I had felt an intense attraction to Devraj!

As I continued walking, so many thoughts rushed through my head. My attitude towards Devraj had clearly changed in the last two days. That was something I had realized earlier. How I enjoyed chatting with him, and how we both had a shared interest in wildlife and the issues surrounding it. He wasn't the egotistical snob I had initially thought he was. Did I have a crush on him? Did I want to take this forward? Was he even interested?

Damn! This shoot was already complicated enough.

We finally reached the lodge. Going up the stairs, I saw Vikram sitting in the veranda with Natasha and a few of the others.

'Hey, I was wondering where you were,' he called out. 'Did you hear about the shoot tomorrow with Zeba?

It'll be great! Me and you versus Devraj and Zeba! Let the games begin! Woo hoo!'

I looked back sheepishly at Devraj, who looked at me curiously.

'Sorry? What's this about?' he asked, sounding confused.

'She didn't tell you? We were looking all over for you. We need you in the shoot tomorrow, please!' said Natasha. 'Sunaina, be a darling. Can you just call Debajyoti so we can discuss this properly?'

I was happy to leave and go find Debajyoti. He was seated at a table in the dining area, chatting with Jaya and Danish. I told him Natasha was calling him as they wanted to speak to Devraj about the shoot.

'Where did you disappear to?' Jaya asked as I sat down with her.

'I just wanted to be by myself for a bit. It's been a crazy day,' I said.

Except I hadn't been by myself. I'd been with Devraj and the most unexpected thing had happened. But I wasn't going to say all that.

'And it will be more crazy tomorrow when we do this tiger-spotting-competition shoot,' she smiled.

'Ugh! When you put it like that, it sounds bad! This shoot has to be done very carefully. At no point can we break any rules in the park. It can't be like we're driving around crazily, looking for a tiger, especially now with so much scrutiny from other media on our shoot.'

'If I remember correctly, it was your idea to do a shoot like this. The safari competition!' Danish said laughing.

'Why didn't anyone stop me!' I wailed.

'You were quite clear about how it would be a great way to put the spotlight on different ways of spotting a tiger: the scratch marks, the pug marks, the alarm call. You said it would be a very informative show and fun.' Jaya rattled off verbatim what I had written in my show descriptor email to the team.

'Argh! Stop it!' I put my hands over my ears. 'This was all before I got randomly linked to a movie star. Now people think there is some kind of a love triangle happening when there really isn't anything at all!'

Jaya and Danish were giggling now.

'Why don't you eat some food? We've all eaten, and it's really good desi khana,' said Jaya sympathetically. Danish got up and fetched me a plate.

'Hello!' said Manju, slipping into the seat next to me.

I looked at her suspiciously. She kept her expression even but I wasn't buying it.

'What lousy update do you have for me now, Manju? Or is it some good news like a star had a wardrobe malfunction, or some hot new affair so the entertainment news cycle can move on?'

'Mmmmm,' said Manju, looking uncomfortable.

'What now? Come on, spill,' said Jaya.

'There's actually a poll now. One of the sites started asking people whom they prefer, Vikram and Sunaina or Vikram and Zeba. So people are tweeting #TeamZeba and #TeamSunaina. The good news is, Sunaina, I think you are winning.'

'How is this good news? NONE OF THIS IS GOOD, Manju! What the hell. There's no Vikram and Sunaina and therefore no need for a "Team Sunaina"!'

Now everyone was laughing.

Frustrated with everyone and with things beyond my control, I decided Jaya's suggestion was the best and I should just eat.

There was rice, chicken curry and yellow dal on the table. I served myself and spent the next five minutes steadily eating. The combination of chicken curry, rice and dal was always comforting.

'Feeling better?' asked Jaya after I finished up.

'Yeah, what a day. So much going on. This shoot with Zeba Khan is great, but I don't want any awkwardness. I'm sure she knows all this stuff online is rubbish, right? Vikram would have told her?' I looked around at everyone to see whether they agreed. From their expressions, they didn't look so sure.

'Mmmm, we can only hope so,' said Manju. 'Because some of the comments she's been getting are not kind. I didn't realize she's not very popular among Vikram's fans, especially the younger girls.'

I decided to bite the bullet and check out what was being said.

'Okay, Manju. Tell me. Show me a few comments, just not the really rude ones that will destroy my confidence forever.'

'Dude, chill. Haters gonna hate! Don't let it affect you. You're good-looking, smart, not fake. That counts for a lot,' said Danish, giving me a side hug. Now that was sweet and unexpected, coming from him.

'Aww, thanks, D. On that vote of confidence from Danish, let's do this.'

We all turned towards Manju.

'Okay, well, here's a nice one, "#VikramSunaina because he deserves someone real, Zeba is such a fake #TeamSunaina".'

'Ooh, but that's not nice about her,' I said.

'I told you some of them were being really nasty about Zeba. Okay, here's another: "I don't even know if it's real but this #VikramSunaina thing is so cute. Cud happen to any of us! #TeamSunaina."'

'See, you're giving hope to all the girl-next-door types,' said Manju.

I wasn't sure if that was a compliment or not.

Manju carried on. 'Here's another nasty one about Zeba, "I hate @Zebakhan because she's the one who got Vikram into that drugs stuff! #TeamSunaina."'

'So typical,' I said, shaking my head. 'Always blame the woman. It's never the man's fault. Isn't it?' Everyone nodded. Even Danish.

'Okay, here's another cute one about your picture, "I love the way he's protecting her! Such a gentleman! I expected nothing less from him #VikramSunaina #TeamSunaina."'

'Then a catty one, "What does Vikram even see in this Sunaina!? Choose me, Vikram! #VikramSunaina."'

'Then, "Vikram! You should be with someone better! #Vikram #TeamZeba." Oops, I shouldn't have read that.' Manju looked up worriedly.

'It's okay. I understand there must be a whole range of comments,' I shrugged.

'Here's another sweet one, "#VikramSunaina is the best thing to have happened recently. For some reason it makes me happy #TeamSunaina".'

'And another, "Now Zeba is going to Chambalgarh. Meow! This will be fun #VikramSunaina #catfight."'

'All right. I think that's enough.' I threw up my hands. 'I get a sense of what's there and it'll be an endless hole if I go any deeper.'

'I'm quite impressed with how you're handling it. Not checking out everything people are saying,' said Manju, as she continued skimming.

'I'm glad I'm not that into it! This stuff can really mess with your head,' I replied.

And it was a fact. It was so easy to feel good for two minutes over some mild praise and then feel so low the very next second because of a vicious comment. Better to keep my equilibrium and not go down that road.

Looking at my phone, I saw that more messages from friends and colleagues had come in. I may as well reply instead of leaving things to their imagination. They were mostly questions about my safety, what was all this stuff online, had our team really been attacked by a mob, was I okay, etc.

I sent short replies along the lines of, 'Don't believe everything you read. All fine,' and, 'It wasn't an attack, just a protest,' and, 'Thanks so much for checking in, I'm fine.'

People were more concerned about the protest and my safety than the gossip.

Reena came up to the table and sat down.

'Are you okay?' she asked me, looking concerned. 'I'm sorry about earlier when I was taking it lightly. It has got a bit much now.'

Wow. I was getting an apology from Reena. Not bad.

'I also thought you should know, some journo friends of mine messaged Vikram asking questions about the protests as well as the shoot. He said he's enjoying himself and learning a lot. And when they asked about you, he said it's a professional relationship and he admires you for your commitment to conservation. I think that's rather nice, isn't it?'

'I hope they believe it and won't write rubbish,' I replied.

'Well, the thing about entertainment writing is you have to leave things a little open-ended, you know what I mean? They will quote him, but they may put pictures alongside and add a little speculation to make it interesting. That's just the nature of entertainment reporting. Soon enough, something else will come up and everyone will forget this.'

She looked at me encouragingly. I wasn't quite sure I agreed with it all but it was nice of her to reach out, all the same.

Debajyoti came in and called out to me.

'Just come and speak to Devraj. He's not too happy with the idea of a tiger-spotting competition. He says we could send out the wrong idea, two jeeps competing with one another.'

I cringed. It did sound bad when you thought about it like that, which was not what I'd had in mind at all.

'Okay, I'll speak to him,' I said, but suddenly had butterflies in my stomach at the thought of seeing him. I'd consciously pushed that whole episode out of my mind. Or tried to, at least.

'Yes, please convince him about it. It'll be such a fun show!' said Reena excitedly.

We all went out on the veranda where everyone was sitting around, chatting and laughing. Devraj stood to one side with Himanshu, just looking but not really participating. He saw me and smiled.

Oh, the tingling feeling again!

'Sunaina, please explain the shoot plan for tomorrow,' said Natasha. 'Devraj had some issues with it, so I thought it best you explain the whole idea behind it. I was just telling him how it was even more interesting now that Zeba was coming and we could have two proper teams competing.'

Everyone turned to look at me.

'Yes,' said Devraj, now looking at me very pointedly. 'Do explain this plan which involves people racing around the park, trying to score points and win a competition.'

'It's not like that at all,' I said in exasperation, getting irritated by his sarcastic tone, but then realizing people had obviously not described it properly to him.

'Yes, it will be two teams, but driving like a normal safari. There will be no racing or anything. Since Zeba Khan will be here as well, we will have two teams with one actor each. I'll be with Vikram and the guide, and you can guide Zeba. So as we drive, we can explain the many ways to spot a tiger or look for signs. Like a pug mark or a tree marking or an alarm call. We can even talk about different types of alarm calls, like a chectal or a monkey or a peacock. And whenever we spot a sign or an alarm call or a tiger, we will earn points. So it will give us a chance to talk about the park and tiger behaviour. Also, how one can feel the presence of a tiger in the park. You don't have to actually see a tiger to know you're in its habitat. There are so many signs that we often miss. So it's a way to make it fun and create awareness at the same time.'

'It sounds great! It will be informative and fun at the same time, right? And I'm sure our team will win,' said Vikram with a wink and a grin.

We all laughed.

'That remains to be seen, but we'll film it very carefully. We don't want any criticism, especially from the environmentalists. And now our shoot is under much greater scrutiny so we need to take extra care,' I said and turned to Devraj to see if he was on board. Everyone else turned to him as well.

After a beat, he said, 'Well, as long as we're careful, then I guess it's fine.'

'Yes!' said Vikram, punching the air, as everyone else looked very relieved.

'Your description was very different from Natasha's,' he said to me, with a one-sided smile.

'I'm sorry if I scared you off. I should have just waited for Sunaina to come and explain it properly!' she laughed.

'Okay, folks! So we're all set for tomorrow,' said a very relieved-looking Debajyoti. 'This shoot will be at 3 p.m. as Zeba gets in by 10 a.m. We'll meet for lunch, and I'll assign jeeps and teams after that.'

'What about the protesters?' asked Zaid, looking worried. 'What if they're outside the gate again?'

'Don't worry about them,' said Devraj smoothly. 'I've taken care of it. Called up a few of their political patrons who've now warned them against showing their faces anywhere near the gate again.'

'Oh thank God for that because I have been worried! They might have enjoyed the five minutes of fame they got today and could be back for more,' said Debajyoti.

'Ravi and Sohan were also stressed about them returning, so I'll let them know they can relax,' said Vikram. 'Also, who did you call? Those are rather helpful connections to have!'

'I called my friend from college whose father was once head of the Bhawani Sena. Then I called the local MLA to make sure they were warned to stay away. Then I called his rival leader in this area, whom I also know well, to relay the same message. So we won't have anything to worry about tomorrow.'

'Yes, they definitely won't come now,' Himanshu emphasized. 'I followed up with calls to some of the local people as well to warn them. All the fellows are known to someone or the other. They've been told off strongly.'

'Whoa!' said Vikram, looking impressed 'That's wicked cool! And all these guys listen to you?'

'My family has had significant influence in this area for decades now. My nana's brother used to live in this baadi earlier, so he was well known in this area. The family had close ties with many of the local families and villages,' Devraj replied evenly. 'Could even be enough to dent or make an election. Especially now that I'm based here, I'm quite involved with local issues and keeping up connections.'

'What work do you do in the area?' asked Debajyoti, looking impressed.

This time Himanshu spoke up, 'The Baagh Baadi Foundation supports many schools around here. We help in the upkeep of the school buildings and ensuring working toilets for girls.

'We also ensure government schemes reach the villages, like funding for *pucca* houses, toilets, hand pumps. Also, most of the staff employed here are from the villages. We train the young men to work here. Devraj sir also gets them employment in other hotels and lodges, and even as drivers. We have a donation option in our final billing to guests, and many of them have been generous.'

Now we were all impressed. This was really quite commendable. This was a great example of tourism benefitting locals.

'Sunaina, we should cover some of this, don't you think? Especially the schools that the foundation is supporting,' said Debajyoti.

'Yeah sure, that's a great idea,' I said. 'And interview some of the staff that are from the villages, to highlight how the tourism industry can be more engaged and benefit locals.'

'I'd love to chat with them,' Vikram gamely volunteered.

'Oh, that would be very nice, sir,' said Himanshu. 'Devraj sir doesn't highlight the work enough, I feel. I keep telling him.'

'Okay, that's enough, Himanshu,' said Devraj with a smile. We discussed a few more issues when Vikram called it a night.

'See you all tomorrow! I'm excited about the shoot,' he said, wishing us all goodnight as he walked off towards his room, with Natasha and Zaid in tow.

I was glad to head back to my tent. I was feeling exhausted now.

'Can I speak to you for a minute?'

I realized Devraj was right next to me. 'Yeah, sure,' I replied as we walked to one end of the veranda, away from the others. What did he want to speak to me? I felt nervous suddenly. Also a little excited.

'Sorry if I put you on the spot there. I was a little taken aback by this safari competition shoot, especially the way Natasha described it,' he said with a wry smile.

'Oh, that's all right. I can imagine how it sounds if it's not explained properly. I had written the proposal back when we were planning this shoot and I had imagined it as an educative show. Little did I know we'd have two movie stars for it,' I said.

I didn't know if I was relieved or disappointed that this was all he wanted to talk to me about. The shoot. What had I expected? Also, what did I want?

'I am also surprised you didn't mention it earlier when we were chatting by the pool,' he said.

'Well, I knew Debajyoti and Natasha wanted to ask you about it, so I left it to them, and I was also a little preoccupied at that time,' I replied.

'Yes, I remember. The social media stuff. All right, just wanted to sort that out with you ahead of the filming tomorrow.' He gave me a smile that made my legs a little wobbly. He looked like he wanted to say something more, but then thought against it.

'Okay then,' I said brightly, before things got awkward. 'See you tomorrow.'

'Are you going back to your tent now? Do you want me to drop you in case there are any more animals lurking around?' he asked.

I looked at his face to see if he was teasing me. He looked back with an inscrutable expression, though I thought I saw a hint of a smile. I couldn't help laughing even as I blushed at the same time.

'Hah. No, that's fine. I'm a big girl, I can take care of myself.'

He stepped a little closer to me and said with a smile, 'I know you can, Sunaina Joshi, but sometimes it may be nice to give others a chance.'

Our eyes locked as he looked at me intently.

I could feel the heat spread across my face. There was no denying the attraction, and this meant he felt it too. As we remained in that moment, I wanted to say something but words eluded me.

Just then, Jaya's voice broke the spell.

'Hey, Sunaina! I'm heading,' she called out from the steps.

Glancing in her direction, Devraj said, 'Well, another time then. Goodnight.'

'See you tomorrow. Goodnight!' I said quickly and turned around to follow Jaya.

Goodnights were said to the other team members, and we started walking back to the tent.

'What a day it's been,' said Jaya as we entered the tent. 'Can't wait to sleep now. What drama.'

I felt like telling her she didn't know the half of it!

12

We took it easy the next morning, since the previous day had been so hectic.

At around 8 a.m. we went to the main building for breakfast. It was quick, uneventful.

We chit-chatted with few of the team members around. I didn't run into Devraj, even though I kept an eye out for him. So much so that Jaya noticed and asked why I was so distracted. It was easy to blame it on the shoot and Zeba's arrival.

I wondered if I should message him. Just a casual 'Good morning'. Then decided against it.

I returned to the tent after breakfast and spent the morning on my computer, working on the script for the episodes, looking at the footage we had on the cameras. Along with Jaya, I identified some good sequences to uplink to the office so that the editors there could get working on the promotional videos for the campaign.

There was such satisfaction in looking at the footage, seeing how well it had come out.

We had managed to get some really great tiger footage; the shots of Mallika were absolutely beautiful. Something for the archives. And the shot of Zalim marking the tree with his paws—just stunning.

Even the incident with the bees was captured on camera. We had some decent footage of the commotion—people yelling, jeeps revving, bees buzzing around, Vikram and I under the scarf, and then Safar holding one side of her face. Along with the doctor's interview, we could definitely make a three- to four-minute segment for the half hour.

Finally, as I skimmed through the footage, I reached the part where we encountered the protesters at the gate. It was strange seeing it from a distance. There really weren't so many protesters at all, when you saw the wide shot, which showed the jeep and the area around it. In the viral picture, though, which was a closer shot, it looked like we had been surrounded by a huge mob.

I saw Devraj get off the jeep and yell at the cops standing some distance away. He looked very worked up and angry, which I also hadn't realized at the time. He was yelling at the men, pushing some of them aside, calling out to the cops. Then there was a point when he glanced back at the jeep, and saw Vikram and me standing together, with Vikram's arm around me. I couldn't see his expression but he seemed transfixed for a moment. Then the camera zoomed in to get a closer shot of us on the jeep, so he was out of the frame.

'Checking out the drama yesterday?' asked Jaya, looking over at the camera screen.

'Yes, it's very different seeing the video and comparing it with what it felt like at the time. It felt quite terrifying, when I had no idea what was happening, how we'd get away,' I replied. 'I'll be honest, I was really relieved when Devraj said yesterday that he had spoken to some people to ensure the crowd didn't come back. I was stressed at the thought of facing this mob again.'

'Yeah, that was some good news. I was wondering if they were feeling chuffed with the sensation they caused and emboldened by it too,' Jaya replied.

We watched the footage of the crowd being cleared and us zooming away. The Bhawani Sena then sloganeered some more in some kind of 'victory'.

I could see Devraj on the sidelines talking in an angry manner with the cop. Almost berating him, it seemed.

'Devraj was very agitated, by the way,' Jaya said. 'I meant to tell you, he really yelled at the police to control the situation. He even threatened them, saying if anything happened, he'd hold them responsible. Danish and I were a little surprised at how worked up he got. He's usually so cool.'

'Really? I didn't realize so much happened.' I hadn't thought so much about how we had escaped.

'Even after your jeep left and we were returning, he seemed very het up. We got the feeling he was more concerned about you than he was about Vikram.'

My face flushed slightly. Looking at me closely as I looked away, Jaya asked, 'What were you two talking about last night on the veranda? I meant to ask.'

'Oh, that. He was just discussing the shoot and how he initially had misgivings about the safari competition,'

I said casually, pretending to go through the footage, wondering how to change the topic. 'I hope the social media hysteria has died down now.'

Almost on cue, Manju came into the tent.

'Hello, I've been looking for you guys. Didn't you see the WhatsApp message? We're all going to the lounge. Zeba is here!'

My stomach knotted in nervousness but it had to be done. I'd been trying not to think about meeting her.

'I have been dreading this but might as well get it over with,' I said. 'I was just telling Jaya that I hope all the social media stuff about yesterday's incident has died down.'

'It has settled somewhat, but now this shoot is going to make things exciting again,' said Manju gleefully (and a little tactlessly I thought), as she scrolled through her phone.

'See here,' she said, showing us some Instagram posts. 'Zeba seems quite excited about her trip. Look at the pictures she's been posting on Instagram. Here's one before she took off from the airport, then here's a story post from the plane, wearing her safari hat! Look! Then she posted a picture in the open jeep. She's getting a lot of engagements. Vikram has also commented on her jeep picture. "Can't wait to see you!"' Manju voiced it in an excited way.

'That comment has got lots of reactions!'

She scrolled more. 'You know, I really think both Vikram and Zeba are enjoying this.'

'What do you mean "enjoying this"?' I asked.

'See this post by Vikram yesterday. He put up a picture of both of you when you were watching Mallika.

And he wrote, "The most special tiger sighting #Mallika #teamtiger #saveourtigers". While that's harmless enough, he's referring to Mallika, but since the picture is with you, and a really nice one, just the two of you on the jeep, it made people talk. And then Zeba is posting so much about her trip here. As much as you're uncomfortable with all this "attention", they're definitely enjoying it.'

'But why? It's such a silly thing for either of them to take interest in. They're such big stars,' I said, taken aback at the idea.

'It's some kind of a social media image-building thing. There's no quicker way to influence Gen Z and the tweens than social media these days, and doing something that interests them. And it's very wholesome, since, after all, it's to do with a tiger campaign too. Soon, others, like mainstream media and advertisers, follow it.'

I looked at Jaya in exasperation.

'Well, it makes sense,' she said. 'And while the gossip has been off the mark, all the sensational events did happen. Bee attack, tiger sightings and mob protests. Nothing has been manufactured.'

'So here I am getting stressed and it's just a laugh for them. Or a helpful way to change the conversation around them.' With this realization, I got up in a determined way, tied my hair into a high ponytail, put on some lipstick, kajal, a little face powder and a peach blush that always helped.

Looking in the mirror and satisfied with my very basic effort, I turned around and signalled to Manju and Jaya to get going.

'All right, then let's go meet her. I'll also play my part. After all, it's for a good cause,' I said with gusto.

'Nice!' said Manju appreciatively. 'Just open up your hair. It's so smokin'! Why tie it up?'

Turning back, I untied my hair, shook it out and then walked out of the tent. Jaya and Manju followed me.

My motives for the campaign to be a success were slightly selfish. If the tiger campaign did well, we would do a follow-up programme to raise money for the villages around the park. We also planned to use the funds for the forest guards in some selected national parks. I was very keen we do the follow-up because it would also mean we could travel more. So this tiger shoot had to be a success!

Fortified with this resolve to keep my focus on work and outcomes, we walked towards the lodge to meet Zeba Khan. Everyone was sitting in the lounge, and, as we approached, it was Natasha who called out, 'Sunaina, we've been waiting for you. Come meet Zeba.'

Everyone turned towards us. Natasha, Vikram, Zaid and Safar were seated on the sofas around the low table at the centre. Zeba was sitting on the lounge chair next to them.

' Hey! Zeba, this is Sunaina,' said Vikram.

'Hi! Nice to meet you,' I said cheerily, with my hand out. 'So glad you could come and be a part of our campaign.'

She smiled and shook my hand.

Zeba Khan looked even more beautiful face to face than she looked on the screen. Oval face, pert nose and almond-shaped, light-coloured eyes. Her face was perfectly done up without being overdone and she had long, wavy tresses. She was dressed in an olive button-down dress, along with a lovely fawn-coloured scarf.

'Hi, finally we meet. Vikram has been telling me what an amazing time he's had here. I'm happy I could get away and see for myself,' she said warmly. She had a sweet, girlish voice that immediately made me feel slightly conscious of my own, which was huskier.

She seemed nice enough on the face of it, and I felt guilty that I had thought badly of her. I introduced her to Manju and Jaya.

'Sunaina, explain what we have planned for today to Zeba. I already have but you do it so much better,' Natasha said.

We pulled up chairs and sat down.

I then explained what we had thought out for the shoot. I also gave her a small talk on Chambalgarh, tigers, conservation and the idea behind our campaign. Vikram too added nuggets here and there.

'It all sounds so interesting! And look at Vikram here! Acting like he's also an expert now,' she teased him, giving him a playful whack on his shoulder.

'These last few days I've learnt so much that I feel like I'm halfway there!' Vikram replied with a grin.

Manju, who had been sitting quietly on one side, stood up and asked if she could take a few pictures for social media.

'Sure,' said Zeba. 'Just show them to Sheila before you post.'

She indicated towards a surly-looking lady who was standing to one side, thin, with long, straight hair, dressed in a dark blue pantsuit. She was furiously typing on her phone. At the mention of her name, she just looked up briefly and gave a tight smile, going back immediately to her phone.

Manju took a few quick pictures. First of Zeba and Vikram. Then she gestured to me to join in, even as I tried to say no.

'Come on! Let's get one of the three of us!' said Vikram as he put an arm around both of us, leaving me no choice.

'This should confuse people,' he whispered in my ear with a grin.

For a second I was stunned. I continued smiling for the picture, but my mind went back to what Jaya had said about Vikram enjoying the social media frenzy around him. She was right!

Satisfied after a few shots, Manju went to Sheila to show her the pictures.

'We're going to have such a great time, Zeba. I think you'll really enjoy it! Hope you get to see a tiger! I didn't on my first safari,' said Vikram enthusiastically. 'And, Sunaina, we HAVE to beat them! Zeba can't just come for one safari and beat me. I'm a veteran compared to her.'

'Wait and see. You never know. I've been known to be very lucky in competitions,' said Zeba as she giggled. 'So where is my teammate? Debajyoti was just telling me he owns this resort, is an expert on tracking tigers and knows the park like the back of his hand.'

'Well, that is true, so, Vikram, I don't think you should be so confident about winning the competition,' I said, and laughed as his face visibly fell.

'There he is,' said Manju. We all turned to see Devraj talking to Himanshu in the doorway of the lounge. Calling out to him, Vikram waved him over to join us.

'What a long life, yaar. We were just talking about you!' said Vikram. 'Meet my dear friend Zeba Khan, who will be your partner in today's competition.'

Devraj greeted her with a, 'Khamagani, welcome to Baagh Baadi'.

She complimented the property and he told her a little about its history.

Then, turning to Debajyoti and me, he said we needed to discuss the filming plan for the day and we had to make sure no rules were flouted. Clearly he was still worried about the shoot getting out of hand.

'Already the protests by the Bhawani Sena have brought a lot of attention to this shoot. Everyone knows Vikram is here, and now Zeba as well. So there's bound to be more excitement and eyes on us,' he said, nodding towards her.

Zeba took it as a compliment and preened.

'Fortunately, as I mentioned last night, I've managed to ensure the Sena protesters won't be back, but we need to be careful. There are umpteen NGOs in the park vicinity that are always on the lookout for some issue to take up. And now we're on their radar. It's so easy to make an issue when movie stars are involved.'

'But why would anyone have a problem? We'll just be driving around the park,' asked Zeba, pouting.

'I just want to emphasize there should be no speeding, off-roading, getting out of the vehicle or making noise during this shoot. There may be people from NGOs or local reporters in the park who would love nothing more than to catch us doing something wrong, so let's be extra careful,' Devraj patiently explained.

Debajyoti tried to reassure him, 'Don't worry, *bhai*. Everything will be fine. I'll make sure the teams and drivers are all briefed. You're absolutely right to emphasize this. We can't have any negative attention on the shoot. It hurts our credibility also.'

'Yeah, we'll make sure. We don't want to get criticized by anyone,' said Vikram.

'Okay sure, just wanted to make this clear to all,' said Devraj with a smile, relaxing slightly with the assurance. 'It doesn't mean we won't have fun on the drive.'

We then stood around chatting as Debajyoti explained the rules to Zeba, with Vikram adding his two bits.

Devraj turned to me. 'Hello, didn't see you all day. Looking forward to the shoot?'

Before he arrived, I wondered what it would be like to see him again, if I'd imagined the whole thing last night and whether now, in the light of day, it would amount to nothing.

Well, it was definitely very much there, whatever this was. I was very aware of his presence, and my heartbeat had quickened since he'd entered the room.

'I was working in the tent, looking at footage, scripting for the shows,' I replied, inwardly pleased that he had looked out for me.

'I see. I thought maybe you were having a good lie-in. I was out of the camp myself, had to meet a few people in connection with what happened yesterday. Just to make doubly sure the message was sent out loud and clear that no one from the Bhawani Sena should venture near the gate today.'

'That's reassuring!' I replied. 'I was telling Jaya how relieved I was when you said last night that they won't return to the gate.'

Just then, Zeba, who was clearly bored of all the serious conversations about protocols that were continuing around her, said, 'Guys, let's take a selfie of the teams! I haven't posted any picture since I got here.'

She whipped out her phone and set it on the self-camera mode. Vikram stood next to her, and she waved at Devraj and me to get into the frame. I stood behind her left shoulder, and Devraj came and stood just behind me.

'Come on, guys, squeeze in,' she said as she tried to angle the frame to get us all in.

Devraj bent down to fit in, his head right next to mine.

I was sure he could hear my heart thudding in my chest as warmth spread across my face again. I was so very aware of his nearness.

Finally, Zeba managed to click a picture she liked.

Surly Sheila had perked up now, and she asked us all to pose for another picture. Again, I was standing next to Devraj, very aware of him close to me.

After the pictures were over, Debajyoti announced that we should all eat lunch as we would be leaving shortly after that. He then began talking to Devraj about jeep arrangements. Vikram and Zeba went off to their rooms, so I walked with Jaya to the dining area.

We served ourselves and sat at a table. It was burgers, oven-fresh pizzas and salads. Yum!

'She seems quite sweet,' said Jaya as we settled in.

'Yes, she was very warm towards me, which was nice. She's very girly girly. Wonder how she'll be on safari,' I remarked, now looking forward to the food.

Devraj came up to the table with a pizza slice on a plate.

'May I join you?' he asked pleasantly.

I had just taken a big bite of my burger and could only nod.

'Yes, sure,' said Jaya quickly, and he sat down beside me.

'So you spent the morning working as well?' he asked Jaya, who was sitting across from us.

'Yeah, it was a comparatively slow day today. So far, at least. After all the excitement yesterday,' she laughed.

'We were going through the footage and planning further shoots.'

'And are you satisfied with the footage you managed so far?' he asked as he started eating his pizza.

Finally I spoke up, 'We have some amazing footage for the shows and the archives. Nat Geo would pay us big bucks to get this footage.'

'Oh really? Nat Geo, huh? Is that the ultimate when it comes to wildlife filming?'

'Yeah, it kind of is, isn't it?' I laughed. 'Must be all those years of thumbing through copies of the magazine as a child. My parents had a collection. And then, of course, watching their amazing documentaries growing up.'

'I used to enjoy watching those too. But the BBC's Blue Planet series was absolutely incredible,' he replied.

'Oh, of course! And presented by David Attenborough. It was mesmerizing!'

I looked at him, smiling, and our eyes locked. He smiled back, and for a moment we were the only people at the table.

'Guys, take a look at these pictures!' We looked up to see Manju, who slipped in next to Jaya.

' I sent all the pictures I took to Sheila,' she continued, oblivious. 'She touched them up with filters, lighting and whatnot, and then sent them back, saying I could post them now. Zeba is very pretty, but after the touch-up, she looks crazy stunning, almost unreal.'

'Ugh, the rest of us, and by that I mean me, now probably look terrible in comparison!' I complained.

'No, she touched you up too, I think! A little, or maybe it was the overall brightening. It would have looked too obvious if she wouldn't have,' Manju laughed, showing us the pictures on her phone. We peered at her phone to see the magic Sheila had done. Zeba did look incredible, and the rest of us (and again I mean me) didn't look too bad either.

Devraj, who had continued eating pizza through all this, now spoke up.

'I'm sure you look great in the pictures. You don't need filters.'

We now turned to look at him.

'You're better off being authentic than faking it with filters,' he shrugged and smiled at me.

I blushed at the compliment and saw that Jaya was watching me.

'Er, thanks, I guess?' I said, trying to act casual. 'Though it's literally her job, so we can't blame her for putting her best foot forward all the time.'

'Oh, she's posted the selfie with you guys on Instagram,' said Manju, excitedly holding up her phone. 'It's so cute, and getting loads of comments!'

Then her face fell. 'Oh damn, she didn't tag the #SaveOurTigers campaign. Let me go tell Sheila.' With that, Manju jumped up to go look for Surly Sheila.

'That's a lot of stuff to keep track of,' said Devraj, watching her go. 'I don't envy Manju's job. Publicity and PR can be stressful.'

'Agree!' said Jaya. 'This shoot has so many more elements than what we're used to, doesn't it?'

She looked at me and I nodded.

'So on a regular shoot, it's usually just you two?' asked Devraj.

'Yes. Jaya, me and our measly budget,' I laughed. 'And not that we got to do many wildlife shoots. Maybe three or four in the last two and a half years.'

'And that's after she pitched twenty ideas, at least,' piped up Jaya.

'That's interesting. You must have been excited then when this project came to you,' he said.

'Oh, we were! To spend so much time in Chambalgarh! It was really lucky, despite the circumstances that led to it.' I said.

'And we're lucky you all came here.' He looked at me and smiled. I smiled back. I could sense Jaya watching us. Oh well.

Then his phone rang. Answering it, he excused himself from the table. 'Fixing up the jeeps for the shoot,' he told us as he took off.

I was watching him walk away when Jaya said, 'What was that about? How come Devraj is suddenly so friendly?'

I shrugged as she looked at me a tad suspiciously. But before she could ask any more, Manju came back to our table with a plate.

'It's done. Sheila was surprisingly receptive when I told her, very professional. Chalo, good.' And she sat and quickly gobbled up her food as we talked about the upcoming shoot.

13

After lunch it was soon time to go to the park. Vikram, Jaya and I were in one jeep along with Ravi, while Zeba, Devraj and Danish were in the other jeep with Sohan.

Danish was all smiles as he'd got his wish of being in Zeba's team. Seated in his jeep, he waggled his eyebrows at Jaya and me, as we tried to suppress our laughs.

There was also a third jeep with Debajyoti, Manju and two camera assistants who would be filming from a distance, which would also be used by either Danish or Jaya when the need arose.

'May the best team win!' said Vikram loudly, as we were all set. 'And by that I mean us.'

He turned to me with a big grin. 'We're going to win, right?' And raised his hand for a high five.

I high-fived him with a 'Let's go!'

While Devraj just smiled, Zeba responded, saying he shouldn't be so sure. They bantered for a bit, as Jaya and

Danish filmed, egging them on. Great, some trash talk before the shoot.

Finally, we were off to the park. Devraj had organized for us to go in a little earlier so we could avoid the crowd. We entered the outer gate of the park and stopped for a shoot with Debajyoti. This was to set up the shoot, a little introduction to the safari competition.

Everyone was miked up, and all three jeeps were parked close to one side of the road. Debajyoti stood in front of the jeeps and explained the rules of the 'competition'. The camera teams filmed the exchange.

Five marks for a pug mark, five for an alarm call, ten for a claw mark on a tree, fifteen for a sitting tiger sighting, twenty for a walking tiger. And thirty if anyone saw a tiger making a kill.

'What if we see a tiger mating?' asked Vikram, eliciting a giggle from Zeba. While she was sweet and all, her giggles were starting to get on my nerves. Glad I wasn't in her jeep.

'Well, that would be fifty, I guess,' said Debajyoti. 'Game over.'

More giggles.

Then Devraj, who had been quietly watching from the front seat, spoke up. 'You know, there's a jungle lore in these parts, that if you can get dust from the place where tigers have mated, you can use it to make a person fall in love with you. It's called "tiger dust" and believed to have magical properties.'

'What? No, you're making that up,' said Vikram with a laugh.

'Is that true? Has it worked?' asked Zeba, wide-eyed, enamoured by the idea.

'I don't know. It's lore, as I said. You can add it to their drink or just blow it on the person you fancy.' He shrugged with a smile and then looked at me for a moment. I couldn't help but smile in return.

Then, addressing Vikram, he said, 'They also say you can sometimes get tiger dust on you while driving through the jungle. You can collect it from your clothes and store it for an opportune time. It's up to you to believe in the magic.'

'Whoa! I'm going to try this!' said Vikram. 'Magic tiger dust!'

'Well, thank you, Devraj, for that little nugget of local lore,' I said brightly. It was time to wrap up this segment. I turned to the closest camera and announced, 'And, on that note, let the games begin.'

With the rules fixed, we set off on different routes. Vikram was very excited and once again spoke about how we had to win this. Jaya looked very amused as she filmed him while he talked about how much he had learnt about tracking in the last couple of days.

We had taken the route through the ravine towards the grasslands beyond.

Suddenly, the driver raised his hand, and we came to a stop.

'Pug mark,' said the guide Kishen, pointing to the mud on the side of the road. Sure enough, there were pug marks for a short distance along the road, and then they disappeared as they went off the road.

'Five marks to us!' said Vikram excitedly as he high-fived me enthusiastically.

'I'm sure Team Zeba hasn't opened their account! Got a good shot, Jaya?'

We conversed a little about the pug marks. About how recent they were, and Kishen spoke about how they indicated the tiger had walked towards the ravine. Also, it was a male because of the size and depth of the pug mark.

'It could be Masti,' he said. 'He's the dominant male in this area.'

We drove on for another fifteen minutes with no more luck. Vikram started getting a little anxious. After half an hour he oscillated between hope and despair.

Jaya and I were quite amused at how invested he was in winning the 'competition'.

'Just be patient. I'm sure we'll see a tiger, and anyway, this game is about the journey, not the destination, and by that I mean winning,' I said, trying to placate him.

'You can say those things after we win, otherwise it just sounds like sour grapes!' he said, peering through the binoculars, willing a tiger to appear.

Soon we spotted another set of pug marks, which we added to our tally. Then just five minutes after that, we saw scratches on a tree which were definitely made by a tiger, though initially Kishen thought they could be by a bear. Some time was spent debating, and then when we got closer, we finally decided it *was* a tiger. We took a good close-up shot to verify later.

As we were moving on from the tree, we finally heard what was music to our ears. The familiar short, sharp bark, a cheetal's alarm call.

'Where is that from?' asked Vikram frantically. 'Which way do we go?'

Kishen looked unsure.

'Let's wait a little longer for another call,' I said.

We didn't have to wait long. Soon, another call sounded, even louder, and distinctly from the right.

We headed in the direction, on high alert, straining to hear anything further. There was another alarm call from farther on.

'It seems that the tiger has descended from the hills and is moving in an easterly direction,' Kishen said with some confidence finally. 'This could mean that it's making its way towards the water hole located there. Let's take the road to the left and see if we can catch a glimpse of it.' He pointed towards the left, directing our attention to the road that could potentially lead to the elusive tiger.

We started driving slowly down the road, all of us peering to the sides to see if there was a flash of orange mixed in the green.

And then the jeep jolted to a halt as a tiger casually stepped on to the road right in front of us.

It turned and looked at us for a heartbeat, and then crossed the road, walking off into the thicket.

'Oh my God!' whispered Vikram loudly, after the tiger had disappeared. It had happened so fast we were all kind of stunned.

'You got that, right, Jaya?' I said, turning to her. As always, it was one thing seeing a tiger, but getting it on camera was more important.

'You bet I did! Though a little after he stepped on to the road because I had been looking to the right side,' she replied.

'Okay. Then let's count up our points!' said Vikram excitedly.

'We still have a few more hours, you know, this is not it,' I replied. 'Zeba and Devraj could have easily seen a tiger or even two. Who knows!'

'It seemed to be coming away from the water hole,' said Kishen.

We continued to drive down towards the water hole. When we got there, we saw there were already a few jeeps. Devraj and Zeba's was one of them, and another with Debajyoti and the rest of the gang.

'Hi guys!' Vikram excitedly loud-whispered as we pulled up next to Devraj's jeep. 'We just saw a tiger!'

'So did we!' squealed Zeba, immediately leading to a shushing and glare from Devraj.

'It's gone now, so how does it matter?' she said, turning crossly to him.

'Yes, but as I explained to you earlier, you have to speak softly in the park. We can't make loud sounds,' he said in a very controlled tone.

Uh oh, this didn't seem to be going well.

'Devraj, you're such a taskmaster. Even my choreographer doesn't scold me as much as you do,' Zeba said, pouting.

'I'm sorry, but you're really going to have to keep it down. You saw those tourists were taking your picture. I just don't want any finger-pointing or bad press. For your sake. They might post a picture or video of you claiming you were creating a ruckus or something. You're an easy target since you're so famous, and people can be nasty.'

Now he was speaking a language she could understand. Well played. All those years working in PR in Delhi was paying off. He really had many layers to him. Safari guide, savvy PR man.

Our eyes met and we shared an amused look. This seemed to mollify Zeba.

'Well, when you put it like that,' she pouted some more, 'I suppose it makes sense. I don't need any negative publicity. Sheila would get mad with me if there was any adverse fallout because of this shoot. She's already not happy with the love-triangle gossip.'

Seeing my face fall, she added, 'Oh, don't worry, Sunaina. Vikram told me all about what really happened, and we've had a laugh at the press getting it wrong again. And we thought it would be more fun if I came and joined you guys for a while. Just to shake things up.'

I was glad it was cleared up, and so effortlessly. It immediately made me feel lighter.

'Well, it's great that you did join us. Tell us about your safari so far?' I asked.

With a glance at Devraj, she took her voice down a notch and told us about the safari.

'We were waiting here because Devraj said a tiger was on the move and it would come here. How crazy, right? How did he know? He could hear other animals calling out, he said.'

'Alarm calls,' said Vikram, in a slightly exasperated tone. 'They were alarm calls.'

'So we came here and were just sitting around in the jeep for a while, swatting flies, and then after a short while, this tiger came down from there,' she pointed to the right. 'The driver, Prem Singh, spotted it first!

'I was so excited I got up in the jeep and, you know, turned to the camera so they could get my reaction, but then Devraj just shushed me and made me sit down. He even left my high five hanging!' She narrated the last part in mock outrage. In front, I could see Devraj was shaking his head.

'Well, we saw a tiger too, and Sunaina did not leave my high five hanging,' said Vikram, nudging me appreciatively. 'We saw it crossing the road. It was a big guy.'

'So you saw a tiger too? And you had fun as well! While I have Mr Super Strict here,' she laughed, indicating towards Devraj.

Then she added a quick, 'Just kidding,' with a laugh, giving Devraj's shoulder a pat.

'Thank God for Danish in this jeep. He's been such a doll.' She waved to the camera that Danish was rolling. I could see him grinning behind the camera and gave us a thumbs-up.

I'm sure Danish was a total doll, I thought to myself, amused. He's on safari with his favourite actor—of course he would be.

'So how many points do you guys have?' asked Vikram, now getting right to it, which I knew he had been itching to do from the start.

Before Zeba could answer, Danish asked Debajyoti to move closer so he could get into the jeep with them.

'I want to take some shots from a distance of you all chatting,' he said.

'So how many points?' Vikram persisted.

'I'm not sure. I know we saw some pug marks and stuff,' said Zeba. All right, that seemed fine, I thought to myself.

But then she added, 'We also saw a tiger earlier, but it wasn't a good sighting. It was lying on its side in the distance. Just kept sleeping! I could only see it through the binoculars, and that too, only its hind leg and tail. Danish helped me see it. That's why I was so excited to see a tiger properly.'

Vikram's face fell. He turned to me and whispered, 'They've seen two tigers! What do we do?'

'Well, let's get out of here and see if we can spot more, I guess.' Vikram's competitive spirit was rubbing off on me. While I had protested earlier that the competition didn't matter, I had been somewhat confident we would win. Now I wasn't so sure.

'Kishen, let's go,' I said.

We started up the jeep to pull out.

Devraj turned to us.

'Leaving already?' he asked with an amused, knowing smile.

'Well, there's nothing to see here, is there? So we may as well move on,' I replied evenly.

'Hmm, so how many points do you have?' he asked, trying to make it sound casual, but I knew he was taunting us.

'We have thirty points at least,' said Vikram defensively.

'Oh cool, so you'll need another thirty to catch up,' replied Devraj smoothly. 'Good luck.'

'Yeah, good luck,' said Zeba excitedly. 'But we're way ahead of you!'

We drove off fuming.

'They don't have sixty points, do they?' asked Vikram, looking panicked.

'I'm sure they couldn't have,' I said, but I wasn't very sure. 'They did see two tigers, but one wasn't a good sighting, like a one-out-of-five type of sighting.'

Now the whole team was charged up to win. Devraj's taunts had got to us. Even Jaya was into it.

'Kishen, where should we go now?' I asked.

'Was there any news of a kill or cubs?' asked Jaya.

'Ma'am, there was a kill two days ago at the Lakda-wala area, near the river bed there.'

'Well, let's try there. Seems a good enough chance. Two days could mean the tiger is still around, depending on the size of the kill.'

So we drove in that direction. On the way we spotted another pug mark so more points for us. Yay!

As we neared the place where the kill had been spotted, the stench of rotting meat filled the air. The deer carcass had been left on one side of the river bed, beneath an overhang of grass and shrubs.

We waited and waited. After half an hour, we saw a jackal sniffing around. It was clear the carcass had probably been eaten up and there was nothing more to keep an eye on.

'Ma'am, I think it was a small fawn. Nothing much left of it. The tiger has moved on.'

'Now where should we go?' asked Vikram urgently.

Poor Kishen was running out of ideas. We also had only half an hour left.

'I think now we need to head towards the exit as it's time to leave the park,' I said resignedly.

So, with an air of defeat, we started heading towards the gate.

Even so, we remained on the lookout. After all, hope springs eternal.

We were ten minutes from the gate when we saw another tourist jeep parked on the side of the road and the people in the jeep standing up and looking at something.

'What's happening here?' asked Vikram.

'They must have sighted something, but what is the question?' I replied. I remembered an earlier time, when I had seen a jeep of tourists parked like this to find they were watching a peacock dance. While it was very beautiful to watch, it was a disappointment as Jaya and I had been very fixated on filming a tiger.

'Fingers crossed,' I whispered.

We stopped alongside the jeep, and Kishen looked at their guide questioningly. He was relaxing in the passenger seat, chewing something as the tourists were gawking.

'Tiger,' he said most casually, after a moment, in response to Kishen.

Vikram and I immediately perked up.

'Where? Where?' asked Vikram. Kishen scanned with his binoculars. On the right side of the road was grass and shrubs and, farther on, thicker foliage.

'Sir, see behind the tree there,' said Kishen.

We looked through the binoculars, and, sure enough, there was a tiger sitting behind a tree some distance away. It wasn't clearly visible at all, just his front paws and a bit of his head.

'Let's wait. Maybe he'll get up,' said Jaya, looking keenly through her camera.

'Did you see it walking?' I asked the other guide.

Again, he took his time to answer, with no regard for the urgency in my voice.

'Arré, Madam,' he started. 'Earlier it was lying down. Last five minutes it sat up.'

'Then it could get up also,' said Kishen.

Now we were very excited!

Just then, another jeep pulled up next to us.

'Hey! What's up guys?' squealed Zeba.

'Aaargh,' groaned Vikram. He clearly didn't want to share the sighting with his friend.

'I think there's a tiger there, Zeba,' said Devraj, pulling out his binoculars and looking in the same direction.

'Yes, there it is behind the tree,' he said after a moment, passing the binoculars to Zeba.

'Oh cool! Our third tiger! So Vikram, I guess I do have beginner's luck! Or maybe I'm just lucky on safaris!' she said excitedly.

Looking through the binoculars, she exclaimed excitedly, 'Yes, I can see its head!' She stood up in the jeep, much to Devraj's irritation. But he decided against saying anything. It was nearly the end of the shoot now.

'Arré, Zeba Khan!' The half-comatose guide from the other jeep suddenly sat up straight, his features transformed in shock. 'Look, Zeba Khan,' he said in wonderment to the guests in the jeep. The family of four— mother, father and two young kids, a girl and a boy— now turned to gawk at Zeba. She smiled and waved.

'Ma'am, I'm a big fan. I've seen all your movies!' said the guide breathlessly.

'So he *can* talk fast when he wants to,' I whispered to Jaya who laughed.

The family started taking pictures of Zeba now, including the guide.

'I don't know whether to be offended or pleased they didn't recognize me,' Vikram whispered to Jaya and me. We both started giggling. What a day for him, losing the 'tiger-spotting competition' to Zeba, and then not being recognized on top of it.

'Must be because of your dark glasses and hat,' I said, to comfort him.

Devraj, who was looking through his binoculars this whole time, announced, 'The tiger is up if anyone's interested.'

Everyone immediately stopped talking and turned their attention back on the tiger.

As we peered at the tree, we saw that the tiger had risen to its feet. Although the tree still partially obstructed our view, we could make out that the tiger was standing and facing away from us. It began to walk diagonally into the dense brush, revealing its full body. We could see a nullah to the right, and the tiger was making its way towards it. Just before it stepped down the embankment, it paused to stretch and marked its territory by spraying a nearby bush. At that moment, Jaya had a clear shot. The tiger then descended slowly, disappearing from view. For a brief moment we could see only its tail, which hung in the air, the tip waving gently from left to right as if it were contemplating its next move. Eventually, even the tail disappeared from sight.

'That was so amazing!' gushed Zeba. 'What a great way to end my first safari!' she sighed.

She gave Danish a big hug, and he looked pleased as Punch.

I saw Jaya filming them. Nice! It was a lovely moment.

'You really do have beginner's luck. Congratulations,' I said with a big smile. May as well be gracious about it. I looked at Vikram, who didn't look happy at all.

'Yeah, Zeba, you really have the luck of the devil,' he said almost reluctantly.

We all burst out laughing, which led to another stern, 'Guys, come on,' from Devraj.

But then looking at Vikram's despondent face, even Devraj softened.

'Hey, you win some, you lose some. Anyway, as Sunaina said, this shoot was more about teaching people about tracking tigers, and we've all been very lucky, haven't we?'

'Yeah, I guess. That last sighting was a bonus,' replied Vikram.

'Oh, don't worry that you lost!' said Zeba. 'It was such a fun day! Even if Devraj was such a grump!' Devraj played along and contorted his face in mock anger.

'Well, that's that. Time to head to the gate,' said Debajyoti. 'Well done, team! We can finish up the shoot at Baagh Baadi.'

By now, several jeeps had pulled up, wondering what we had stopped for and whether it was a sighting. The tiger had left but they did get a sighting—Zeba and Vikram, and there was a lot of excitement.

To Devraj's dismay, soon all lenses were pointed at our vehicles. For the next five minutes, Zeba primped and preened as people took photos of Vikram and her, and then his patience ran out.

Time was also running out, as everyone had to exit the park.

'Let's move it now,' Devraj ordered all the drivers. 'The last thing I want is a fine for exiting the park late. How would a shot of that look in your documentary?'

That didn't sound good at all, so we all quickly settled down in our jeeps to leave the park. Fortunately, since the gate was close by, we were out in less than two minutes.

Back at the resort, we filmed Reena interviewing Zeba and Vikram by the pool. They recounted the experience, and there was banter and leg pulling.

Reena did a really great job of getting the best out of them.

Devraj and I joined the interview towards the end, and it led to more fun moments. Zeba accused him of being a stern taskmaster during the shoot, with some muted protests from him. He spoke about the tourists who stopped to see the tiger but got to see Zeba instead and weren't disappointed, which made us all crack up.

Devraj had been reluctant to do the interview but had finally agreed, after much persuasion by Reena. But once in it, he was very relaxed. He even spoke about how great it was to have a news channel focus on such a vital issue as conservation and tigers. And how he appreciated the fact that we had gone in depth and got the perspective of the forest guards as well, as they were often overlooked during this kind of coverage.

We had half an hour before assembling again for dinner after we wrapped up. We all went back to our respective tents and rooms to freshen up.

Back at the tent, I had a quick bath and washed my hair. Using the hair dryer, I tried to set my hair in soft waves with my round brush. I had carried a button-down olive shirt-dress just in case, and this seemed like the right time to bring it out. After I was dressed, I added some make-up: kajal, eyeliner and lipstick. My usual routine. And then added some peach blush to round it off.

Jaya walked in just as I was putting on my small gold hoop earrings.

'Oh, look at you,' she said teasingly. 'Zeba is making you up your game! Looking nice!'

I smiled at her compliment. It's always nice to have a friend who's a cheerleader as well. 'Thanks, I may as well put my best foot forward. For what it's worth,' I winked at her.

The evening was a relaxed affair, with everyone gathered around at the outdoor bar. Dinner would be served by the pool. The entire crew was relieved with the shoot having gone off so well and without any controversies, unlike the previous day.

Manju was showing me our social media traffic. She had shared some fun pictures of the shoot after checking with Sheila first. I felt relieved that the hyper speculation surrounding Vikram, Zeba and me had settled down.

There was one picture of an excited Zeba looking at the tiger, with both her thumbs up.

There were various pictures of the tigers. Of Vikram looking sad, with Jaya posing with her camera behind him. Another of me looking pensively into the jungle. There was one of the four of us making a V sign, so cheesy. I couldn't believe we had let Manju talk us into it. It had generated quite a lot of interest on social media. There were lots of comments on the dynamics among the three of us, some speculation obviously, but mostly positive reactions and interest in the campaign.

'So many people are commenting on the tiger pictures as well. They came for pictures of Vikram and Zeba, and the gossip, but learnt about the campaign too,' said Manju.

'Okay, okay, I'm trying to not let the chatter bother me, so please just show me positive stuff,' I laughingly told her.

I was feeling quite buoyed by the success. Looking around, I wondered where Devraj was.

He had been fun during the interview and had afterwards told me he would see me at dinner as he had to wrap up some work. He wasn't here yet. I checked my phone to see if there was any message from him.

Earlier, I had fielded more messages from my sister and Devika, and assured them that everything was fine. That we all got along well, and I reiterated that the triangle gossip was rubbish. I also told my sister that Zeba was actually very nice, and despite what she felt, had not thrown me any attitude.

Somehow, from social media and the pictures, she had got that impression. I put it down to 'elder sister syndrome', always looking out for me.

Devika, on the other hand, had also asked about Devraj. She told me he was quite the eligible bachelor in the Rajasthan circles and added that one of her husband's cousins, whom we used to refer to as 'Babe Baisa', had been very keen on him. 'Baisa' is a term for a Rajput woman, usually sister or sister-in-law. Devika and I used to call this particular cousin 'Babe Baisa' as she was very good-looking and would constantly post glamorous pictures of herself on Instagram. She even had quite the following online and each post was accompanied by a slew of comments from her admirers.

Devika said Babe Baisa had been shocked that her overtures hadn't been reciprocated.

Now that was an interesting nugget of information.

I had simply replied to Devika that Devraj seemed very nice and Baagh Baadi was a beautiful property.

I was chatting with Manju and Jaya when I saw Devraj arrive at the gathering. While I continued chatting, I was acutely aware that he was making the rounds, greeting people and slowly approaching us.

Manju was showing us some of the other pictures from the shoot.

'Hello! Are those pictures from today?' asked Devraj as he appeared by our side.

'Yes, some really good shots of the tiger and candid shots of all of us,' I replied casually, as my heartbeat picked up.

'I saw you had put up some online. Himanshu is pleased as Baagh Baadi has been mentioned quite prominently.'

Turning to Manju, he said, 'A lot of my journalist and media friends have been calling thanks to your pictures. Everyone wants to know about the shoot, they want to know about Vikram and, of course, whether they can visit. I've had to really fend them off to the point of being a little rude. We've also had paparazzi at the gate and walls. Security is on high alert.'

'Oh gosh! That's quite a lot to handle!' said Jaya, to which Devraj shrugged.

'Well, the whole idea of the social media push was to get attention. To create interest in our campaign message. And with Zeba also here, it's had a major boost. There's been so much chatter and gossip. Even the protest yesterday led to more attention. What's the saying, "There's no such thing as bad publicity!"' said Manju.

Devraj's face tightened slightly at the mention of the gossip. Trust Manju to bring that up.

'For a campaign like this, around issues related to environment and tiger conservation, bad publicity would not be good at all, but thankfully there's been none of that. And let's face it, "bad publicity" is what led to this campaign in the first place,' said Jaya with a wicked smile.

'Very snidely put, Jaya,' I said, and we all had a laugh.

'So what's the shoot plan like now?' Devraj asked, looking at me.

'Well, it depends on Debajyoti. We have to discuss how much more we need. Some interviews are still pending. But I should think in a few days we'll be out of your hair.'

'Oh, I wouldn't put it like that,' he said with a smile.

Manju and Jaya walked off to where Danish was showing pictures to another group.

'So your little competition turned out to be quite fun in the end, despite all my reservations about it,' said Devraj.

'I saw you thoroughly enjoyed beating us at it,' I smiled at him, but then looked away. There was a bit of an awkward pause.

'Sunaina, why don't you tell me a little about yourself? We've been going on all these shoots together, but I don't know a lot about you,' he said.

'Well, I don't know much about you either,' I replied evenly, trying to keep it light.

'Would you like to know more about me?' he said softly, looking straight into my eyes.

My heart started beating faster.

'I would. You do have a fascinating life here,' I answered, indicating the property with a sweep of my hand. 'It must be fun living like this, next to a national park, going for safaris whenever you please.'

'That's not what I asked, but yes, it is. I admit I have a lot to be grateful for.' He gestured towards some chairs nearby so we could sit.

'Though I didn't always live here, you know, only the last five to six years. Before that I was a Delhi boy too,' he said when we had settled down.

'I heard that. Reena said you were in PR in Delhi,' I replied.

'Yes, advertising and PR. I was working with a friend. It was hard work but fun. Lots of travel, lots of events and lots of partying as well.'

'What made you shift back to Rajasthan? Baagh Baadi is wonderful but it seems you had a great time at your work.'

'I'd like to say I burnt out and came back, but it wasn't quite that simple. I was in a road accident. It was on the Delhi–Gurugram highway, a friend was driving. She was someone I had been seeing on and off. She had insisted on driving as I'd had a few drinks. It was one of those foggy nights and she hit a stationary truck on the highway. Luckily, she only got a few minor injuries, some bruises, but I smashed my leg.'

'Oh God! That's terrible!'

'I know but we were lucky. Ashima wasn't driving very fast. But because of the broken leg, I came home to Jaipur. My parents, who had been worried about my hectic Delhi lifestyle, were happy to have me home, even in those circumstances. It was during those months, when I was recovering, that I started visiting this property with my sister. She's older and lives in Jodhpur. In fact, my father's side is from near Jodhpur. So she suggested it would be great to develop it and for me to connect with our family ties in this area. This property is my mother's as her uncle left it for her. Since I had always loved this place as a child when I would visit, and loved wildlife, I decided to go for it.'

'Just like that? You gave up your Delhi life and work?' I asked.

'I had a lot of time to reflect when I was recovering. I'd worked hard for six to seven years but it wasn't what I wanted to do with my life. I spoke to my friend. He was understanding but on the condition I helped him out whenever he was in a pinch. Which, fortunately, has been only four or five times since I left.'

'You're very lucky you could do this,' I said wistfully, looking around.

'Absolutely. I realize I had the luxury to leave it all. And I like spending time here, being next to the park and going on safaris. Though it's hard work as well.'

'Do you miss living in the city though?'

'Not really. It's not like I'm a hermit here, I go to Jaipur, Delhi and even Mumbai once in a while for work. And to catch up with friends. But enough about me, tell me about yourself,' he said, turning to me expectantly.

So we continued to speak. I told him how as children, Didi and I travelled a lot, as my father was in the administrative services. Then how we eventually attended boarding school in Dehradun for our senior years. How I enjoyed travelling to the mountains and national parks for school trips. That piqued my interest in nature and wildlife. After graduation in Mumbai, I got a postgraduate degree in journalism from a college in Chennai, and then got a job at NNTV, where I had been for the past six years. I had always wanted to work for the channel because I had grown up watching it.

'And is that something you plan to continue with now? News reporting?' he asked.

'In the foreseeable future,' I said. 'Then I want to do special programming around India's wildlife. We have so much to offer. I'd love to make documentaries or a series on India's wildlife reserves. There are also so many options to showcase such shows now, with OTT platforms like Netflix, Prime, Disney, etc.'

'That's true. I had an uncle who used to make documentaries when he was younger. He stopped by the time I was a teenager, but he loved telling me stories. He talked about how he had to pitch the films to Doordarshan as that was the only option in those days. Even then it was frustrating, as he had to cater to the whims and fancies of the bureaucrats. One documentary series he made on Indian tribes and their practices never got shown, as the government that commissioned it changed and the next one felt parts were too controversial.

'How frustrating!' I said.

'It really was. He had featured various tribes from the hills, Jharkhand and the North-east and their very distinct practices. How the Khasis of Meghalaya practise the matrilineal system, interviews of old surviving headhunters of Nagaland, animism practices, the polyandrous tribe of Himachal. It was a huge effort to film it all, but it scandalized the bureaucrat who was newly in charge, as it didn't fit in with his ideas of what is acceptable in society. It was soul-crushing for my uncle and he just gave up after that.'

'That's so sad. What a terrible thing!' I exclaimed. 'I wonder if the series is still there!'

'Yes, under mounds of dust in some old Doordarshan archives, I'm sure.'

We shared a laugh.

'Well, I do hope to have a more fulfilling career than that!' I said.

'I'm sure you will. You seem so driven. Most people I meet these days are so jaded and cynical. Or uninterested in things that matter. Which is why I find you so interesting.' He said the last line softly, looking at me.

Our eyes met, gazes locking as the silence between us stretched. The weight of his words lingered in the air. My cheeks felt warm as I tried to come up with a response that would show my interest as well, without appearing too eager.

I opened my mouth to say something, anything, when Vikram and Zeba walked up to us. They had arrived a short while ago and had been chatting with the others.

'Hello, hello, you two!' said Vikram. 'It's so nice to have everyone together like this. What a fun day we had!' He was in an upbeat mood.

Devraj and I stood up to greet them. The matter between us would have to wait till later.

'Zeba had a really great time, especially since we let her win, didn't we, Sunaina?' Vikram winked at me.

Laughing, I picked up his cue. 'Totally! We had tracked a few more tigers, heard the alarm calls but didn't follow up because we didn't want to score more than you,' I said, grinning. 'We're very generous that way.'

We all laughed, though Zeba looked a little confused but laughed along anyway.

'I'm going back to Mumbai tomorrow, but it's been an amazing short trip. I'd love to come back again at a later date. Bring some friends. Everyone is so amazed that I saw three tigers on my first safari!' She said excitedly. 'When do you return, Vikram?'

'I think in another few days. I still have a week before any other commitments,' he said.

'We'll make a forest ranger out of you by the time this shoot is done,' I said with a laugh.

'Jokes aside, stepping into this tiger park has been an eye-opening and humbling experience. We're so caught up in our own lives, we don't even know the kind of work being done to protect the country's forests and all the animals in them. Like here in Chambalgarh. My father constantly lectures me about broadening my horizons, "beyond the glittering lights of the Mumbai film industry" is how he likes to put it. He reminds me that there's so much more to India, that it's rich with history, diversity and challenges. I get what he means now. It's important to constantly try to understand and appreciate the world around us.'

Wow, that was such a profound and empathetic thing to say. 'That's so nice to hear,' I said, touched by his little speech.

'My father said such experiences would help me as an actor as well. By meeting different people, watching them, listening to them. I was speaking to Jaya earlier, and she was telling me about her family and her tribe in Jharkhand. So interesting. I understand what my father meant about broadened horizons.'

'Which of the experiences affected you? The bee episode? Seeing the tiger for the first time? Getting mobbed by protesters?' I asked.

'Well, all of those were definitely experiences to remember. But what really affected me was the evening we spent with the forest guards. They have such a tough job and you never even think about it. They patrol the forests with just their lathis, making sure no poachers or timber mafia are around. Just a lathi in a forest teeming with tigers. And away from their families for days on end. Seeing that was very moving. It will stay with me.'

Devraj was visibly impressed with Vikram's speech; he patted his back and shook his hand. He, like me, had probably judged Vikram earlier on and slotted him into the 'vain Bollywood actor' category.

'That's great to hear. Every time we get visitors here who are not regular safari folk, the hope is they will take a little bit of the jungle back with them in their hearts. I'm happy to see we have converted you.'

'I'm officially a convert,' said Vikram, as he did a little half bow which made us laugh.

'Zeba, I hope you too will take a little of the jungle back with you, even if we haven't managed to convert you fully,' Devraj said to Zeba.

'Don't be so sure you haven't. You were quite a taskmaster but it was fun, and I did see three tigers on my first safari, so woo hoo!' she punched the air.

Turning to Devraj, she added, 'And now you can't even shush me!'

Danish, Jaya and Safar walked over to us, and there was more ribbing and joking about the safari.

It was a lovely night with the sharpness of a chill, but not too much. A clear sky allowed us a fabulous sight of the stars glittering in the inkiness above us. There was a faint hum of insects and the clicking of bats all around.

Himanshu soon announced it was time for dinner, and we all walked towards the poolside.

The scene before us was breathtaking. Long tables had been elegantly arranged by the shimmering pool. The warm glow from the lamps, hanging from the branches of the surrounding trees and tall poles, illuminated the entire area with a soft light. The tables were adorned with exquisite white flower arrangements, serving as the centrepiece. Intricate silver-toned tiger, deer and bear figurines were artfully placed between the centrepieces, along with white twisted candles on glass stands. The finishing touches were added by sophisticated white plates and cutlery. The napkins had silver tiger stripes. The overall effect was nothing short of magical, and everyone was enchanted.

'Wow, this is so gorgeous!' said Zeba, and immediately insisted on getting photographed next to the table. She was wearing a lovely khaki-and-black wrap dress, with a collar and lapels. It had sequinned tigers sewn on the skirt.

Manju obliged and many pictures were taken before we could all be seated.

Danish and Jaya filmed the table and then the team being seated. We planned to use the dinner shots in the credits of the episode.

There were name cards on the table, with our names written beautifully in calligraphy. I found myself seated between Natasha and Reena with Vikram, Devraj and Zeba opposite.

'Well done, all of you,' said Natasha, beaming. 'My phone has been ringing off the hook, so to speak. Just inundated with calls. So many magazines, online sites, advertisers and agencies are calling up to talk, ask, offer, inquire. You've all managed to generate so much interest in the campaign.'

'I know!' Reena gushed. 'My journalist friends have also been asking me about the shoot, wanting interviews and reading up on tiger conservation, trying to weave it into their stories. Sunaina, you should be happy about that!' she turned to me.

'I think we all should be, shouldn't we?' I smiled at her. 'A campaign on conservation that raises awareness. That's what we were aiming for. We had a few scares, with the bees episode and the Bhawani Sena protest. But thankfully it didn't derail the shoot. And Safar has fully recovered.' I raised my glass to her. She beamed back, sent me a flying kiss.

'Well, I've thoroughly enjoyed my guest appearance in this lovely campaign,' said Zeba, with a laugh. 'I've faced none of the troubles, had a wonderful safari and even beat Vikram at the sighting game. All in all, it's been win-win.'

'Yay!' said Danish, clapping enthusiastically, making everyone laugh and applaud.

'Yes, yes, Zeba. How wonderful for you,' replied Vikram with a comical eye roll, as the clapping subsided.

He then stood up to address everyone.

'I just want to thank everyone who's been a part of this absolutely amazing experience. What a great team and a great campaign,' he raised his glass as did everyone.

'To all of you!'

With that, more applause and enthusiastic cheers erupted. Everyone was filled with exuberance, and it created a warm and celebratory atmosphere. Moments like these brought the team together, fostering a strong sense of camaraderie and team spirit. Although Vikram and, to a lesser extent, Reena and I were the public faces of the campaign, there were others who had done so much work behind the scenes. An evening of togetherness like this was great motivation for the team, lifting the spirits of all involved.

'Let's get down to eating now!' said Vikram, to more claps. Clearly, the team was hungry!

'I thought you'd never ask,' said Devraj, getting up with an air of ceremony. 'In honour of our guests and this wonderful campaign, Chef Satbir and Himanshu have planned a truly extraordinary meal for everyone. This dish is a result of a meticulous and time-honoured cooking process, a speciality of the state. It's called khadd meat, as it's prepared by leaving the goat roasting inside a pit or *khadd* all day. The goat was marinated with a blend of the most delectable spices, then enveloped in a massive, uncooked roti, wrapped in a burlap sack, and buried in the ground with glowing coals. The meat was then roasted for fifteen to sixteen hours, slowly infusing with the flavours of the spices and smoke from the fire. After a full day of preparation, the mouth-watering feast has just been brought out for all of you.'

He indicated with a sweep of his arm. We all turned to see the waiters bringing a huge platter with the goat wrapped in a roti.

'The tale of "khadd meat" is steeped in the rich and turbulent history of Rajasthan,' continued Devraj. Everyone was mesmerized by his speech. It was dinner with a dash of drama.

'This land was a battlefield, where the rajas were constantly engaged in conflicts, both among themselves and against the Marathas, and then either for or against the Mughals. The loyalty of the rulers shifted with the changing winds of power, and many vied for the favour of the emperor seated on the Peacock Throne. Many were even related through marriage. In this volatile environment, the soldiers on the frontlines of the many battles had to be vigilant and keep a low profile. They couldn't risk the smoke from their cooking fires giving away their positions or spend time after the battle cooking. So they resorted to an ingenious solution—burying their meat in the ground to cook all day while they fought. At night, after a long day of battle, they would dig out the succulent, flavourful meat and have a well-deserved feast. Later this method became popular with hunting parties.'

As he was talking, the platter was placed on a large side table, so we could all watch. Everyone had turned to face him, in complete silence, waiting for the next step in this dinner drama.

'Chef Satbir, please do the honours,' Devraj called out.

Chef Satbir came up next to the table with a big knife. He greeted everyone and then began cutting through the roti. Some of the staff came up and helped part the roti. He then started cutting through the crispy meat exterior. Aromatic steam rose out, carrying the fragrant scents of the spices and smoke from the fire. The chef cut in deeper, using a bigger fork to take portions of the meat and put them on smaller platters to be served to us.

Some of the waiters carried the platters to our tables while others brought the rest of the food—roasted vegetables, steaming dals, aromatic curries and a garlic chutney, along with plates of fluffy naans, crispy tandoori rotis and the special red chilli parathas of Baagh Baadi. It was quite a feast, with a medley of aromas to tantalize us.

As we helped ourselves to the food, all conversation came to a halt as everyone was lost in their own sensory experiences. The star of the show was, of course, the khadd meat, a dish that I had only heard about but never had the opportunity to try. The moment I took the first bite, I was blown away by its tenderness and fragrance. The meat had been marinated and roasted to perfection, resulting in a flavour that was as rich and amazing as I had heard it would be.

An hour later, everyone was in varying states of food coma, their bellies full and spirits satisfied. A lovely, tranquil atmosphere had settled over the gathering, the kind that only comes when one is satiated with good food. The feast at Baagh Baadi had been nothing short of extraordinary, and its memory would linger long after the last crumb had been devoured.

The staff was serving a variety of after-dinner options. There were crumbly motichoor laddoos from a famous shop in Jaipur, freshly brewed coffee or green tea, or a glass of chilled Sauternes, a sweet dessert wine. One waiter was taking around a small silver platter with paan neatly piled on it. All good for digesting the massive meal we had consumed.

'This was divine,' said Natasha, sipping her glass of Sauternes in appreciation.

'Oh my goodness. I've eaten so much I'll need to be wheeled to my room,' she laughed.

'Me too,' said Vikram. 'I'm not even bothering to check my calorie intake. This was too amazing for that.' He reached out for a paan off the proffered platter.

'The roast meat was unreal!' exclaimed Zeba. 'I might come back only for this meal. Please promise you'll make this again when I come.'

'Of course,' said Devraj. 'But only if you take a picture with Chef Satbir and the team. I've recently been informed you have many fans here at Baagh Baadi.'

Zeba happily obliged. The staff were called from the kitchen and many photographs were taken. Manju was only too happy to do the honours. Vikram also joined her for a few.

More pictures were then taken at the table, with Vikram and Zeba moving around, posing behind various groups.

'Does anyone want to go for a drive tomorrow morning?' Devraj asked, rising from his seat. 'I'll be going in a little later, around 8 a.m.'

'I'll go,' I said quickly. Maybe a little too quickly, I suddenly realized, my face reddening.

Devraj shot me a smile.

'Count me in,' said Jaya. 'My FOMO [fear of missing out] is super high during wildlife shoots.'

'I'll go too,' said Vikram, to my surprise. Clearly he had developed a passion for safari life. 'I have FOMO as well!'

We all laughed at that.

'I can't as I'm leaving in the morning, but I would have liked another safari. Next time,' said Zeba, giving Devraj a big smile and wink. 'That is, if you'll take me on safari again.'

Devraj smiled and replied, 'It would be my absolute pleasure!'

'I'm going to sleep in,' said Natasha. 'But you enthu-cutlets have fun.'

'So I guess Jaya, Vikram, plus Ravi or Sohan and I,' I said, after waiting a few minutes to see if anyone else wanted to come. But everyone else looked zoned out, and clearly getting up early was the last thing on their minds.

'Okay, great, we'll all manage in one jeep then. I'll fix the permissions,' said Devraj, and wished everyone goodnight. I felt a twinge of disappointment as he was leaving, but it seemed he had some official work to wrap up. Himanshu was hovering, waiting for him.

After Devraj left, the evening started wrapping up. There were a few more anecdotes shared, a few more laughs and soon enough everyone was set to call it a night.

Debajyoti took the opportunity to address the gathering and express his gratitude towards everyone present. He acknowledged the hard work and dedication of all the team members and thanked Zeba again for joining the campaign.

As we walked back to the tent, Jaya asked about Devraj. 'I saw you two chatting for a while,' she said with a smile. 'Actually, I didn't notice at first, but Manju pointed it out. By the way, she thinks he has feelings for you.'

'What do you mean? Why does she think that?' I asked, curious to know why Manju had sensed this.

'She said he keeps looking at you when he thinks no one is watching. And then those long chats. Also, he joined us for lunch, chit-chatting with everyone but especially you.'

'Well, we were just chatting about this and that. The shoot and whatnot. Nothing specific,' I shrugged. I didn't feel comfortable talking about this just yet, considering I didn't even know if there was anything.

'Okay, just asking. This has turned out to be quite an interesting shoot,' she said as we reached our tent.

My phone beeped as I entered the tent.

I saw it was a message from Devraj.

'Goodnight. Sorry I had to leave dinner, had some urgent work to finish off. Would have liked to chat further and walk you back to the tent. Just in case there were any animals lurking about.' He added a smiley emoticon.

I was chuffed to hear from him, and my face showed it.

'What are you looking at your phone and grinning for?' asked the ever sharp Jaya. 'Haven't seen you do that in a while. You usually look so grim when you're on the phone.'

'Oh, just something funny,' I replied, turning away.

I typed back, 'Luckily, the walk back to the tent was uneventful. We can continue our chat tomorrow! See you for the safari. Night night.'

And on that happy note, I turned in.

14

The next morning Jaya and I arrived at the front porch at 7.45 a.m.

I was stretching, trying to get the night kinks out of my system when Vikram walked up looking rather cheerful.

'Hello, hello! Had a good sleep?'

I must admit I was surprised to see him. I had half expected him to give it a miss. We greeted him and a very sleepy-looking Ravi.

As we were chatting, Devraj emerged from his office. He must have arrived earlier.

'Good morning, everyone, good to see you all here,' he said, as the jeep pulled up.

We all clambered in. I sat in the seat behind the driver. Devraj, who was sitting next to the driver, diagonal from me, turned and gave me a warm, friendly smile. A smile that went all the way to his eyes, lighting them up with a burnished intensity. I smiled back, and, in that moment, it felt as though the rest of the world faded away and it was just the two of us, alone in the jeep. The familiar fluttering in the pit of my stomach had returned. I couldn't help but wonder if Devraj felt the same way. The air between us was charged with an energy I couldn't quite put my finger on.

'DO YOU MIND?' said Jaya, loudly, breaking into the moment. I realized she was waiting to get into the jeep, and had been holding out the camera stand for me to take.

'Yes, sorry. Here, let me help,' I said quickly, my face reddening. I wondered if she had noticed Devraj and me locking eyes.

Vikram and Ravi settled into the back seat, and we were on our way.

'I'm feeling quite excited about going into the park again. This is all so new for me. Who would have thought something like this could be so fun! Ravi, are you enjoying yourself? Have you developed a taste for wilderness like me?' Vikram asked a still sleepy-looking Ravi, who tried to muster up some enthusiasm.

'Wow. We really converted him, didn't we?' whispered Jaya to me, amused by Vikram's enthusiasm.

We reached the park entrance, and stopped for the quick formality. The gate was fortunately not crowded at all since all the jeeps had gone in earlier. Just then, one of the forest guards came running up.

He spoke to Devraj urgently, and after a short discussion, Devraj turned to us. 'There seems to be a situation in one of the villages. A cow was killed and the villagers are angry. It may be a tiger who killed it, and the villagers are turning on the forest department. If it's all right with all of you, can we go there for a bit?'

'Okay,' I said quickly. And then turning to Vikram, asked if he was fine with it.

'Yeah, sure,' said Vikram. 'But what will you do?'

'The forest department asks me to help out sometimes to calm things. I'll offer money to the villager who has lost his cow. It takes a while for the forest department to give the official compensation because of red tape. And the locals all know me and listen to me.'

'This would be really interesting for us as well. Especially since we are focusing on the issue of man–animal conflict as one of the challenges facing the country when it comes to tiger conservation,' I said, looking at Jaya who nodded.

'All right, thank you. I'm not sure how long it will take but let's get there first,' said Devraj, nodding at the forest guard. 'And when we get there, Vikram, can you just pull your hat down and sit low in the jeep? Don't want to create another situation.'

'Yeah, sure man. I'll be totally low-key. Let's go help the forest department!' said Vikram, though Ravi didn't look very happy at the prospect of a crowd.

We drove off to a village called Tikri, where the incident had taken place.

When we arrived, we were directed to one end of the village, where the open fields stretched out before us and the dense, verdant forest loomed next to them. As we approached, we could see a throng of people gathered towards the far end of the fields, surrounded by an expanse of untamed scrub and the beginnings of the dense forest.

There was a lot of shouting.

We pulled up next to forest department jeeps that were parked at the end of the dirt road, and Devraj jumped out to see what was happening.

Jaya picked up her camera and stood up to film the crowd. I watched the action from my seat, not wanting to draw too much attention by standing up.

'What's happening?' asked Vikram in a stage whisper, sitting low in the back seat, with his hat pulled down, just like Devraj had instructed.

'There's a big crowd, and they do look very angry. I can see some forest department guards in the crowd, but can't see the cow. Devraj is there now, speaking to an elderly man.'

'Sunaina, I'm going to have to go closer to get better visuals. This will be a great element in the show.'

'Okay, let's do it. You go ahead, and I'll get the tripod,' I told her.

'Be careful, man,' said Vikram from the back.

'Don't worry. You just make sure they don't realize who you are.' I gave him a wink.

Ravi scowled. He was clearly uneasy with this situation where he felt out of his depth.

It was then that the yelling became more aggressive. I could make out shouts of 'Tiger, tiger!', and the mood of the crowd abruptly changed.

Some people started running away from the crowd as Jaya and I ran towards it. Jaya stood up on a mound to get a better look.

Turning to me, she waved frantically. 'The tiger is there!' she yelled.

I brought the tripod to her as she started rolling. I got to the mound and fixed the tripod, and she deftly placed her camera on it, all the while rolling.

It was only then that I looked to see what was happening.

At one corner of the field was the dead cow, its body half-submerged in the thick undergrowth that surrounded a large, gnarled tree. The villagers, who had gathered at a safe distance, were shouting and brandishing their lathis, their faces contorted with anger and fear. As I gazed upon the scene, I could see the large paws on the cow's body, while the rest of the tiger was obscured from view by the dense foliage.

The air was thick with tension, and I felt a shiver run down my spine as I stood witness to this uneasy confrontation between man and beast.

The forest guards were trying to push the crowds back; they were dressed in body protectors and helmets, which was probably their conflict gear. They were determined to keep the situation under control, and I could see Ram Tiwari exhorting the people to step back and remain calm. He wasn't wearing a helmet, though, maybe so the villagers could see his face and hear him clearly in the confusion.

Meanwhile, at the fringes of the crowd, I spotted Devraj, who was trying to make his way to the front, his voice raised in a chorus of shouts and calls as he sought to move the people back and defuse the tension. His determined demeanour was a stark contrast to the panicked expressions on those around him. The shouting and gesticulating of the crowd only heightened the sense of chaos and confusion.

'My God, just look at that!' said Jaya. It was chaotic and incredible.

There was a tiger just sitting there, with this big, agitated crowd seething in front of it.

I had read articles on man–animal conflict in India, that crowd control was one of the big challenges in such situations. For the authorities, that's the forest department, the problem was not only the animal they had to manage but all the people as well, who were determined to watch despite the danger.

And this was exactly the scene in front of us.

As the tiger had made its presence known, some of the people had scattered in terror, running back towards the road for safety. However, others had stood their ground, seemingly emboldened by their numbers. Despite the best efforts of the forest guards, who were working tirelessly to clear the area and ensure the safety of all those present, these determined individuals had refused to budge.

There were two trees near the dirt road on the other end of the field. A handful of people, who had retreated in the face of the tiger's appearance, had climbed these trees, and now clung precariously to the boughs, peering down at the scene below with a mixture of fear and curiosity.

We saw one of the forest jeeps was being driven through the crowd towards the front. It helped disperse some of the people.

I took out my cell phone and started filming some of the action as well. You never knew what might be usable.

The jeep was now in the front and there seemed to be an urgent discussion underway.

'I think they're moving the jeep there to use it to scare the tiger off,' said Jaya. 'I remember reading an article where they used a tractor, or a JCB, to scare off a tiger that wasn't moving. In that case, it was a villager's body it was sitting on.'

I was about to respond when an enraged roar echoed through the air.

The sound was like nothing I had ever heard before.

My heart raced and my blood ran cold. I was momentarily paralysed, frozen in place by the sheer power and intensity of the roar. The entire scene before me seemed to have come to a standstill, as if time itself had stopped in response to the tiger's call!

The instinctual fear that gripped me was unlike anything I had experienced before. It was a primal reaction, rooted in some deep, ancestral memory that knew to fear this sound. Despite being at a safe distance from the tiger, the sound went deep into my being and evoked a biological response beyond my control.

I had read that a tiger's roar was not only loud, but also had a low frequency that could be felt as much as heard. Now I understood this first-hand, as the sound seemed to vibrate through my entire body, causing an overwhelming sense of fear and awe.

If there had been chaos before, it was nothing like the pandemonium that erupted now, when people were finally able to move, after being rooted to the spot.

In another second, there was yelling and terror all around. People started running helter-skelter.

I looked towards Jaya with a horrified expression but she seemed to be calm, or was she frozen? Whatever the case, she continued to look into her camera and film.

Just then another snarl filled the air, and I was witness to a scene that would haunt me for the rest of my life.

With lightning speed, the tiger lunged forward and headed straight towards the jeep. Ram Tiwari, who had been giving orders on what to do next, was right in its path.

He saw the animal coming and leapt back just as the tiger took a swipe at him. I saw him fall back, as if in slow motion.

Two other forest guards, dressed in protective gear and armed with sticks, reacted quickly and bravely, shouting and brandishing their weapons. Despite the chaotic and frightening situation, they had the presence of mind to react quickly.

I could see Devraj, now near the front of the crowd, also yelling and waving his hands.

The tiger snarled once more, as it remained in a somewhat crouched position. However, as it surveyed the loud and intimidating crowd, it must have decided it wanted no further confrontation. With a final low growl, it bounded into the thicket and was gone.

I felt my body relax. I hadn't even realized how tense I had been this entire time. It was like my entire body slowly unclenched.

Jaya finally left the camera and shook out her body. She must have been rigid too during the whole incident.

'My God! What a scene! I got the whole thing on camera! Unbelievable!' she said with a shake of her head, her expression incredulous. She took another long, shaky breath and composed herself, bending down, resting her hands on her thighs.

'Let's go and help! Poor Ram Tiwari!' I said, still dazed and stunned by everything we'd just seen.

Jaya detached the camera and ran towards him, as I picked up the tripod and followed. We reached the spot where Ram Tiwari was lying on the ground, his entire face covered in blood. He had a massive gash on one side.

Devraj had taken off his shirt, that he was wearing over a t-shirt, and was gently pressing it down on Ram Tiwari's head. He was also yelling to people to help carry him. Some of the villagers were standing around looking quite dazed, just as I had been moments earlier.

'How bad is it?' I asked, kneeling next to him. 'What can we do?'

'Have to get him in the jeep! We need to take him to a hospital now!'

One of the forest guards who had yelled at the tiger earlier was kneeling next to Ram Tiwari, who was awake and groaning gently.

'These stupid people! Half the problem is managing the damn crowds. It just creates so much unnecessary confusion and agitates the animal,' said Devraj angrily.

'Do you know which tiger that was? It was the most frightening thing I've seen in my life!'

'That tiger was Zalim. He's the one who comes to the villages looking for easy prey. Any other tiger faced with a mob would have run off, but not him.'

Devraj seemed to be talking more to himself than to me.

Turning to me, he said, 'Can you hold this down, please? I'll go organize these people.'

Ram Tiwari was trying to talk.

'Tiwari ji, please relax, don't say anything. We're taking you to the hospital,' I said to him, trying to comfort him.

Suddenly, he went limp, likely due to the shock and pain. The gash on the side of his head, I realized, was actually a big flap of torn skin, exposing a part of his skull. Devraj had put the skin back, and the cloth was being used to hold it in place.

'He's lucky he moved back just in time, otherwise his head would have rolled off. This way he just got a nick of the claw,' said Devraj. He held Tiwari's hands and squeezed them for a moment, in a gesture of reassurance. He then spoke to the forest guard to call the others.

Good lord, this was just a 'nick' by a tiger claw, but it was the worst thing I had ever seen in my life. I took in some deep breaths just to calm myself.

A villager, who had been the most vocal while arguing earlier with the forest guards, came running with water.

'Tiwari ji, please have some,' he said as he tilted the pitcher towards his mouth. I was relieved to see Tiwari taking a few sips.

I looked up to see Jaya at a little distance filming everyone.

Devraj returned with several of the forest staff, and Ram Tiwari was gently helped up. I kept holding the cloth on his head. He was taken to the jeep and placed at the back. One of the guards took over from me, holding down the cloth, and sat at the back with Ram Tiwari lying on the seat, his head cradled in his lap.

I stood on the side with a few of the villagers. Jaya moved around, trying to get different angles without coming in anyone's way or being too obvious.

I glanced back to see Vikram and Ravi standing a little distance away. I had completely forgotten about them. Ravi was looking around nervously as there were quite a few people around. Vikram was watching what was going on very closely. He had his hat pulled down low on his brow and was wearing dark glasses.

Jaya walked up to them and they started conversing. She was probably filling them in on what had happened.

Devraj spoke to the guards and the driver. They started the jeep and very slowly moved towards the road. Jaya began filming the jeep driving away as I joined them as well.

A few of the villagers surrounded Devraj to discuss what had happened. I could hear him berating, almost scolding them. They seemed like the more senior members of the village. He was telling them how they should have helped the forest department calm the situation since the tiger was still in the area. Their issues and grievances could have been dealt with later. No one was denying their loss or refusing to help.

'And when the forest department is unable to, haven't I always helped you out?' he said to them, almost shouting.

They looked shamefaced and quite sorry about what had happened.

'Hukum, hukum,' they murmured in appeasement.

'And if anything happens to Ram Tiwari, it will be your fault! Pray he comes out of this all right,' he said to them harshly, before finally walking off.

Approaching us, Devraj indicated we should all also move back to our vehicle.

'Come on, let's go. We'll go to the hospital,' he said.

You could tell he was still very angry.

Jaya took one last shot of villagers standing huddled together, and then put down the camera, following us back to our jeep.

'I can't believe a tiger attacked Ram Tiwari! And we were right there!' said Vikram.

'Did you see it?' I asked.

'Just about. We were waiting and waiting, and Ravi just wouldn't let me go and check it out. But when we heard that roar. My God! It was the most powerful thing I've ever heard! Then I had to see, so I jumped out and just as we were running towards you all, I saw the tiger dart out and attack.'

'I managed to film the entire thing,' said Jaya with some satisfaction, as if in awe of what she had managed to do.

It really was rare to have a tiger attack on camera. I had seen a few online in the past.

There was the one of a tiger leaping out of a field near Kaziranga at a person atop an elephant. They had been searching in the field for the very same tiger.

Then another, somewhat similar to the scene today, where a massive crowd of villagers was yelling and running, and a tiger darted out in their midst. One person fell and the tiger ran away.

There was one from the Sundarbans of a tiger attempting to cross a wire fence that had been put by the forest department to protect the village. It snarled and growled and then moved on.

On the other hand, the video Jaya shot that day would be one of the rarest, since we had got there before the actual attack and had a good overview of the scene.

Then I felt a pang of guilt. Here I was thinking about the footage we'd shot, while poor Ram Tiwari was badly injured. Ugh, selfish, I berated myself. Though there wasn't anything Jaya or I could have done in that situation. That was small comfort.

'Shouldn't you have called for an ambulance to take Ram Tiwari?' asked Vikram as we got into the jeep.

'No time. It would have taken too long, and I want a doctor to look at his wound as soon as possible,' said Devraj. 'In fact, I think I'll have to make arrangements for him to go to Jaipur. I don't think the hospital here can manage his injuries. He needs plastic surgery as well.'

He dialled someone on his phone and began giving instructions.

'The hospital here must be a district hospital, with limited medical facilities,' I explained to Vikram. 'Jaipur is the closest big city with good medical care.'

Vikram seemed to go deep in thought.

We drove ahead of the jeep carrying Ram Tiwari, as it was driving slowly and carefully, given his situation.

Devraj kept speaking on his phone. It seemed he was calling up ahead to make arrangements at the hospital.

Vikram suddenly sat up, as if something had just dawned on him and patted Devraj on the shoulder urgently.

Devraj turned around, looking a little irritated.

'I have a chopper on standby in Jaipur! I can get it to come here to take Ram Tiwari,' said Vikram.

'What?' Now he had Devraj's full attention.

'Natasha had called for it after the bee incident because she was worried if anything more serious happened, in case someone else got injured, we should be able to evacuate the person quickly. It's just stationed there in Jaipur with a pilot on standby.'

'That would actually be incredible. Could you ask Natasha to call it here? I'll speak to the park director for permission. I'll even speak to the chief minister's office for any clearances from there. Please call for it!'

Vikram called Natasha and explained the situation to her, and asked her to urgently organize the chopper to come to Chambalgarh. She asked him a whole bunch of questions, and I could hear him reassuring her that he was fine.

Devraj asked for some details of the pilot and chopper. He then called up someone in Jaipur with the details and contact numbers.

I saw that the ever-diligent Jaya was filming the interactions. Good girl, never know what may be useful.

We arrived at the hospital, a drab and shabby building with a sprawling porch at the front. Its former grandeur was a distant memory, as it had succumbed to the neglect that plagues many small-town institutions.

We parked our jeep off to one side, a short distance from the entrance, so as to leave room for other vehicles to pull in.

Already there was a bit of a crowd at the porch area. I could make out some forest department personnel also in the crowd.

Clearly, word of the attack must have spread. There was some local media as well. Devraj jumped out to help with the arrangements and speak to the forest department officials there. Vikram slunk down in the seat, still on the phone, as Ravi again looked worriedly around.

Jaya also got down from the jeep and started filming the hospital and the officials as unobtrusively as she could.

The jeep with Ram Tiwari arrived and there was a flurry of activity. A stretcher was brought, and he was taken out very carefully and placed on it. One doctor yelled at the people around to stop crowding. It wasn't some tamasha or entertainment taking place.

The stretcher was quickly taken inside and things settled down.

I called up Debajyoti and told him what had happened and where we were now. He was horrified, asked several questions, asked whether we had been in any danger and if anything more could be done for Ram Tiwari. I told him about Vikram and Natasha organizing the chopper from Jaipur, and he was happy to hear that.

Looking up from his phone, Vikram said the chopper was leaving and would arrive in half an hour or so.

Jaya and I decided to go find Devraj to tell him about the helicopter. There were still some people loitering near the entrance. Some of the media, now standing at a distance, looked at us with interest.

On entering the hospital, it wasn't clear where they had taken Tiwari, but on asking a peon, we were directed to the first floor. There we found Devraj standing in a corridor outside a room, along with some other officers. He looked up at us as we approached.

'Sunaina, Jaya, meet Mr Mir Ali Khan, the deputy director of the park.'

We greeted him, and then I told them the chopper from Jaipur would hopefully arrive in half an hour.

'Great! They're doing some preliminary work on Ram Tiwari, but he needs to be shifted to a better facility as soon as possible. There could be damage to his eye and that's worrying,' Devraj said.

'We should get the ambulance ready to take him to the chopper landing site,' said Mr Khan.

He gave some directions to his junior officers who went off to make the arrangements.

'I've also requested the chief secretary and wildlife warden for the special task force from Jaipur to come immediately to handle T35,' he said, speaking to Devraj.

'A letter has also been sent to the National Tiger Conservation Authority informing them. We don't have time to wait on their approval.'

'Yes, I think it's for the best,' said Devraj, looking very grim.

My ears pricked up. What was happening here? They spoke some more about the task force and forest officials needed at hand.

Finally, I had to speak up and know what was happening.

'So what is this about? Is Zalim going to be removed from the park?' I asked.

Mr Khan looked at Devraj questioningly. Devraj nodded, as if indicating 'go ahead'.

With a deep sigh, he then spoke to us. 'There have been concerns about T35 for a long time. He's killed at least ten cattle in the last two years,' he said. 'The villagers have been agitated by this. A year ago a villager who had gone in the park illegally was killed, but his body was found in a highly decomposed state. I had wanted to send it for detailed testing but the family protested, wanting to conduct the final rites. The local MLA also put pressure so we released the body. T35's role was suspected by us.'

'So now what will be done?' asked Jaya.

'Look, I know you're the media, but this is not for reporting,' said Devraj a little forcefully. 'Zalim will be tranquilized and shifted to a special zoo in Udaipur. It has a very large enclosed area where he can be kept. The locals are so angry over the cattle killing, the next time they could poison the kill. The forest department staff are upset and angry as well, and reluctant to patrol if he's still in the park. There have been several instances of him chasing jeeps. For their sake and the sake of the other tigers, it would be better to remove Zalim. It would help the department with the locals as well, in building trust with them.'

'My big fear is a pilgrim being killed. We have groups that sneak into the park to visit a mandir there. If something were to happen, it could lead to more agitation,' said Mr Khan. 'Unlike other tigers, he seems to seek out confrontation.'

That made sense. I'd seen pilgrims walking in the park myself during the last shoot. All the wildlife conservation specialists I had spoken to in the past on such issues had said it was important to avoid conflict and keep the local population in the area on the side of conservation.

Removing one problem animal was in the larger interest of the tiger population. I remembered reading a piece that had argued how India's practice of waiting to see if an animal would kill again and again was highly questionable. And in some cases, three to four people were killed before the National Tiger Conservation Authority ordered action.

The article had spoken about how, in the US, while their policies were usually on a case-to-case basis, if an animal attacks a person and is considered dangerous, it is often euthanized. This was done in order to protect the public and prevent future attacks.

After what I saw today, I was more inclined to the case-by-case basis. People on the ground needed to be able to make those decisions.

'Once the operation to remove him is complete, you can go ahead and report it. Right now, we'd like it to be as smooth as possible,' said Devraj, looking at me expectantly.

'Yes, sure, we don't want to create trouble,' I assured him. And I really didn't. This could be twisted into a sensational story, but that wouldn't help the situation at all. In fact, once done, I could do a story on why it's important to be pragmatic in conservation.

An ambulance was organized to take Ram Tiwari to the helipad. A doctor and a nurse would also travel with him, and in Jaipur the administration had been informed. Jaya and I decided we would go to the helipad and film Ram Tiwari leaving because we already had pictures of the morning incident. We hurried out to our jeep. When we got to it, we found a few people hanging around, looking curious. Vikram was still slumped in his seat and Ravi looked irate.

'Sorry for leaving you here for so long. The ambulance has come to take Ram Tiwari to the helipad.'

'Okay, let's get going because more and more people are coming to ogle but they can't quite put their finger on it. A trick I've learnt is to not make eye contact, though that doesn't stop the staring,' said Vikram.

He spoke too soon because suddenly a photographer popped up, and started clicking pictures of Vikram. Ravi glared at him, but there was nothing that he could do. We quickly got into the jeep.

I looked back, and to my relief saw Devraj approaching.

'Hey, please stop,' said Devraj irritably to the photographer, as he got into the jeep.

'Arré, Devraj sahib, how is Ram Tiwari?' said a man standing next to the photographer. 'I heard the top of his head is gone? Is that true? It's what the villagers are saying, so I wanted to get the right information.'

Must be a local press guy. How word travels and stories are created.

'Oh, it's you, Anil,' said Devraj, still glaring at the photographer, who was now filming a video.

'Please put that down!'

Anil gestured at the photographer to stop, who did so reluctantly and stepped slightly away.

Looking at the photographer and then back at Anil, Devraj spoke, 'It's the skin on top of his head that came off. He's badly injured and we're shifting him to Jaipur. That's a lot of information I've given, so please go now.'

'So you were there when it happened? How come?' asked Anil, not ready to let go so easily.

'I was requested to come talk to the villagers by the forest department. They were agitated because of the cattle kill,' said Devraj as the jeep started up.

'Oh,' said Anil, writing in his notebook. 'Where were you at the time?'

'We were headed to the park then. Anyway, khamagani, I have to go now.'

'Oh, so Vikram ji was also there when it happened?' he asked, glancing at Vikram, excited to add a Bollywood element to his story.

After a beat, realizing he'd revealed far too much by recounting the entire sequence, Devraj just shrugged.

'Anil, please, we have to go now, thanks.'

We reversed our jeep, driving out of the hospital compound and headed towards the helipad.

'I guess the local media's going to have a big, fat story on their hands now,' I said to Vikram.

'It's all right, as long as it's nothing negative. Devraj, can you please ask your friend not to give any negative spin? You seemed quite friendly,' said Vikram.

'Sure, I will. That Anil Gehlot. He's a wily one. He keeps pushing with subtle questions and before you realize it, you've revealed everything,' he said with a grimace.

'The mark of a good reporter,' said Jaya, with grudging admiration. 'And speaking of a dedicated reporter, look who,' she indicated behind us.

Vikram and I looked back. Talk of the devil. It was the intrepid Anil and his photographer on a motorcycle following us. Devraj followed our gaze.

'Argh. Trust him to follow the story through.'

'Can't blame them though,' I replied, turning back. 'It's a great story to follow. I would have done that too! That could have been Jaya and me, if one of us could ride a motorcycle, that is.'

'Yeah, if we were reporters in this small town, this would be quite a scoop,' she laughed.

'That would be a sight,' said Vikram, also joining in with a laugh as we continued to giggle.

'He's one of the main reporters in this area. A big fish in a small pond so to speak, but very committed as you can see,' said Devraj.

'Well, it's turning out to be a pretty big story for us too. Vikram, we're going to be filming a sequence with you also at the helipad. We've covered the events of the day, so it's only fitting we get that last bit as well.'

Seeing Devraj give me a look, I turned to him and shrugged.

'Sorry, Devraj. We're the media, can't help it. We'll add it to our show. In fact, Vikram, you should give them an interview. Clearly there are a lot of wild rumours, and they know you were there, so why not talk to them since they will be reporting this anyway›?

Ravi did not look happy, but Vikram agreed.

We reached the helipad but the chopper had not arrived yet.

There were some boys playing cricket next to it, and a woman with a small herd of goats walking across it.

'What is this?' said Jaya. 'How is the chopper going to land here? There are so many people.'

'Don't worry. This is very normal,' said Devraj, sitting back to wait.

The ambulance with Ram Tiwari arrived, along with a jeep which had some forest staff.

The driver jumped out of the jeep and went to chase the boys away from the helipad.

Now we could see a speck in the sky and hear a slight humming from the chopper. While the kids had been cleared out, the woman with her small herd of goats was still too close.

Another forest staff member joined in to help the driver clear the landing area.

Now the chopper was clearly visible, with a loud whirring sound.

The last goat was shooed away, and within five minutes the chopper landed. We all watched and were fascinated. Amazing how things in India work out.

Jaya, who had filmed the chopper landing, now jumped out of the jeep and filmed Vikram and all of us getting out. There was a lot of activity. The medics in the ambulance were organizing the stretcher to take Ram Tiwari to the chopper.

Devraj walked up to the chopper and spoke with the pilot, probably about the arrangements. One of the officers also approached them to discuss logistics. Two personnel went into the chopper to make room for the stretcher.

Vikram, Ravi and I stood on one side, watching. I saw Anil's photographer taking pictures as he spoke with one of the forest department personnel. Another journalist had also arrived with a camera person, who got busy filming. After ten minutes of sideways glances, they teamed up and approached us.

'Hello, Vikram ji. We wanted to ask you a few questions, please,' said Anil.

Since he had been expecting it, Vikram agreed.

'Is it true you organized this helicopter from Jaipur?' they asked, getting right down to it.

'Yes, I did,' he replied. 'Luckily we had it on standby in Jaipur for any emergency. I'm happy it could be used for Ram Tiwari.'

Jaya came up and started filming him as well.

'Were you there when the tiger attack took place?' Anil asked.

'I was. The tiger had killed a cow and was sitting on it. The forest department was trying to clear the crowd of people, but they just wouldn't move. There was also a lot of noise, when suddenly the tiger roared and jumped out!' Vikram used his hands to make a pouncing move. 'It was the most frightening thing I had ever seen! He swiped at Ram Tiwari who moved out of the way at the last minute,' Vikram made a ducking motion. 'Thank God. Otherwise he was a goner!'

I was smiling watching his exuberance. He told a compelling tale.

They spoke to him for another five minutes. Vikram told them about how he had filmed with Ram Tiwari earlier in the park, so he knew him and was shocked by what had happened. He was willing to do whatever he could to help and was happy the helicopter could take Ram Tiwari to Jaipur, and he hoped he would get the best treatment to recover at the earliest.

Anil and the other journalist were so pleased with their chat, they still couldn't believe they had managed it. They shook Vikram's hand and thanked him. Then the photographer asked them to stand together for a photograph.

'Please join us, madam,' said Anil.

'Yes, come on, Sunaina, since it's a photograph with the reporters,' said Vikram.

I happily obliged.

By this time, they were ready to move Ram Tiwari to the helicopter. He was brought out on a stretcher, heavily sedated and with his head bandaged up. He was safely transferred to the chopper. A nurse and a doctor from the hospital also got in as they were accompanying him to Jaipur.

We all stood to one side as the helicopter started up again. The rotors began whirring and the bird took off. After all the excitement, stress and events of the day, it was oddly reassuring to see the helicopter lift up, into the air, and then slowly fade into the distance. Everyone just stood there watching for a while.

'Well, that's that, I guess. Now I hope the doctors in Jaipur can take good care of him and he'll get the treatment needed,' I said, more to fill the sudden vacuum after all the hectic activity earlier.

'I really hope so. This morning has been unbelievable. Poor guy,' said Vikram.

'Thanks to you, he will soon be getting the medical treatment needed. Good call,' Devraj nodded at Vikram. We started walking back to the jeeps.

Jaya and the photographers took a few more shots, we said bye to the other officers and finally left.

On the way back to the resort, the mood was very sombre. It had been more than an eventful morning, and we hadn't had a moment to just think, to process everything that had happened. Poor Ram Tiwari nearly losing his life while trying to negotiate with irate villagers for the sake of the tiger. The tiger, oblivious to the trouble he'd caused, attacked the one person who was, in a sense, pleading his case.

As we drove in from the gate, approaching the lodge, we saw Debajyoti was waiting on the main porch. They had all been in touch through messages and wanted all the details.

'It's been quite a day, guys,' said Vikram, as he got out of the jeep. 'I'm exhausted, so I'm going to take a nap. I'm sure Sunaina can fill you in on all the events of the day.'

Vikram and Ravi left for his room while the rest of us sat in the dining lounge. Devraj went off to his office with Himanshu.

Jaya and I recounted the day's developments to the group. They had many questions and we spent the next half hour answering them. Sandwiches and coffee appeared, and we realized how hungry we were. We went through the footage Jaya had recorded

'This is incredible to see, Jaya!' I exclaimed as everyone ooh-ed and aah-ed.

The footage showed the villagers gathered and the forest guards talking to them. The tiger paws were visible on the carcass of the cow. You could make out the tiger head behind the grass. Jaya zoomed in on animated faces arguing. She began pulling out the shot, getting more of the crowd. In the centre of the frame was Ram Tiwari. Now the jeep pulled up right next to him.

And then, you heard the roar. The camera swung back to the tiger, and you saw it rise up and charge towards the crowd. The quick swipe at Ram Tiwari who was already falling backwards. The frame pulled out more and you see the tiger bounding away, with Ram Tiwari on the ground, people running, shouting and screaming.

We slowed down the footage to watch again and again. Just before the attack, you could see the expressions of the people change when the tiger roared. And then when Ram Tiwari tries to move away, as he sees the tiger coming in for a swipe, saving his life.

As Devraj had said, if he hadn't moved back just then, the tiger's paw could have easily taken his head off. When you froze the image, the paw looked as big as his head! Jaya kept the shot surprisingly steady given what was happening. I remarked about that to her.

'I really don't know what kept me filming the scene. I was stunned by what was happening but I just kept going. Much as I wanted to look up and watch what was happening, I just kept fixated on what I saw through the lens.'

Looking at the footage, we also realized there was an ant mound next to the gnarly tree near the attack site, which, along with the tall grass and foliage, could have blocked everyone's view of the tiger as it had stealthily returned to reclaim the cow.

It was incredible footage to have but our concern was about Ram Tiwari. We were all wondering about him when Devraj came to the lounge to have a bite and sat with us. He told us he was awaiting an update. We showed him the footage as well.

'Just look at that. So much noise, commotion. Any other tiger would avoid this crowd. They're not fond of humans or interested in having any kind of interaction. But Zalim came to get the cow despite the crowd. And then just bounded up, took a swipe and made off,' he said, shaking his head.

'This just makes me realize again how close it was. Ram Tiwari or anyone else could have died. Zalim won't stop. He's become extremely bold and aggressive. Also, he prefers the easy kills from the villages rather than hunting.'

As the others were discussing the events of the day, I asked Devraj, 'So, when are they moving him? Do you know yet?'

'Well, let's not talk too much about that just now. We'll have to wait and see what decision comes from Jaipur on that front. But I expect soon. There were ongoing discussions about moving him even before this incident.'

We discussed the events of the day for another hour as Devraj got an update that Ram Tiwari had been safely taken to a hospital in Jaipur and was being treated by a top doctor. I wrote out a short script for the news report and online. Debajyoti said he would uplink the footage.

We had footage of Vikram recounting the incident as well, when he was speaking to the reporters at the helipad. It fit in quite well with the report. It was 2 p.m. by this time, and we were all exhausted. Jaya and I went back to our tent and crashed for a few hours.

15

I was dreaming about being chased by a tiger, running towards a jeep ahead of me, and Devraj reaching out to pull me up, when Jaya shook me awake.

'Wake up! Debajyoti is calling us to the lodge. Also, why are you looking so agitated?'

I sat up, relieved to be awake.

'Now I'm even dreaming of tigers! I was being chased and the fear was palpable,' I said, shaking my head.

'Well, it's good I woke you when I did. Let's go.'

We freshened up and went to the lodge where everyone had gathered. Manju was sitting in the porch area and jumped up when she saw us. 'I know this is getting a little routine,' she said, laughing. 'But you're going viral! Again!'

'Well, I was expecting the story to get reported,' I said.

'It's become a sensation. Slow news day, I guess. The local news carried videos that were picked up by other channels. Good thing you wrote out the copy and we uplinked the footage! We carried it on the channel as well. And everyone is going gaga over the fact that Vikram arranged a chopper for Ram Tiwari. Come see. Oh, and you'll have to do a live report for the 7 p.m. bulletin.'

We sat on the porch and looked at all the online coverage. Besides the report I had sent in, we checked out the local news coverage.

Anil and the other reporter had done quite a number with the story. It was almost a mini movie by the time they were through with it. It had been picked up by various entertainment portals. A few of them had even interviewed Anil, who spoke like he was right there when the tiger had attacked Ram Tiwari! He also made it seem like Vikram had helped carry Tiwari after the attack and rushed him to the hospital. And then he described how Vikram had organized the helicopter. He ended with a piece to camera, where he said that just a few days earlier, when Vikram was filming with Ram Tiwari in the park, he had never imagined that he would soon be saving his life. Talk about hyperbole!

All in all it made a captivating story, and clearly the media could not get enough.

I was amazed at the extent that Anil had embellished the story. As journalists, yes, we all exaggerate and sensationalize a little, if I'm being totally honest. After all, we have to make it interesting—it has to captivate the audience. So if I'm doing a story on water shortage in the city, I'll find a case study, some family where the daughter, who is a Class 12 student, is forced to wake up at 5 a.m.

every morning to ensure the water tank is filled, which in turn means she's sometimes late for school or unable to spend enough time studying for an entrance exam. Or if it's about rising food prices, it would have to be from the angle of a housewife, a mother, who is forgoing a meal so that her children can eat. It was always best to have some such angle to create sympathy and hook the viewer.

Anil, on the other hand, had taken an already dramatic story and created a total thriller with a happy ending of sorts. He had got his hands on some mobile footage taken by a villager at the scene. There was a shaky shot of Zalim sitting on the dead cow. Then chaos and yelling, after the tiger had attacked. Ram Tiwari could be seen on the ground. He even interviewed some villagers who were there, who talked about the attack and described in great detail how Vikram Khanna had been there and had helped carry Ram Tiwari to the vehicle.

The power of suggestion. So many times, when interviewing people who had just witnessed something, I found they would agree with leading questions, even when you simply wanted them to tell you exactly what they had seen. They would readily agree with another version suggested to them, despite having witnessed something else.

Vikram had just been standing to one side, dazed, when Ram Tiwari had been transported to the jeep. But now, thanks to Anil's probing and suggestive questions, the villagers believed he was at the centre of things.

Jaya and I watched the report our channel had done, and even though it was more truthful and had the footage of the actual attack, Anil's report was far more gripping.

'You're going to have to up your game!' said Jaya, teasing me as I remarked on the differences in the reports.

'These local channels can do this level of sensationalism,' I laughed. 'Not us at NNTV.'

It was soon time for me to do my live piece for the channel. I went outside, where Debajyoti had set up the camera. I put the earpiece in my ear so the director in the news studio could speak to me, and miked up. Once the checks were done I was ready, facing the camera.

My report on the tiger attack was carried first. A sober account with dramatic footage of the tiger jumping, which we had slowed down for emphasis. And then a great shot of Vikram seeing off the chopper rounded it up nicely.

After that they cut to me and the anchor, Priya. She asked about what had happened. I described the situation, as well as explained the issues involved in such man–animal conflicts.

'Were you or Vikram ever in any danger?' she asked.

'No, no. We were a little distance away and watching the events unfold. We were heading to the park for a safari when we got news of the tiger killing a cow.'

She asked a few more questions and finally ended the report.

I took off the mike and earpiece and joined the group seated on the porch.

Reena had also arrived by then. 'My phone won't stop ringing! You will not believe the kind of attention this story is getting. It's all kinds of sensational! A tiger attack, a wounded forester, a superstar who helps save his life, chopper to the rescue. The good thing is everyone seems to have forgotten about your love triangle,' she said with a laugh.

Debajyoti joined us, looking preoccupied as usual. As he sat down, the waiter brought a pot of coffee to the table.

'I really need that,' he said. 'It's so strange, how so many things have happened during this shoot that have been totally out of our control. Some have been negative, like the bee sting, protesters at the gate or this latest, Ram Tiwari being attacked. But they've all been so newsy and have brought so much attention to the campaign. Strange how these things happen.'

'Must be a sign from the heavens. What do you think it means, Sunaina, since you're a great believer in the fates?' said Jaya, smiling at me.

'I hope it means everything will be all right in the end,' I laughed.

'Sunaina, you have another live spot at 8 p.m. This one will be with Vikram for PrimeTime news. I've informed Natasha who'll tell Vikram,' Debajyoti said. 'By the way, she's over the moon with all this coverage. I don't get why, since he's such a big star and doesn't really need additional attention, does he?'

'Oh, Debajyoti, my sweet, naive boy, have you forgotten about the drug scandal? Hopefully everyone else has as well—now that Vikram has emerged like a hero in all this,' Reena said with a laugh.

'Not so loudly, Reena,' shushed Manju. 'His team is around.'

'Oh pffft. They know we know,' she replied, raising an eyebrow.

'Well, what I know is we're going live at 8 p.m., and we should be all set,' said Debajyoti.

Later that evening, we were all set up for our live piece from the lodge. The anchors from the studio were going to chat with us, after playing the video report.

Debajyoti had created a perfect set-up for us. We were seated on chairs in front of the building, spotlights lighting up our faces. And behind us, a series of lights had been carefully placed to light up Baagh Baadi and make it look stunning in the background.

Finally we were on air, as Rajiv and Priyanka, the two anchors of the show, chatted with us about what happened. Vikram spoke about the shock he had felt, and how he was in awe of the forest guards and rangers who put their lives on the line to protect wildlife. I talked about the man–animal conflict that needed to be handled delicately, and also emphasized the dangers the forest staff often faced.

It was all going smoothly when Rajiv suddenly asked about plans to shift the tiger out of the park, and how this had upset many animal lovers, who were protesting the move.

'Well,' I said, taken aback, since I hadn't expected this to be general knowledge, 'you understand that there's a threat to the tiger as the villagers are angry because he killed several cows. Also, there is a fear among the forest staff. So in the interest of conservation and for the safety of the other tigers in the park, this decision may have been taken. We can't get overly emotional over one animal. The conservation picture involves many factors like the local population, the other animals and the forest department.'

'It's certainly been quite an experience, one you didn't bargain for, hasn't it, Vikram?' Priyanka said, thankfully changing the conversation.

He nodded and then added, 'It's been an amazing and humbling experience. While we all love the tigers, let's not forget the people who work hard protecting them.'

Priyanka then wrapped up the segment.

'Thanks for joining us, and for our viewers, let's take one more look at the attack and hope for Ram Tiwari's quick recovery.'

I was removing my mike and earpiece when Devraj came stalking up angrily. 'I had told you in confidence about Zalim being moved. Now you spoke about it on the news,' he said angrily.

I was taken aback by his tone and my temper shot up immediately. 'Well, I didn't tell the office. I have no idea how they knew,' I said to him, quite forcefully. 'You had asked me not to tell anyone and I agreed. I'm not the type to go back on my word!'

Now Devraj looked a little taken aback at my tone.

'Hey, hey, what happened?' said Vikram, looking at both of us in surprise. 'Relax, guys! What are you two going on about?'

'The forest department is shifting Zalim to a zoo, it's supposed to be a secret, and Devraj thinks I told my office about it,' I said irritably.

'Look, I'm sorry for accusing you but when you were discussing it on the news, I thought you must have informed them,' he replied, looking a little contrite. 'These things are very sensitive and timing is everything. In fact, the operation to move Zalim is happening as we speak.'

'But why? Why are they shifting him? Because of the attack today?' asked Vikram, seemingly perturbed. 'You know, today when those local journalists were speaking to me, they were saying something about how Zalim would definitely be shifted now. I didn't pay much attention at the time.'

'Well, he's being shifted for his own safety and the safety of the locals. He was creating too much tension between the forest department and the villagers. He was killing cattle and then sitting in the fields. It was just a matter of time before he killed someone or was poisoned. That used to happen frequently around five years ago, but after a lot of effort by the forest department and because of paying compensation, we haven't had a case in a long time,' said Devraj.

'And, while he's very popular, there are many other tigers besides Zalim here. The forest department has to think about all the other animals that could suffer if the villagers stopped supporting conservation efforts,' I said. 'Many former poachers now work with the forest department as trackers.'

I was still a little irritated by Devraj's accusations earlier. He kept looking at me but I ignored him and avoided meeting his eyes.

'Hey, I think I know how the office knows!' said Manju, walking up with her iPad. 'Look at this Twitter trend, #savezalim. So many people are tweeting about "Justice for Zalim", "Save Zalim and don't let them punish a voiceless tiger", "It's their land, we're the encroachers", and on and on.'

We all peered at her iPad as she scrolled through and showed us all the tweets.

'Hmm, it's those NGO guys who must have outed it. I recognize some of the names.' Devraj grimaced. 'There's this photographer who comes here now and then, Bharat Singh. He started an NGO called Friends of Chambalgarh, basically to get perks in the area. He pays some locals for information and runs a Facebook and Instagram page with updates. He's also friends with many journalists in Jaipur, so he keeps feeding them all kinds of stories about the park. Save Zalim indeed! He's basically zoomed in on an issue that appeals to the city's tiger lovers who don't know anything about the ground reality.'

'Ugh! The do-gooder variety who have no clue about conservation. I know exactly what you mean,' I said, forgetting my earlier anger with a new anger.

This was an old peeve of mine. The 'bunny huggers' or dog lovers. Not that I didn't love bunnies or street dogs. But there were these groups of people, with the best intentions, who didn't realize the harm they were doing with their tunnel-vision love for animals. It was often unbalanced. The rights and safety of the poor should matter too, but somehow that didn't figure in the crusade for animals which, in the cities, was often centred around street dogs.

I had covered stories of children being killed or mauled by packs of stray dogs. There were so many 'dog bite' incidents involving the poor, who could not afford medical help or miss a day of work. But, if at any point, the authorities took action or removed some dogs, these groups of dog lovers arrived from their privileged positions to oppose it.

So while they do it ostensibly out of love for animals, they actually harm their fellow human beings who aren't privileged enough to have a safe place to live.

Similarly, they were now jumping in on this issue with a misplaced 'love for tigers', and specifically Zalim, without any understanding of the big picture and ground realities.

'This is like a whole new world I've been introduced to,' said Vikram, shaking his head. 'And I thought Bollywood politics was getting too complicated.'

'Now I hope Zalim is shifted out quickly before the situation gets out of hand,' said Devraj.

'Like what, exactly?' I asked.

'They have a lot of locals on their payrolls and could mobilize them to do a *dharna*,' he said.

'Dharnas seem to be quite popular here,' said Vikram with an eye roll.

We all laughed.

'There are more positive comments about the day and Vikram coming through for Ram Tiwari, so don't worry about it,' said Manju.

'Well, I'm calling it a night. It's been an exciting day and I really pray Ram Tiwari will be okay. Let me know if anything else can be done for him,' said Vikram, yawning slightly. He said his goodbyes and walked off to his room.

The rest of the team was wrapping up after the live spot. A table had been set up with finger food for all of us—tikkas, kebabs and rolls. We'd been eating all evening so there was no need for an elaborate dinner.

Seeing Vikram go off made me realize how exhausted I was too. It really had been a long and exciting day. An emotional whirlwind. I yawned loudly.

'I think I'll turn in as well. What a day it's been,' I announced. Everyone said goodnight to me.

'Yes, best you go and rest. We'll meet tomorrow to discuss the plan for the day,' Debajyoti said.

'I'll drop you to your tent,' said Devraj. I suppose it was a conciliatory gesture after our angry words earlier.

We walked back in a slightly tense silence. Outside my tent, Devraj finally spoke. He turned around and faced me. 'Look, I'd just like to apologize again. I saw the broadcast and thought it was a pre-decided question. I assumed you must have told them about the plan to move Zalim, and it upset me because I had specifically requested you to not tell your office.'

While I had been determined to remain in a sulk, I was impressed with his apology. It was a sincere one, well-articulated. I decided to forgive him.

'I guess I can understand how you jumped to that conclusion. I hope the transfer goes off well. We'll have to see how to deal with the fallout tomorrow,' I said, looking up at him. I gave him a smile to show the earlier incident was now a bygone.

'I just don't want there to be any misunderstanding, especially between us,' he said with some feeling, looking down at me intently.

We were standing very close to each other, at the entrance of my tent. I felt the butterflies in my stomach again as the mood suddenly changed. The air between us seemed charged.

There was a lamp hanging outside the tent that lit up his face, and I could see the intensity in his eyes as our gazes locked.

I found myself leaning in towards him, as he bent down and we kissed.

Before I even realized it, my arms were around his neck and his arms were around my body, pulling me closer.

I don't know how long the kiss lasted, it seemed to go on and on, though it must have been a minute, when I heard a cough behind me. We quickly jumped apart to see Jaya standing there with her camera slung across her shoulder, looking sheepish.

'Sorry to interrupt but I really need to crash,' she said with a grin.

'Oh yeah, me too. What a long day! Time to call it a night. God knows what surprises tomorrow will bring,' I found myself yammering on, sounding ridiculous even to my own ears. Jaya gave me a look and darted into the tent, leaving us outside.

Devraj looked at me with a barely suppressed smile. 'I've been wanting to do that for so long,' he said.

I blushed and looked down. He put his hands on the side of my face, and leaned down to give me a gentle kiss on the lips and then the forehead.

'Goodnight then, Sunaina, I'll see you in the morning. Sleep well.' And he left.

I watched him walk away, dazed. Just before he turned, he looked back and gave me a smile and a wave. And then he was gone.

I went into the tent to find Jaya sitting cross-legged on her bed, clearly waiting for me.

'Soooooooo then? I was wondering when this would happen! I could totally sense something was up,' she squealed.

'Nothing was up, you know. This was the first time we kissed!' I said, my face red as a tomato.

'Oh, damn. And I interrupted it. Sorry about that,' she said, but her face seemed to say, 'Sorry not sorry.'

'You and Devraj! This is so funny, especially when you think back to all the run-ins you two have had. So what's going on?' she called out as I went into the bathroom to change.

'I don't really know. I guess we'll figure it out,' I replied from inside. 'Like I said, that was the first time anything really happened.'

When I came out she was still sitting up, looking at pictures on her phone. 'So you have no idea what's happening between you two?'

I shook my head.

'Gosh! What a shoot this has been,' Jaya laughed, now lying back on her bed. 'Something or the other keeps happening. But this, by far, has been the most exciting thing. No rush, you can always figure out things later. Goodnight.'

She switched off the lamp and settled down to sleep.

Settling down in bed myself, I thought about it some more. What had just happened? How were we going to 'figure it out'? This, 'whatever it was', didn't feel like a flash in the pan. It seemed like something more. But the question was, did he think it that? With this troubling thought, I drifted off into a fitful sleep.

16

I woke up feeling very happy the next morning. And then I felt anxious. And then happy again.

The agony and the ecstasy of infatuation. I decided to focus on the joy as I stretched lazily in bed. Then I remembered the nagging doubts of last night and the joy was dampened a little.

Anyway, there was no time to ponder on my personal business. I jumped up and began to get ready. I made coffee and woke Jaya up. Drinking her coffee in bed, a rare luxury, she started scrolling through her phone.

'Oh God!' she said, sitting up. 'The Save Zalim campaign has really taken off on Twitter.'

'And your clip from last night is also going viral among the campaigners! People are criticizing you and Vikram because you supported shifting the tiger out.'

Ugh. This damn social media would not leave me alone.

'What rubbish! These people have nothing better to do than sit in their homes far away and play finger warriors! Anyway, Zalim has been shifted now and there's nothing they can do. He's safe, the locals are happy and the forest guards are safe. I'm sure their attention span lasts like a minute, and they'll move on to some other bleeding-heart issue.'

These misguided do-gooders were really a bane. They had no idea about conservation and would get sucked into an issue based on emotions alone. Emotions that could be easily manipulated if someone wanted to.

It was the last thing we needed now that we were nearing the end of our shoot, and I really did not want them spoiling the good vibes and happy buzz.

Speaking of a happy buzz, I thought about Devraj again, and a warm, happy glow grew inside me. Thinking of our kiss, my face felt warm and my toes curled.

When we arrived at the main building, most of the crew had gathered already. They were sitting around in groups, eating breakfast in the courtyard. It was the last day or so of the shoot with Vikram. The Mumbai contingent planned to leave the next day, if nothing more was needed of them. I was scanning the dining area for a place to sit when Devraj suddenly showed up beside me.

'Good morning,' he said with a half-smile.

Oh lord, the butterflies in my stomach.

'Hi!' I said, grinning like an idiot. I couldn't help it. I couldn't stop.

'Um, hope you slept well?' he asked.

'Yes, very well, thanks. Have you had breakfast?' I replied, a little awkwardly. Talk about a formal conversation.

'Actually, I was waiting for you.'

He was waiting for me! This was moving in the right direction. The warm glow inside me spread around my being. We both smiled at one another.

'Hey, good morning, you two! What's cooking?' said Vikram, as he came up next to us.

The sudden interruption made me start. Devraj gave him a tight smile.

'What happened?' said Vikram, looking at both of us suspiciously. 'What did I miss?'

'Nothing at all,' I replied casually. But I could feel my face reddening. 'You two are keeping secrets from me and there's something cooking here, I can tell, but right now I'm really hungry and need to have breakfast. Didn't feel like having it in my room. Come, let's eat,' he said, putting his arm around my shoulder and directing me towards a table.

I could sense Devraj stiffen, and I looked at him with a helpless shrug.

He mumbled something about joining us in a minute, how he had to check something, and walked off.

We went and sat at the table that had been set up for us. Drinking his orange juice, Vikram looked at me appraisingly.

'So spill the beans. What's going on between you and Mr Sunshine?'

His nickname for Devraj made me laugh. It's true on most days Devraj was anything but Mr Sunshine. That was how I had thought of him too for the longest time. How things change.

I realized Vikram was still looking at me as I was caught up in my reverie.

'Nothing is up!' I replied, trying to sound exasperated.

'That was too long a pause,' he said with a grin. 'Okay, don't tell me but I can figure it out. I've seen the way Devraj looks at you sometimes. I know you all think actors are really self-absorbed, but I have actually studied the craft, and we were taught to observe people a lot—especially interesting characters—because you may pick up something, like a mannerism you can use. Anyway, I noticed something was up and was wondering when you would realize.'

'Realize what?' Now I was just curious about Vikram's observations.

'He's into you! I can totally see it. He thinks he's got this cold, aloof thing going on most of the time, but I am very perceptive.' Vikram nodded sagely as he buttered a croissant. Then biting into it, he asked me, 'Do you like him? From what I saw this morning, I think you do.'

I felt my blush coming back. Vikram gave me a big grin and a wink. 'I think I got my answer.'

Fortunately, Debajyoti joined our table just then.

'Just wanted to run you through the plan for today. We just have some additional shots we need to take. Things that we may have missed earlier, like more shots of driving in the park. Shots of the jeep. A few close-ups,' he said.

Reena had just entered the dining room and, seeing us at the table, made a beeline for us.

'Hi, you all! Have you seen the kind of rubbish people are saying online? They are saying that the tiger was shifted because of Vikram. Since he was visiting the park and the forest department didn't want any trouble for his shoot, they decided to shift out the "problem" tiger!' Reena said as she slid into a chair. 'What nonsense, yaar. That's not why they shifted this tiger, na, Sunaina?'

I was shocked she could even ask me that. But then, in all fairness, Reena didn't really know the whole story or even understand the conservation aspect.

'No, no, not at all. We had nothing to do with the transfer of the tiger. That was totally the forest department's decision, and we didn't even figure in the scheme of things. If any of your reporter friends ask you, please say that.'

'How stupid, yaar. Why would I want a tiger moved out? In fact I was a little surprised at the move, but then Sunaina explained how it's for the safety of the locals and the forest guys. That made sense. I'm gone in a day or so. These people have to live here,' said Vikram, barely even looking up as he ate his egg-white omelette. It looked really good so I decided to have one myself.

I was calling the waiter to order one when Natasha entered the dining room. She looked quite agitated, and I sensed there was trouble in store. 'What is this damn thing about a tiger being moved because of Vikram? I'm getting calls from various journalists looking for the next juicy story. What is wrong with these people! Yesterday's story was so good. Why can't they be happy with that?' she wailed.

Turning to me, she asked, 'What is this all about? I can't even respond because I don't understand it.'

I explained what had happened, how they had moved Zalim from the park because of various issues prior to our trip, and how the attack on Ram Tiwari was the last straw.

But now we were being blamed by the wannabe tiger saviours as we were a soft target.

'Okay, I get it,' said Natasha, shaking her head. 'Now how do we fix this? I can't have my man Vikram getting all this bad press. Especially since he was getting such positive press earlier. Right now, it's still limited to social media, thankfully. Do we just ignore it? Should I tell my people to get the word out that Vikram had nothing to do with this?'

She looked really sorry, while the man in question, Vikram, seemed more interested in the pancakes in front of him. I guess he was done with the social media scrutiny.

'Well, hopefully this will blow over,' I said. 'The mainstream media has covered yesterday's news, which was good. If we don't give this any attention, maybe it will die down. Also, you have all those Vikram fan clubs, right? Activate them. We can also push back on social media.'

'That's an excellent idea. I just needed to figure out the details so we're all on the same page,' said Natasha.

Then Manju arrived to add to the drama. 'I guess you all have seen this trend on Twitter, #VikramFakeTigerLove and #JusticeForZalim,' she said.

'What?' said Vikram, finally reacting and looking away from his food. 'That's really taking it too far.'

'Such lies are being passed around, I can't believe it!' said Manju. 'As if Vikram forced them to move Zalim. Unbelievable!'

'And now they're setting the narrative with this online campaign, and the media may think it's true! Natasha, we need to move quickly to counter it,' I said.

We discussed a plan. Manju had some suggestions on handling social media. We had to also get journalists on board from other publications, and the forest department as well.

I saw Devraj standing near the entrance to the courtyard, speaking to someone. I decided to talk to him about how to tackle this issue. And it was an excuse to go speak to him. I wondered why he hadn't joined us like he'd said he would.

'Hi,' I said, walking up to Devraj who was speaking to Himanshu. 'You were supposed to come back and join us.'

'Yes, sorry, something came up,' he said. His tone had a slight chill in it as he looked at me and then looked away.

'Is something wrong?' I asked, genuinely puzzled by the blow hot, blow cold.

'Look, I have to ask you something,' he said. He indicated we move a little away, to a more secluded part of the veranda.

I was curious about what was going on, so I followed him.

'This may seem a little ridiculous,' he said, running his hand through his hair. He seemed uncomfortable. I waited.

'But I just needed to know if there is something going on between you and Vikram? I don't want to assume or presume anything.'

I was taken aback. How could he possibly think something was going on between Vikram and me?

I thought I'd made it clear there were just rumours, nothing more.

'No, no, nothing at all. He's just been really friendly and we're working together on this campaign. How could you even think there's something going on? Especially when you saw how upset I was about the rumours!' Now I was feeling slightly agitated.

'I'm sorry, I didn't think so initially. But then I wasn't sure, especially since you two are so friendly, and, after all, he's a big star. I thought he liked you.'

'Well, he just told me he thinks you like me,' I said, a little too loudly.

Now Devraj looked surprised.

'Okay, that's unexpected,' he said, raising his eyebrows.

Then after a moment, he added, 'And I do like you. I just wanted to clear the air before we take things any further. That is, if you want to,' he said and looked at me intently.

'Well, I would like to get to know you better, but right now I'm a little ticked off by this,' I said.

I was irritated about him thinking there was something up between Vikram and me, but one part of my mind appreciated that he had told me what the issue was instead of the confusing passive-aggressive treatment.

He took my hands in his and squeezed them.

'I am really sorry. I didn't mean to upset you. But at least it's out of the way.'

I could feel my irritation dissipate. I gave him a smile. 'Well, thank you for asking instead of giving me the cold treatment.'

As we looked at each other, I could feel this magnetism between us. He looked like he was going to kiss me again.

'Hey, lovebirds!'

The moment was broken and we both turned around to see Vikram standing there with a grinning Natasha and a bemused Zaid behind him. I said a small prayer, thankful others from my team weren't with them. I wasn't ready for that.

'I was looking for you guys! I'll be damned if I'm leaving this shoot with these people trolling me and spreading lies. Especially since I've really developed an understanding of the issues involved. So, do we have a good plan to counter this?' he said.

Now Devraj looked confused so I quickly filled him in on the latest developments, how Vikram was being blamed for Zalim's shifting.

'I'll put some information together after speaking with tiger conservationists I know, to forward to a few journalist friends of mine. I'll pass it on to Reena as well. Manju is looking at social media, and now Devraj's on board also, so let's figure out what else we can do,' I said.

'Great!' said Natasha. 'We can delay our departure by a day, but Vikram really wants to get this done. So let's get down to it.'

'I was informed a short while ago that some of the local members, and some Jaipur members of Bharat Singh's NGO, will be protesting at the gate with banners,' Devraj said. 'They basically want to take pictures and post on social media to amplify their campaign. I was going to ignore it, but I can rustle up a counter-protest by village groups and the forest department association.'

'And we can ask the local media to cover it. We'll also do a piece for our channel. People need to see the ground realities and not fall for this fake campaign,' I said.

'But what do I do? I need to do something too,' said Vikram.

'I was just thinking of that. Maybe you can interview the park director. That was something we'd planned anyway, and this is a great chance to talk about the reasons for shifting Zalim, what the forest department does and how they need to manage the sentiments of the locals. We also have footage of you walking in the park with Ram Tiwari. We can speak to his family and put it all together.'

'Okay, great! I like the energy. This sounds good,' said Vikram enthusiastically. 'So let's get moving.'

We planned to meet in an hour after making some calls and fixing up the shoots and interviews. I had to go to my tent to pick up my computer, and Devraj said he'd accompany me.

'We'll see you all here in a bit. Don't go AWOL on me now,' said Vikram with a wink as we walked away.

'He's not a bad guy,' said Devraj with a laugh as we set off down the path to my tent. 'I have to admit I was sceptical about him at first, and then just plain irritated and angry when I thought there was something going on with you two, but now, since that's cleared up, he's okay.'

'Oh, really? It's funny that you thought something was going on. It's ludicrous, really. He's so not my type,' I said with a shake of my head, looking up at him. There was a slight wind and my hair blew across my face. He reached out and brushed it away.

'So what is your "type" exactly?' he asked, abruptly coming to a stop. He looked at me expectantly, with a smile on his face.

'I'm not sure I had a defined "type" up till now, but tall, rugged, with a passion for wildlife could be my type,' I said with a grin.

'I'm glad to hear you say that,' he said as he pulled me to him and kissed me.

Surfacing from the kiss after what seemed like a long time, he said, 'I've been wanting to do that all morning. Finally got a chance to get you alone.'

We kissed some more when I heard a shuffling sound.

We turned to see Jaya, along with Manju, standing behind us on the path. Manju's mouth was wide open.

'Get a room, you two! I can't keep bumping into you like this,' Jaya said with a laugh.

'Apologies, Jaya,' said Devraj, seeming unruffled.

'I'll see you all later then,' he said to me with a smile. Then he gave a nod to Jaya and Manju, and walked back to the lodge.

We began walking to the tent, and the moment he seemed out of earshot, Manju burst out, 'What was that? When did that start happening? Oh my God! Colour me shocked!' she said.

'And you knew about this?' she turned to Jaya, who just shrugged with her hands out.

'It just kind of happened,' I said weakly, by way of explanation. 'It's been surprising and we're still figuring it out.'

'Actually, now that I think about it, I had an idea something was up,' said Manju, thinking aloud. Turning to Jaya, she said, 'Remember? I told you how he would look at Sunaina. I was on to something.'

We reached the tent and walked in.

'I'd appreciate it if you didn't tell anyone, Manju. We're here on work, in the middle of a campaign, so that's very awkward for me and I hate being gossiped about.'

'Oh, absolutely,' said Manju. 'I won't tell a soul.'

She then sat down on Jaya's bed and proceeded to interrogate me.

'Have you thought about how this is going to work out? The logistics. He's here and you're in Delhi.'

Before I could even say anything, she continued, 'I guess it will have to be a long-distance relationship. But those are really difficult, you know. You'll have to talk all this out. I had a friend whose boyfriend moved to Mumbai, and they had all these rules about how to keep in touch and not let the distance matter. But in the end it really does.'

Manju went on and on about her friend's hopeless long-distance relationship. Jaya was trying hard not to laugh, I could tell.

'Manju, it's really sweet that you're so concerned, but don't stress me right now with so many questions, I haven't even thought so far,' I said as calmly as I could in the face of her rapid-fire questions and unsolicited advice. 'Right now, we have to do a counter campaign against this attempt to vilify Vikram, so let's put our energies there.'

I changed into safari clothes as I filled them in regarding what we were planning. A counter-protest being organized by Devraj, interviews with the park director and Ram Tiwari's family, and a well-edited report explaining the ground realities. Jaya had some suggestions, while Manju said she would discuss the online coverage with Reena.

17

An hour later we all met up in the lounge to decide on the coverage.

Devraj informed us about the counter-protest, and how he didn't need to make much effort as the villagers were already planning one. They had heard from the local media about how people wanted Zalim to be brought back to the park and were enraged. They were also upset that Ram Tiwari, who was a local, had been injured.

Zalim had been tranquilized and moved safely to a botanical garden-cum-zoo on the outskirts of Udaipur. Several acres had been allotted solely for his enclosure. The National Tiger Conservation Authority had been informed of the move, and they were planning to send a team down to file a report. The state government had also been kept abreast with all the developments and was completely backing the forest department.

The NGO that was fighting for Zalim's return was apparently planning to approach the court with an urgent petition for a hearing on the matter at the earliest.

Candlelight vigils were also being planned by some of the members in various other towns. I couldn't help but feel very irritated at this piece of news. Candlelight vigils for a tiger, but if any villager or forest guard would have been killed, they wouldn't even have blinked. That would have been a routine news article. Such insensitivity towards the people who actually work to make our parks and wildlife safe. I really wished more people would put in the effort and go beyond loving tigers and wildlife, to understand how they were managed and what went into conservation.

Devraj was seated next to me during this discussion and kept his arm on the back of my chair. Despite the serious discussions underway, I was very aware of him next to me. It was all so new and exciting. I had to make a real effort to concentrate on all that was being said, as well as keep the grin, that kept creeping up, off my face.

We divided up the work, with Danish, Manju and I headed for the protest coverage, and Devraj, Vikram, Debajyoti and Jaya for the interview with the park director. Reena and some members of the Mumbai team were working on social media, while Natasha, now armed with all the information she needed, was going to make some calls to journalists and editors she knew, to put the correct story out there.

'I'd really rather go with you,' said Devraj in my ear, as we all started to disperse.

'I'd rather you came with me too, but it's important you go with Vikram since you know the park director well,' I said, moving my head slightly away, but smiling as I did. His face so close to mine sent a frisson of excitement through me.

'Yes, yes, I know that. But I'm not happy,' he said, looking very 'not happy'. 'Call me in case you have any problem whatsoever. It should be straightforward enough but you never know with these protests and counter-protests. Wouldn't want any trouble.'

'You know I've been doing this job for a long time, right?' I replied laughing. 'And I know how to handle these situations.'

'Of course I know you're a thorough professional, an ace reporter, very passionate about your job. That's what attracted me to you in the first place. So driven,' he said, brushing away a strand of my hair.

How sweet, I thought. My best qualities.

I suddenly felt someone's eyes on me—the creepy feeling when you know you're being watched.

I subtly took a step back. 'Well, that we can talk about later today,' I said with a smile. Glancing sideways, I saw Reena watching us intently.

Following my glance, Devraj saw her too, and realized I was feeling awkward. 'It's okay, I get it. You're at work. We'll speak later,' he winked and walked off.

It didn't take even two minutes for Reena to sidle up to me. 'Soooooo. You and Devraj, huh?' she said, wiggling her eyebrows.

'Yes, me and Devraj,' I said weakly, resigned to the interrogation.

'That's a surprise. You're so intense about work, didn't realize you had any time for extracurriculars,' she said with a grin.

'Reena, I always have time for extracurriculars,' I said cheekily, grinning back. That would give her something to think about.

'Well, good for you. Just be careful. You know he had quite the reputation as a ladies' man back in the day. So I wouldn't get too involved or anything,' she said as she walked off.

Argh. Trust her to try and get into my head. I really didn't have time to think about all that, I had a job to do. But now she had gone and planted doubts in my head before I had even had a chance to think things through. First, Manju asking all those questions about how I'd manage a long-distance relationship, and now Reena implying Devraj was a player.

I didn't get to stew for too long as Danish called me, since it was time to leave for our shoot. The jeep was waiting and the equipment had been loaded. Still a little preoccupied, I got into the jeep.

'What's up?' asked Manju. 'All okay?'

'Yes, all fine. Just want this to go well. Don't want Vikram to leave this shoot feeling misrepresented.'

'Yeah, true. By the way, Reena asked me about you and Devraj. I didn't say anything,' she whispered to me.

'Oh, thanks for that.' I was a little irritated now. The last thing I wanted was chit-chat about me in the group. Anyway, there was no time to obsess over it as we had to get down to work.

We headed to the park gate where the protest was planned.

When we got there, we saw that a small group of protesters had gathered, as well as the local media. We parked a little away from the crowd to put some distance between us. We were readying our equipment when I heard a greeting. Turning around, I saw Anil Gehlot standing beside our jeep.

'Hello ji. How are you, ma'am?' he asked.

'Anil ji, I saw your piece. Impressive. You made it seem like Vikram single-handedly rescued Ram Tiwari,' I said with a smile.

'Oh, thank you, ma'am. It did very well. Got many hits online.' He looked chuffed, though my comment wasn't meant as high praise. But just as well, since he was a helpful person to have on your side, to help suss out the local dynamics.

'So, what is your view on this lot?' I asked, indicating towards the crowd of protesters.

'These people are rubbish, ma'am. Some of the locals are paid off by the NGO to do these events. Some NGO members have come down from Jaipur also. They take pictures and share on social media. We've seen it so many times. To outsiders, it looks like some big activity, and they get donations. It's an old game, ma'am.'

'But you all help them, don't you? By reporting on it?' I asked.

'What to do, ma'am? Not much happens here. We also have to have something to report on,' he said with a shrug. 'Is Vikram ji coming here, ma'am? Now, that would be an A-one story!'

I laughed at the A-one phrase. It was a curious phrase, extremely popular in small-town India. Even back home, some of my relatives used it.

'No, I don't think he'll be coming here, but I believe there's going to be a counter-protest by the forest department association and some local village group?'

'Yes, ma'am. I heard that too. Good, na? These NGO people are just trying to appeal to their foreign donors and the city folk. I'm glad Zalim is gone. He was very aggressive! One night he blocked my path on the road right there. I've never been so frightened in my life. He charged at the scooter in front of me. I went back to my friend's house and waited. The forest department had to come and move him off the road. This was just a few months ago.'

'Hmm, interesting. Oh, the NGO crowd has grown a bit now,' I remarked, as we started walking to the protest site.

'Yes, more locals are joining in, ma'am. If you look closely, some of those people you saw at the Bhawani Sena protest will be there also. Like those three on the side. They come for every protest. Sometimes for and against an issue on different days.'

'You're right,' said Danish, who had been following our conversation. 'I remember those guys from the other day. I have footage of them sloganeering. That's hilarious!'

Seeing our cameras, the 'Save Zalim' gang got energized. They started sloganeering loudly, jostling among themselves, trying to look more active.

There were a handful of city-types among them, the 'outsiders', who must be the NGO members from

Jaipur, and then there were the locals mixed in, and the 'mercenary' protesters, who had been at the Bhawani Sena protest. Despite Anil's very jaded view of them, I knew there were some in the crowd who genuinely felt very strongly about the issue. Who felt Zalim had been treated badly by authorities and it was their duty to highlight it.

Armed with the mike, I started taking some sound bites.

'What is this protest about?' I asked

One young man in front said, 'This protest is against the dictatorial action of the forest department removing Zalim from this park just because of their own failures. These jungles belong to the tigers! The villages were also jungles earlier. We are the encroachers who have taken their space. And now, when one tiger doesn't behave the way we like, we are punishing him! We want justice for Zalim! We want him to be brought back and set free! Free Zalim!'

The crowd started chanting 'Free Zalim' slogans.

When they settled down, I managed to ask more questions.

'So where are you from?'

'Some of us are from Jaipur. I come to this park all the time. I love this park and all the tigers here! It's a shame we have to punish the animals for roaming freely in their own territory!'

'Arré, sahib, what about the people here? They also need somewhere to live. They've lived in these villages for decades now. Your city was also a jungle once, by that logic,' said Anil, standing behind me.

A few of the other local journalists also murmured in agreement.

'What about the forest guard who was attacked?' I asked, pressing on.

'First, the tiger was in his right to be there. It was a part of his territory,' the young man went on, ignoring Anil's argument.

'The forest guard should have been more careful. They should be better trained to deal with these situations. He let it get out of hand. He shouldn't have allowed the crowd to gather next to the carcass,' he said self-righteously. It was easy to have these views from afar. It all sounded logical enough, but having been right there and seen the chaos up close, I knew how naive he was.

Another woman in the group piped up, 'I've seen how forest rangers in Africa are trained to deal with conflict. They don't let their guard down, they are thorough professionals!' she said forcefully and a few people nodded in agreement.

This very privileged reply took my breath away.

'You do know in Africa, on the reserves, most rangers have guns and are allowed to shoot if the animal threatens them? They do it from time to time. It's out of the question here,' I told her. 'And the situation on the ground was very different from what you're imagining.'

'They are blaming poor Ram Tiwari!' said Anil angrily, with more angry murmurs from the other local media.

'It could have been handled better!' said the young man again. 'Now Zalim has been punished for the lapses. Sent to live in a zoo! That's no life for a tiger.'

There were more 'Free Zalim' slogans.

'And what about Zalim's cubs? He has two cubs with a tigress and now they have been left without protection!' This was said by the same annoying woman who gave the Africa example.

Again murmurs of agreement from the crowd.

'She doesn't even know those cubs are sub-adults and about to leave their mother anyway. Not that Zalim cared,' said Anil next to me.

Just then, the counter-protesters started arriving at the gate and placed themselves on the other side of the current protest.

It was a large number, mostly villagers and former forest department employees, who had gathered to show solidarity with the department.

We took shots of the counter-protest, which also included women and children. Whoever Devraj had got in touch with had managed quite a decent turnout.

One of the men, an elderly gent, took a mike and started addressing the gathering.

'Brothers and sisters, today we have come to make ourselves heard by those who live in cities far away from these forests,' he said.

'They want Zalim to be brought back! Why? So he can live in our midst once again, kill our cattle and attack our people? He attacked Ram Tiwari! Some of you were there that day! You all saw what happened!'

There were loud murmurs in the crowd, with some people yelling 'hai hai'.

'If these people in the cities want Zalim back, they should come and live here first! We are not against tigers, we love this jungle and we worship here! Those living in cities will not dictate to us!' he said forcefully.

This was followed by more chanting and sloganeering.

Quite an orator, I thought to myself.

'He is the former sarpanch, very active in local politics and a good man,' Anil filled me in helpfully.

With all this sloganeering and shouting, those on the other side, with the NGO, now felt the need to assert themselves, so they too started shouting and sloganeering. It was fairly chaotic.

In a few minutes the mood shifted, and it suddenly seemed that there was a lot of aggression on both sides. The young men belonging to the Bhawani Sena who were campaigning for Zalim were the ones getting aggressive and taunting members from the other side.

The local reporters started filming them and that seemed to encourage them to behave even worse.

Manju was also taking pictures, and I got a sense it seemed to excite them further.

'Things are getting a little heated here,' said Danish, in an obvious understatement. He was moving into that protective mode with his camera when he feared something could happen.

Now a handful of people from the Save Zalim group moved closer to the other group, calling out and challenging them. The man with a mike made an appeal to both sides to move back.

Before things got out of control, I decided to jump in and try and calm things down. Anil also joined me in trying to get the men to return to their respective sides. Even as I thought some semblance of calm was returning, two men started brawling and everyone gathered around them. Lathis appeared from somewhere and they really went for it.

'These two are sworn enemies. There is some family bad blood, a land dispute, so they fight any opportunity they get,' said Anil, as he simply watched them with no inclination to get involved.

'But do something! They might crack their heads!' I said, hoping this violence would stop.

'Don't worry, ma'am. They will stop themselves. No point getting in the middle of the lathis,' said Anil sagely.

'But let's call the police at least?' I said, exasperated with how everyone was so matter-of-fact about this violence. Now some of the locals from both sides had surrounded the two men, and seemed to be egging them on! It had become a full-blown tamasha!

The Jaipur members of the NGO looked very shocked at the turn of events. Some started taking pictures, while others seemed to be retreating.

Just then, two jeeps pulled up, one of them with Devraj, Vikram and the crew in it, and the other a forest department vehicle.

Devraj jumped out and some forest guards from the other jeep also got off. They strode headlong into the brawl, and the two men were separated immediately. The men stopped fighting the minute they saw Devraj and the others arriving. I heard him berating them and telling them to move along, otherwise they would be locked up. They both retreated meekly.

Protesters on both sides were now wondering what to do. The young man and woman who were part of the

'Save Zalim' group started rallying the others to restart their sloganeering.

The former sarpanch also began speaking on his mike again.

Devraj now walked up to where I was standing.

'I told you to call me if something happened!' Devraj said to me in exasperation. 'These things can get out of control sometimes.'

'It just broke out minutes ago. We were trying to calm things down but Anil said these two fight all the time. I thought it would settle down,' I replied, though a few moments ago I hadn't been so sure.

'We were returning to the resort when one of the guards got a report on his radio that some trouble was happening. I immediately made the jeeps rush here,' he said grimly, looking around.

'Thank you for that,' I said, almost hugging him but then, conscious that we were in public, I simply gave his arm a squeeze.

That seemed to mollify him, and I was genuinely relieved to see him.

'I think we're about done here. I got my shots and sound bites before the brawl. How did your interview go?'

He told me about their shoot, how Vikram had turned out to be a great interviewer. The director had explained the issues very clearly, and overall it went well.

We started walking towards the jeeps when Anil spotted Vikram.

Vikram had tried to sink into the seat, with his cap and sunglasses on. But after having seen him outside the hospital, Anil was on to his trick.

'Arré, Vikram ji. Please say a few words here. It will mean so much to everyone,' said Anil, approaching him.

'I don't know, Anil. Things look a little heated here. Not sure what I can do,' said Vikram. He looked at us questioningly. But now other reporters had also approached the jeep.

Seeing him there, the villagers and forest association members now started cheering for Vikram. Realizing it was no use trying be low-key, he waved at them. Jaya, Danish and Manju started filming the scene. Debajyoti and Ravi, who were seated in the back of the jeep, were looking worried. I was sure Ravi was wondering whether the situation could spiral!

Devraj gestured to the forest personnel to help manage the crowd that was moving closer. They quickly ringed the jeep so the crowd couldn't get closer. I could see Ravi was getting agitated now, fearing a mob.

'If you're fine saying a few words, it would be nice,' I whispered to Vikram, leaning into the jeep.

'Do you think I should?' he asked, looking at me anxiously.

'You know what to say, right? Stuff that we've been discussing over the last few days, your own experience? You also just spoke to the park director,' I whispered urgently to him. He took a moment, then seemed to relax.

'Totally, don't worry, I've got this.' He flashed me a wide smile.

We asked the people to move back slightly as Vikram stood up in the jeep.

On the other side, some of the 'Save Zalim' campaign people started booing, but most of them had their phones out and were taking videos.

I asked Anil to call the man with the mike to come up to the jeep. He was most happy to do so. Anil even encouraged him to climb into the jeep next to Vikram, though Ravi did not look pleased.

Taking the mike, Vikram launched into a speech in a mixture of Hindi and English.

'These last few days that I have spent in Chambalgarh will stay with me my whole life. I have always loved tigers and wildlife, and have been proud that our country has so much to offer. Most of the world's wild tigers live right here, in India,' he said with gusto. The crowd cheered him on.

'But I never realized the effort that goes into protecting tigers, keeping the forests and the wildlife safe. This is what the forest guards do! Like the jawans at our borders keeping the country safe, here it is the forest guards who protect our green wealth, armed with only a stick!'

He was on a roll now, and I have to say I was impressed! The crowd was loving it, and even the other side was mesmerized.

He spoke about how he had experienced walking in the forest with the guards, with Ram Tiwari himself. How he had seen Ram Tiwari that day talking to the villagers, putting his life on the line to save the tiger. How, even after he was attacked and rushed to the hospital, his primary concern was the tiger.

Then, looking across at the crowd that was earlier booing him, he said, 'We're all on the same side. We want to save this forest and all the tigers in it, and for that we need to respect the people who live here as well as the forest department that works day and night. We can't protect tigers without their support and we need to support them!'

It was all very powerful. The media was filming the whole time as were many people with their phones. And then, to top it all off, the man who had given the mike to Vikram called a young teenage boy up to the jeep. He whispered something in Vikram's ear.

'And here is Ram Tiwari's young son. His father is in the hospital, fighting for his life as we speak,' Vikram said, putting his arm around the boy's shoulder. 'We owe it to him and all the other children of the forest guards to help make their lives a little safer. I want to announce here that I will sponsor this child's education, and I will help set up an insurance fund for the forest guards and their families.'

People clapped and cheered. Even the crowd on the 'Save Zalim' side started clapping.

'Thank you, everyone. Again, we're all on the same side. We want to see the tigers and wildlife in this park flourish, and that's only if we take everyone along. We need to imagine ourselves in their shoes and understand their position,' said Vikram to finish it off. More cheering followed. He sat down and chatted with Ram Tiwari's son, which was duly recorded by all the cameras.

'Wah! A-one, ma'am,' said Anil, appearing at my side. 'I told you it would be a blockbuster.'

I almost felt a sense of pride. As if he were my mentee. Vikram had spoken so passionately, had made so much sense, I couldn't have done it better. And that was saying a lot.

'That was . . . unexpected,' said Devraj, standing behind me. 'I must say, I did not realize he could go so deep. He really learnt his stuff here.'

'Well, he had a great teacher,' I said with a wink, grinning up at him.

'Yes, clearly he did,' he smiled back, putting his arm around my shoulder.

We got the crowd to clear out and sent Vikram's jeep back to the resort. Devraj joined me in my jeep with Manju and Danish.

'I just put that on Facebook live!' squealed Manju. 'It's already been seen 20,000 times. Can you imagine that? It's jumped to 30,000 now. Oh my God! Working with celebs is a different league altogether.'

'Which is why it helps to get them to promote these issues,' I said, looking pointedly at Devraj, who smiled back. 'Usually our videos get a few thousand hits after a few hours. But having a superstar support your cause, that's priceless!'

18

As expected, Vikram's speech went incredibly viral. People were watching it, commenting on it and sharing it. There were memes as well, always a sign of success. There were fan pages, there were articles. Someone even remixed a few lines with a rap beat and that went viral as well.

Even the 'Save Zalim' brigade cooled it, with some admitting they had been wrong. Though others still remained firm, who would just not stop, fortunately they were in a minority.

Manju was on a roll. She edited different clips, made montages and used various pictures on our web page and official handle, and each post was getting massive hits and shares. She sat with the Mumbai team as they also shared clips and pictures, and responded on the official Vikram social media sites.

And, of course, the channel wanted more from us that evening during prime time.

Vikram and I did another live TV spot from the resort. This time I had prepped the anchors according to the message we wanted to send out, and we played out clips from his afternoon address as well as his interview with the park director.

What made it even better was that top environmentalists, who are usually so difficult to please, had praised Vikram's stand. They lauded his clear statements that had highlighted an important aspect of conservation—the local population, their welfare and support, as well as the forest department.

We had two of them on the show with us, and it made for a good interaction on the channel.

Natasha was fielding calls from international media now, who wanted to interview Vikram. It was such an eye-catching story—young movie star talking passionately about protecting tigers. He had just seen a conflict situation first-hand, helped in sending the injured forest guard for treatment and taken a bold stand on the controversial issue of shifting the tiger. It also tied in with the role forests played in preventing climate change, which was a hot international issue.

All in all, it was very exciting and a great finale to our shoot.

Dinner that evening was a fun, celebratory event. Devraj had organized a big barbecue and bonfire. Everyone sat around chatting, drinks in hand. Natasha, who looked the happiest I had ever seen her, had announced champagne for everyone. She had apparently had two crates brought in from Jaipur to Baagh Baadi.

'This has been quite amazing, I have to say, Sunaina. You really pulled it off,' said Reena, holding up a champagne glass in a toast, as she joined us near the bonfire.

'Well, a lot of the stuff just happened. It wasn't staged—it's the reality of conservation. We just happened to be there and then Vikram said all the right things. I'm glad he's promised to help Ram Tiwari's family. That was really nice.'

'That would be great to follow up on, down the line,' said Manju.

'Yes, it would,' said Reena. 'Good idea! Hopefully Natasha would help make it happen. Her boy is now back on top of things.'

'Boss is very pleased with it all!' said Debajyoti, joining us. 'I just got off the phone with Lata and she was saying everyone in the office is so excited we had this amazing, super exclusive! They want us to get back so we can edit the shows and put them out as soon as possible! When it's still fresh in everyone's minds.'

'Oh, okay,' I replied, feeling a little taken aback. I guess I knew we were going to leave soon. I hadn't thought it was going to be quite so immediate.

'So you and I will leave tomorrow, Sunaina. Jaya and Danish can stay here with the rest of the team and finish up filming any more footage we may require. Reena can be here and coordinate with the Mumbai team. They will also be leaving by the afternoon'

Whoa, tomorrow! I nodded, though I was feeling a little agitated at how fast it was all happening.

I looked around for Devraj because I had been waiting for a chance to finally talk to him. I had thought we'd have more time to talk and figure out things. But now I was about to leave.

'Hey everyone, come here. Vikram wants to say something!' Zaid called out.

We all gathered round as Vikram stood up on a chair to address everyone.

'I just wanted to thank you all for the incredible time we've had during this shoot. And I can say that for my entire team. Even Sohan and Ravi!' he said waving to where they were standing, arms folded, generally looking big and tough. We all laughed as they cracked a shadow of a smile.

Vikram continued, 'We had challenges, from the bee attack to Bhawani Sena, to a tiger attack and then being blamed for the forest department's actions, but we persevered!'

Some laughs and cheers from everyone ensued.

'I'm sure we'll always cherish the memories from this trip. I know I will. It's been completely out of my comfort zone but so enriching!'

He mentioned each member of the team by name and thanked them.

I was so surprised. It was really quite remarkable he remembered everyone's name, down to the production assistants. That was a gift that so few had and went such a long way in making someone feel appreciated. I remember him telling me how he had a really good memory, which helped when he had to cram his lines for film shoots. He wasn't kidding!

When he came to me, he asked me to come up next to him. Everyone clapped and cheered. I gave a theatrical wave.

Debajyoti put another chair next to Vikram for me and he helped me get up on it (not that I really needed it, but more to do with playing to the gallery).

'A whole lot of what I learnt here has been thanks to Sunaina,' he said, holding his glass up to me. 'Everything you told me during our drives was told in such a passionate and fascinating way. It's thanks to you that I was able to talk about conservation with any authority. You didn't treat this as just a shoot with a star, but took the effort to educate me, so thank you for that.'

Everyone cheered.

'And, finally, please raise your glass for a toast to the entire team and to this amazing, successful shoot!'

'Hear, hear!' everyone said, as we all raised our glasses to each other.

I spotted Devraj standing towards the back, smiling. He raised his glass to me with a wink.

I felt a warm glow inside.

There were more short speeches and toasts made, and everyone was rather jolly. It was a perfect celebration to end our time together.

As soon as all the farewells were over, Devraj came up to my side.

'Can I steal you away for a bit? It seems everyone wants your time this evening,' he said with a smile.

'Well, it is my final night here,' I said, looking at him carefully.

'What?! What do you mean? You're leaving tomorrow?'

There was some satisfaction in seeing his distress.

'I just found out, actually. Debajyoti informed me that the office wants us back in Delhi to start working on the show edit.'

'That's disappointing. I had thought we'd have more time to spend with one another now that the pressure of your shoot was over,' he said, looking slightly crestfallen.

We walked to one of the sit-outs, away from the others.

'I knew you were leaving soon, but tomorrow is too soon!' he said as we sat down. 'We need to talk, to work something out.'

'Yes, even I thought we'd have more time, but this is it as far as the shoot goes,' I replied, a little unsure of what to expect. Also, what Reena had said was playing somewhere at the back of my mind.

'But not for us,' he said, taking my hand. 'I really hope you'll let me see you in Delhi and we can then see where this takes us.'

'I thought you had given up on Delhi and the city life,' I replied.

'Look, I won't lie. I do prefer being here to city life, but it's not like I don't go. And now I have a reason to,' he said, looking at me intently.

I felt my heartbeat quicken. I was feeling excited and nervous at the same time. I decided I had to make my feelings clear, otherwise things would just be left unsaid.

'I would really like that. Frankly, I didn't really know what to expect. We barely know each other. I believe you were quite the heartbreaker during your Delhi days, and I don't want to get serious if you're not. I've had my share of dead-end relationships, and that's not what I want here.'

'Who said that? Please don't believe any Delhi gossip,' he said, his eyes narrowing. 'People in the city have nothing better to do! And I don't want a dead-end relationship either.'

Saying that, he pulled me closer and kissed me hard.

When we pulled away, he said forcefully, 'This is something special. I just feel it! Sunaina Joshi, you will be seeing me in Delhi, don't doubt it for a second.'

Feeling a little breathless from the intensity of his kiss, all I could do was nod at him.

'There you are, you lovebirds!'

We both turned around with a start

We'd been so wrapped up in one another I'd forgotten about everyone else.

I turned to see Vikram walking towards us, with a grinning Manju right behind him.

'Come on! We're taking group photos, and we can't get one without you,' said Manju.

'And from tomorrow, you won't have to worry about me pestering you for pictures!'

I laughed at that. 'You know, I think I'm going to miss you clicking pictures constantly. Now see what you've done! You've created a monster.'

We returned to the group and joined everyone for a final snap. Or should I say snaps, as many pictures were taken. Everyone was getting sentimental with the shoot now more or less over.

Natasha gave me a big hug.

'This has been just great! And don't be relieved. You haven't seen the last of us. We're now planning a fundraiser for the forest guards so Vikram can really put his money where his mouth is. I'm counting on you for help,' she said.

This was great news. The channel would be so happy with a follow-up. It was what we were hoping for.

The rest of the evening passed by in a haze of goodbyes and 'let's keep in touch' being said on repeat. I didn't get a chance to talk to Devraj again. He got called away for some work, and shortly after that we all called it a night.

Vikram gave me a big hug and said I must visit him in Mumbai.

'And I don't mean it in that "we must do lunch" kind of fake way, which everyone knows won't happen. You have to come visit me in Mumbai. Natasha will follow up. Promise?'

'Yes, I promise,' I said with a laugh. It was touching how genuine he sounded.

Jaya and I walked back to the tent. I was feeling a combination of emotions. On the one hand, I was deeply satisfied and happy with the campaign. On the other hand, I was a little low and uncertain about Devraj and me. I didn't even see him before I left, and he last said he'd be in touch. But would he?

Jaya sensed my pensive mood. 'Hey, so what happened between Devraj and you? When will you see him again?'

'He said he would come to Delhi so let's see,' I replied with a shrug.

'Don't worry. It's been a great day, and if he said he'll come to Delhi, I'm sure he will. You should be so happy right now about everything!'

'Reena said he's a player.' I finally let her in on what was bothering me.

'Since when do you listen to Reena? Devraj seems very nice, and he seemed quite smitten by you. Don't let gossip bother you!'

She was right, I thought. '*Que sera sera*, whatever will be will be.' And with that, I turned in for our final night in the tent.

The next morning I got up with the alarm going off at 5.30 a.m. I was still feeling exhausted but forced myself out of bed and was ready in half an hour by the time Debajyoti pinged me to come to the main porch.

Standing there with my bag, I looked around, hoping Devraj would come say bye to me. Who knew what the future had in store for us. He had messaged me late last night, wishing me goodnight and apologizing for having left the party. I had replied to him this morning but he hadn't read the message, so perhaps he was still asleep.

Disappointed, I got into the jeep and we headed for the station. Debajyoti chatted about the shoot and the programming, the upcoming edit, and script timelines. While I kept nodding, I was not really focusing. I was more focused on thoughts of Devraj, and I was feeling despondent about our situation.

At night everything had seemed so romantic. He had said the right things, and the idea that we could have a relationship had seemed doable. But now, in the morning, I was feeling doubtful. Sure, I had felt emotions and a kind of excitement with Devraj that I hadn't experienced before. But was that enough? Would it just fade with us being apart? At the thought of that, I felt something clench inside and a sinking in my chest.

Now I was feeling slightly depressed, and to distract myself, I engaged with Debajyoti's chatter about logistics and timelines. He'd been involved in a one-sided conversation for the last fifteen minutes.

We got to the station and walked along the platform. The train we were catching came from Bikaner and was headed for New Delhi. The stop at our station was just about five minutes, so it didn't give us too much time. We figured out where our particular coach would arrive on the platform and waited for the train.

I kept glancing at my phone to see if I'd got any message from Devraj. Nope. I felt even worse.

The train pulled into the station and there was the usual scramble to get in. There weren't too many people boarding from this station so it wasn't too bad. We found our seats, put our luggage overhead and sat down, awaiting departure. I told Debajyoti I was going to try and sleep. It was a five-hour journey, and I could use the time to rest. I unlocked my phone again, invariably went to Twitter and scanned some of the tweets about Vikram and our campaign. It was all good stuff, the occasional criticism and trolling. At least the campaign was a success.

I had messages from friends and family. Didi had congratulated me on the campaign and then followed up with several questions about Vikram and whether she'd be able to meet him when she was next in India, given we were friends now. Trust her to think of something like that, I laughed to myself. Another message from my friend Devika, also asking about the events yesterday and about how long I was going to be in Chambalgarh.

I got busy replying to all the messages.

'How come the train hasn't started?' said Debajyoti, after several minutes had passed. He looked around, and added. 'It stops so briefly here. The compartment's quite empty. I think it has four more stops before Delhi.'

'I believe this train is usually very punctual, though,' I commented, as I continued to look through my social media. Now I was looking at the campaign's Facebook page. Manju had done a good job. Nice videos, engaging descriptors. Lots of engagements. I started looking at the comments on the various posts and videos.

'Maybe it's a VIP. You know, they do that in these small stations. It's like making the plane wait for a minister,' said Debu after another five minutes, looking at his watch.

'Hmm. Maybe.' I was now looking through Spotify for a podcast to listen to before I slept. Maybe a 'true crime' one, (my guilty pleasure) or maybe a TED talk (more educative).

Much as I was trying to distract myself, my mind kept going back to the fact that there was still no message from Devraj. How sad. That sinking feeling in my stomach was not going. I didn't want to spend my time like this. Wondering, second-guessing, waiting for calls and messages. What was I even thinking? Irritated with myself, I chose a juicy crime podcast to distract myself, closed my eyes and started listening. Better to try and shut out all the self-doubt. It could be dealt with later.

'Oh, hi!' I heard Debajyoti say loudly, suddenly sitting up in his seat. Hearing this and feeling him move, I casually glanced up. And did a double take!

To my shock, Devraj was standing there next to our seats, smiling at us.

'Do you mind if I ask you to move?' he said.

'Oh yeah, of course, no problem!' said Debu with a grin and got up.

Sliding into the now vacated seat, Devraj turned to me with a smile. 'Good morning,' he said.

'What are you doing here?!' I asked, still in shock.

The train was finally pulling away from the station.

'Did you delay the train??' I asked in disbelief.

'Pfft . . . me? No way. I was just lucky it was delayed and I managed to make it. Himanshu had called the station manager to check and he said I'd manage to catch it, so here I am.'

Not at all convinced, I scrutinized his face, but he kept a bland expression, raising his arms in an exasperated way. I decided to drop the inquiry into the train delay since I was so happy for it.

'Why didn't you reply to my message in the morning?' This was the question that had been troubling me for the last hour or so.

'Sorry about that. I had to quickly wrap up a few things before leaving. Hey! I thought you'd be happy to see me,' he said smoothly, taking my hand in his and giving it a squeeze.

'I am! I'm just a little stunned,' I said, grinning from ear to ear. This was so amazing. I just couldn't believe it.

'Well, the thought of spending five hours with you on a train and getting to know you was so tempting, I couldn't pass it up. Also, I didn't want you to have second thoughts. You know, out of sight, out of mind kind of stuff,' he said, turning towards me.

'Oh no. That's silly.' I shook my head like that was the most daft idea.

Then, after a moment, I added, 'But having said that, we didn't really get a chance to know exactly what this is, this thing between us. So we can manage expectations, know where we stand.'

'See, you were having doubts,' he squeezed my hand. 'All I can say is I've been intrigued since I met you and want nothing better than to get to know you, and we can take it from there.'

'The first time you met me, you yelled at me,' I said, giggling.

'Okay, maybe not from the very first moment,' he said with a smile. 'Though I remember you weren't really bothered by my yelling. In fact, you answered me right back.'

'Of course I did. Would you expect anything less?' I answered. 'So how did you manage to leave everything to come to Delhi? Was Himanshu okay with you leaving?'

'I have to head back soon, maybe tomorrow or the day after. But that's fine. I couldn't let you go just like that.'

And so we spent the next five hours talking and getting to know one another. It was the best train ride ever.

19

THREE MONTHS LATER

'This is so exciting, Sunaina! What a great show it's been!' gushed Reena.

'We've managed to raise Rs 30 crore so far! How amazing! And we still have the pledge of 5 crore each from Sharad Bajaj and Dinshaw Mistry to announce!' said Manju excitedly, looking into her laptop.

We were in Mumbai, backstage, for the special fundraiser telethon we had organized along with Vikram and his team for the forest guards. The money raised would help with the education of their children, as well as pay for life and medical insurance for forest guards from the top ten tiger parks in the country. Certain amounts would also be set aside for each park to provide forest chowkis with amenities to help the guards.

Natasha had gone all out and managed to get some of the top names in the film industry to commit time or perform for it, while everyone from Daleep Varma to Boss had reached out to all the corporates and philanthropists to pledge money. Some of the big donors were flown to Mumbai to share the stage with the stars for the various segments. The whole show was televised and playing out live on our channel.

We were now nearing the finale.

'Are you ready? Feeling nervous?' I asked Devraj who stood beside me.

'Me? Nervous? Nah, I'm fine. I'll just follow the professionals,' he winked at me, squeezing my hand. I beamed back.

'Aww, you two, this is so cute. Let me take a picture,' said Didi, who was also backstage with us. When she heard we were having this big event in Mumbai with Vikram as well as other stars, no one could stop her from flying in.

'A visit was due anyway,' she had said. I didn't complain—at least she got to meet Devraj as well.

It had been an amazing three months for Devraj and me. All my worries about long-distance, being stressed and second-guessing had been unfounded.

We hardly felt the distance. He came to Delhi every two weeks or so, as there was always some work or the other he had in town. Earlier he would send someone else for it, but now he did it himself.

I guess this was what you call the honeymoon period of a relationship, but it was incredible. We had so much to talk about, many common interests and really enjoyed each other's company. Occasionally we'd socialize with friends, sometimes his, sometimes mine. His friends were really happy that, because of me, he was spending more time in Delhi.

And now he was here in Mumbai for our special show, where in a short while he was going to get onstage.

Priyanka and Rajiv from NNTV were hosting the telethon, with Vikram on and off as a guest anchor. Then there were several guest appearances and performances by actors, segments with environmentalists, activists and even a handful of political leaders across party lines.

I had been on at the start of the show, along with Vikram, to talk about our shoot for the campaign. We had played clips from the various adventures, the bee disturbance (which is how I wanted it referred to), the first time Vikram saw a tiger and seeing the park's legend, Mallika. It had been fun and Vikram had been charming. The clip of that interaction had already had thousands of viewings within an hour, Manju had duly informed me.

Now that the telethon was drawing to a close, for the finale we had the big-ticket donors on stage, and the anchors would announce their donations for the cause. Vikram and Zeba were on stage as well. She had sung in the previous segment. I had no idea she could sing so well. The audience loved it and there was much cheering.

'She's been recording an album,' Reena told me excitedly. 'It was all hush-hush, but I'd heard about it. She just dropped her first single during our telethon! That's huge. I'm getting so many messages and calls about it.'

Before the final announcements, we had a surprise in store for Vikram. Ram Tiwari was joining the telethon via video link from Jaipur.

Or so Vikram thought! What he didn't know was that Ram Tiwari was actually here backstage with us!

Devraj had organized to get him here safely and he was coming on stage as well, along with Ram Tiwari. We had currently made him sit in the adjoining green room.

'Sunaina, it's time for you to go on again!' said Debajyoti, running up, talking into his walkie-talkie.

I gave Devraj's hand a squeeze and went up on stage. In this final segment, Boss was also joining us onstage.

We were going to bring back the focus on the man–animal conflict issue and the risk the forest guards take in patrolling the national parks. We were also going to talk more about our experience the day Ram Tiwari was injured.

Boss asked Vikram and I various questions about our experiences. A few jokes here and there, but then we got serious when we spoke about the attack and the aftermath.

It was all going to plan. The conversation was engaging, and then the director cued Vikram to introduce Ram Tiwari. We had earpieces on so the director could instruct us onstage.

Vikram then walked up to the plasma screen that was set up at one end of the stage. It was on this screen Ram Tiwari was meant to appear via video link, so they could interact. Vikram told the viewers and audience how he was glad Ram Tiwari had made a good recovery, and was looking forward to introducing him.

He turned expectantly towards the screen, but no Ram Tiwari appeared. It remained on the generic video of the Save our Tigers campaign.

'Vikram!' I called out from where I was seated on stage.

He turned slightly towards me, but remained more focused on the screen, wondering why Ram Tiwari had not appeared, especially since the director speaking in his earpiece had told him to look at the screen.

I stood up and called to him again.

This time, he turned just as Devraj and Ram Tiwari walked on to the stage.

His face registered shocked surprise and then delight.

He rushed across the stage to meet Ram Tiwari, who was folding his hands in a namaste before Vikram engulfed him in a bear hug. It was so genuine and emotional. Everyone was clapping, and I could imagine the crew being thrilled backstage in the control room. It was such a wonderful moment as all the emotions were completely genuine.

I introduced Boss to Ram Tiwari and Devraj. They shook hands and he chatted with them as well.

Ram Tiwari, who had red, visible scars on one side of his face, broke down as he spoke of his ordeal and long recovery in hospital. He thanked everyone who had helped—Vikram, Devraj, and even me and the channel. The doctors had saved his eye, but the skin around it had been grafted and would take more time to completely heal.

The most touching part was when he said he couldn't wait to get back to the field and continue doing what he loves best, patrolling Chambalgarh and making sure it was safe.

This led to applause from the audience and another hug from Vikram. It was the perfect finale for the show.

Vikram and I wrapped the show by thanking everyone for their donations and reiterating the cause we were raising funds for.

Later, we were all backstage after the show had wrapped up. Everyone was upbeat with how well it had gone off. I was tired of hearing Manju tell me how many hits various videos and pictures were getting. Boss came backstage as well and met everyone, to congratulate them on a job well done. I introduced Didi to Boss and of course she got a photo with him.

Jaya and I were chatting about the show when Zaid came looking for us. He informed us that Natasha had invited everyone to come to a nearby restaurant that she had booked to hold a celebration for the success of the campaign and event. He also added that it was Vikram who was keen to do this for the team. This sounded like a lot of fun and the production team that had worked so hard on the show today would be thrilled.

Jaya and I informed everyone and sent out a message on the WhatsApp group as well, with details of the location.

Didi was most excited. She couldn't believe it! Not only had she met Vikram Khanna today but was going to actually 'hang out' with him.

'My friends in London are not going to believe it!' she added, her eyes wide with excitement.

Devraj had gone to see off Ram Tiwari, to make sure he was sent back to the hotel quickly as he was exhausted by the events of the day. He would leave for Jaipur the next morning.

When Devraj returned, we headed to Tamarind Court, where the wrap-up party was taking place. Luckily it wasn't too far from the telethon location, and Vikram and Natasha had clearly reserved the whole space, as there was security outside the restaurant, screening the people going in. I saw Ravi there, in charge of the entrance. He smiled on seeing us and waved us in.

Inside, it was full of our team from NNTV as well as several other people who must have been invited by Vikram and Natasha.

Zaid spotted as and took us to Natasha's table where we met Safar, Maya and several others from the Mumbai team. It was a nice little reunion.

Soon enough, Vikram arrived at the restaurant with Zeba. Their entrance caused quite a sensation and many NNTV colleagues mobbed them for pictures. He happily obliged.

'I can see your friend Manju is also taking pictures,' said Devraj, looking amused. We were now standing near a pillar next to Natasha's table.

'Yes, she clearly never stops. Anyway, this is the final day so she may as well go all out,' I said with a laugh.

'It's a nice gesture. To have this party for all of you,' he said, looking around. 'I'm just glad I finally got to meet your sister. Even if she's more excited about meeting Vikram Khanna than me.'

As we watched Vikram was slowly making his way to our table.

'Don't be silly! She's been so excited to meet you. Meeting Vikram is just thrills but meeting you was a big deal,' I said, giving him a hug, as he put his arm around me. Being with Devraj still made me a feel a little giddy sometimes.

'Well Sunaina Joshi, since I've met your sister it's about time you met mine,' he whispered in my ear.

'When did I say no?' I replied, smiling at him.

'Great, because she's been after my life and I'll set it up once we're back in Delhi. This might involve a weekend in Jodhpur if you can get away.' He gave me a kiss on my head. The thought of meeting Devraj's sister made me a little nervous, but I was also thrilled she wanted to meet me. Was this a 'next step' in our relationship? Meeting each other's siblings seemed quite significant.

I didn't get a chance to ponder this any further as Vikram had finally arrived at the table.

'Hello, hello! Great to see everyone again!' he said, beaming at us.

'Hi, Devraj!' Zeba squealed as she gave him big hug. He looked a little bemused by her enthusiasm as he asked politely 'And I hope you've been well, Zeba?'

After meeting everyone else, Vikram gave me a hug.

'Isn't this nice! he said. 'All of us together again, though no jeeps or tigers.'

'And no shushing me, right Devraj?' said Zeba laughing. 'I hope you heard my new song?' She looked at us expectantly.

Both Devraj and I said we had and followed up with the requisite praise.

I could see Didi standing behind Vikram, signalling to me with her eyes.

'Vikram, my sister would really like another photograph with you since she was too starstruck in the last one to smile,' I said.

'Yes, of course. Anything for Sunaina's sister,' he said graciously, posing with Didi, who looked absolutely thrilled.

'Please don't encourage her,' I said, laughing as I clicked a few pictures.

'I'm glad you were able to make it,' he told Devraj after the picture taking was over, as Didi feverishly pored over the photos I'd just taken.

'I'm glad I did. It was really interesting watching it all behind the scenes and on screen. The show went off quite well. And of course, anything for Sunaina,' Devraj replied, putting his arm around my shoulder and giving it a squeeze.

'Well, look at that,' Vikram said with a big smile, as he turned slightly to Natasha, who had come and stood next to him.

'Natasha, I'd like to believe I played Cupid in this relationship.'

'You? I thought it was me,' she laughed. 'Sunaina, this campaign has been so fun and at the same time done us a world of good! And today's event was so moving that I had tears in my eyes, especially in the end when Ram Tiwari came on. Despite knowing he was coming!'

'So did I!' said Didi. 'It was so emotional and I knew you weren't acting.' She gave Vikram a big smile.

'I believe the clip has gone viral,' I said to all of them. 'And hopefully now that this campaign is over, I will not have to hear that for a while. Whew!'

Everyone laughed at that.

'I have to come back to Chambalgarh soon!' said Vikram. 'I must say I really enjoyed the experience so much that I miss it. And, Sunaina, you must come when we visit.'

'Of course, let us know. Baagh Baadi would be pleased to host you again,' said Devraj.

'I'll come too! But we won't compete this time, so don't worry, Vikram,' said Zeba with a laugh.

'So it's a plan then. All of us together again in Chambalgarh! During the next tiger season,' said Vikram, smiling all around.

And so we all raised our glass in a toast: 'To the next tiger season!'

Acknowledgements

It is impossible to adequately thank everyone who has helped me conceive, begin and complete this book. My gratitude to the team at Penguin Random House India, especially Gurveen Chadha and Saloni Mital who worked with me and guided me on the manuscript, and Milee Ashwarya for accepting my proposal in the first place.

Prannoy and Radhika Roy for giving me the chance to report on wildlife and environment at NDTV, more than twenty years ago, and for giving space on the channel to these vital issues so consistently over the years.

Swati Thiyagarajan, my companion, friend and guide in wildlife reporting, throughout our years of working together on India's first wildlife shows 'Born Wild' and 'Safari India'. Thanks also to Sumi Deogam who accompanied me on various adventurous shoots.

Thanks also to my husband, Yusuf Ansari, for all his help and advice and to Arkaja Singh for reading the first draft.

Last but not least, thanks to The SUJÁN Life for the exceptional safaris and glamping experiences at their camps over the years.